Harrows Gate

by Neil Colby

Harrows Gate

Editor: D.S. Williams (The Pedantic Punctuator)
Cover designer: Domi at Inspired Cover Designs

ISBN: 9780994406606

Neil Colby,
PO Box K712
Haymarket
New South Wales 1240
Australia

neilcolby.com

In memory of Gertie

1

The rhythmic thump-and-hiss of the barge's steam engine could be heard about a mile down-river. Its large metal water pipes gleamed dully in the twilight, and the steam that escaped from its central chimney swirled, ghost-like above the barge. It was heading towards the prison, and as it sailed closer, the prison's large metal gates slowly opened. Two men stood guard on the walls near the prison gates. One of them carried a Martini-Henry rifle, while the other had a service revolver tucked into a leather holster on his hip.

The tall lookout tower near the gates looked more like a lighthouse, with two large spotlights on its circular roof. The spotlights pointed at different areas of the prison yard. In the small windowed office near the top of the structure sat the duty officer, dressed in a black leather jacket which was buttoned up to his neck. He picked up a pair of binoculars and turned a brass wheel on them, which adjusted the focus and sharpened his view of the 'death barge', as it was known at the prison. He saw nothing unusual. The barge's lights had been switched on and the skipper stood at the wheel, guiding the vessel towards the prison wharf. Two other men stood on deck, waiting patiently by the landing ropes near the bow.

In the prison yard, in a small nondescript building about fifty feet from the wharf, two men lifted a body off the garrotte-chair – a solid wooden chair with a high back that had a leather cord threaded through it. Condemned criminals were forced into this chair, the wire placed around their neck, and their hands tied. Once the sentence was read out, the garrotter pulled a metal lever and the mechanised garrotte would do its work, snapping tight around the person's neck with such force that it would sometimes crack the vertebrae and cause the head to flop limply to one side.

At the old Ironworks Prison, notorious for its executions, the guards were efficient at getting prisoners in and out of the chair. During its busiest times, up to four people—men, women, and occasionally children—were executed in a single day.

On that particular day, the prisoner Fryman Sellers was led into the execution room, and made to sit on the chair. He was strapped in by the waist and had his arms tied, so that he could barely move. He resisted feebly for a moment, and then sat motionless, watching the other faces in the room under the dim light. His expression was not malicious, but rather showed a certain curiosity, as if the others were beings from a different world.

The judge, an elderly and somewhat sickly-looking man, cleared his throat, and with trembling hands, rifled through the papers on the small desk in front of him.

"Fryman Sellers," he said finally, in a voice that still carried the authority of law. "It is… my duty…" His voice faltered for just a moment, until he cleared his throat again. "It is my duty before the court, and according to the rule of law, to reiterate your sentence, so that you shall understand your punishment before the community and before God. You are accused of stealing from your former employer, and of the most vile act of murder of an innocent young girl."

In the audience, Dame Margaret Lafroste, once Fryman's employer, dabbed at her eyes with a small'kerchief. She sat upright on one of the chairs set out for the small gathering, her back held ram-rod straight. She wore a formal, long black dress with a starched collar, buttoned to the top, and a small brooch, which reflected dimly in the light.

"For these crimes, you have been condemned to death by means of the garrotte," the judge continued, his voice rising.

Fryman Sellers watched passively as the judge read from

the sheet of paper before him. "You have been found guilty of stealing a freshly prepared turkey, six candles, and a jar of pickled onions from the kitchen of your employer. But your actions were observed by the housemaid, who is also the niece of your employer. Once you realised that your actions had been discovered, you murdered the witness in cold blood."

The judge paused, his old, but sharp eyes peering angrily at Fryman Sellers. "It was a crime most vile," he said after a moment. "An innocent girl, as yet unmarried, and related to your employer, was bludgeoned to death by yourself. It was a crime without mercy, and one that demands the ultimate penalty."

Dame Lafroste's face was impassive, although she dabbed at her eyes once or twice before crushing the 'kerchief into a small ball in her hand.

The man in the chair next to hers, the Sherriff Emilio Ducanti, took notice. He sat stiffly, his red leather jacket creaking slightly with every movement. It was unusual for women to attend the garrotting executions, and Ducanti was uncertain how he should react.

At last, the judge reached the end of his speech. "I command that the execution to be carried out without delay. May God have a measure of mercy on your despicable soul." He closed a large book on the desk, then nodded at the garrotter, who had taken up a position behind the garrotting machine, with his back up against the wall.

The garrotter was an unnaturally large man. He wore a leather cap and looked fierce, a scar disfiguring part of his face. His expression was a steady as a rock, his actions slow and deliberate. He slipped a black cloth bag over Fryman Sellers's head, and tied it loosely to keep it from falling off. Then he positioned the garrotting wire in front of the condemned man's throat. Finally, he took a step back, his hand resting on the lever... and waited.

The judged nodded, and the garrotter pulled the lever. There was a sharp, snapping sound as the wire was released. Fryman's head was pulled back sharply. For a moment, he seemed to wriggle, then he grew still, his head tilted to one side.

The judge cleared his throat. "Ladies and gentlemen. I bid you good day." He stood up and left the room, ahead of the onlookers.

There was a brief murmur of voices, as the small group stood up and shuffled towards the doorway. "Ghastly," Dame Lafroste muttered. "Utterly ghastly."

The Sherriff, who was still at her side, spoke. "I apologise that you had to witness such an act, madam. The application of the law is brutal sometimes, but necessary in a civilised society."

Margaret Lafroste nodded agreement, as she continued to walk. She did not make eye contact with the Sherriff. She heard him say, "Madam, may I show you to your transport?"

She paused and turned, studying the small, gold-rimmed spectacles that pinched the sheriff's nose, before replying. "Please do so, sir."

He held out his arm, and she accepted, touching it near the elbow and allowing him to lead her towards the exit.

Once the guests and officials had left, two of the prison guards entered the room to do their work. They and the garrotter lifted the body into a battered metal crate mounted on a trolley, which made it easier for them to wheel it towards the treatment room. This was the last part of the process, before loading the body on to the barge.

However, as the men reached the treatment room that day, Fryman Sellers suddenly sat upright in the metal crate, his eyes wild and his breathing rapid. The man closest to him opened his mouth to shout a warning to the others, but he was hit from behind by the other guard, and fell forward towards the crate, groaning loudly.

The garrotter closed and locked the door behind him. Fryman leapt from the metal crate, invigorated by his newfound freedom, but clawing frantically at an attachment around his neck. He struggled with it and finally removed the raw hide collar, which had protected his throat during the garrotting.

He took a closer look at the man on the floor. "Job well done, lads." He smiled crookedly and rubbed his neck where the garrotte had left its mark.

Together, they loaded the unconscious guard into the crate and wheeled him towards a large funnel-shaped object near the oven. They undressed the guard down to his underwear, then positioned the crate underneath the funnel and pulled a lever, and a large amount of thick, muddy liquid was released on the unconscious man's body. Both the guard and the garrotter began to smear the clay over his face and body, until the man suddenly regained consciousness and clawed at his own face to remove the sticky clay. The garrotter grabbed the hapless man by the throat and applied great pressure, to push him down and cut off his air supply. Moments later, the man no longer struggled.

Fryman Sellers swiftly dressed himself in the dead guard's uniform, while his accomplices finished the job of covering the body with the thick clay and pushing the crate into the oven. The crate moved slowly forward on metal rollers. As it entered the oven, they shut a large metal door behind it and waited.

About fifteen minutes later, the metal crate emerged at the other end of the oven, with the body encased in a cocoon of hard clay. The men lowered a chain with large metal claws attached, and positioned it so that the claws hooked onto either side of the clay sarcophagus. Sweating in the heat from the nearby oven, they hoisted the body out of the metal crate and swung it over to a waiting wooden trolley, before finally wheeling it out of the room and towards the waiting barge.

The air outside was cold and moist. The garrotter stayed behind and watched the other two continue. A nervous Fryman Sellers checked his uniform, to ensure it was in order. He knew that the slightest mishap could give him away, and destroy their carefully laid plans. As they approached the barge, he drew his cap tighter around his ears to avoid showing his face to the barge's crew. The two men half-pushed, half-carried their cargo across the gangplank and towards the aft end of the barge, then off-loaded it on to a flat metal platform created specifically for the purpose. The barge crew took over from the two men wordlessly, and secured the cocooned body with ropes, while the deliverymen made their own way off the barge.

Fryman Sellers walked back towards the gangplank at an even pace, following closely behind the guard. As soon as he was out of the view of the two crewmen, Fryman ducked into a shadowy corner on the barge and crouched down behind a large barrel, which had been tied to the deck with thick rope. The guard who had helped him to deliver the body walked on as if nothing had happened, stepping back onto the wharf and heading back to the guards' quarters.

The barge crew released the mooring ropes, and the barge's engine started with a loud clanking noise before settling into its usual rhythm. As the barge sailed past the prison gates, the guards in the lookout tower watched it curiously. Once the barge had passed through, the large metal gates closed behind it, the hinges whining as the gates swung shut.

Fryman Sellers peeked out from behind the barrel where he was hiding. It was too early to relax, but he was relieved that the barge was out of the prison enclosure and steaming freely down the river. He looked out for the crewmen, and could see both of them walking towards the bridge. Even though the bridge was dimly lit, he could make out the skipper at the wheel. Fryman clenched at the collar of the uniform he was wearing. He was cold and shivering. The air that hung over the river could chill a man to the bone.

It took the barge nearly half an hour to reach the Isle of the Dead, as it was known by the city dwellers. The islet was a barren, black rock that jutted out above the water's edge, less than 500 metres from the river bank, where a large and smelly paper factory stood at the water's edge, a few dim lights casting shadows behind its dirty windows. Fryman was unable to keep himself from shaking violently with the cold. He peered over the barrel and watched as the crewmen slowly made their way to the aft deck. The skipper switched on a bright gas light, which illuminated the aft deck. Fryman ducked out of sight, fearful that he might be exposed by the light. For a few heart-stopping moments, he waited. There was no response. No alarm.

The noise of the barge engine changed in pitch and the barge slowed to a near-stop as the two crewmen loosened the ropes around the cocooned body. It was the moment Fryman had been waiting for. He moved quickly across the deck and clambered over the side of the barge, hanging on to a mooring line with near-frozen fingers. He could hear noises as the two crewman grunted and heaved, and finally shoved the body overboard. Fryman waited for the loud splash, then let go of the mooring rope and plunged into the freezing water.

He came up for air moments later, his body aching from the cold and his chest so constricted that he could hardly breathe. Did anyone hear him? Would they be turning in his direction?

He listened intently, but there were no shouts, no voices. All he could hear was the steady, rhythmic noise of the barge's engine. The engine noise changed pitch again as the barge slowly turned and steadily began to turn away from the islet.

As soon as the light was switched off, Fryman began to swim. In the distance, he could see his goal: the paper factory on the shore.

2

On the south bank of the Thames, in the industrialised quarter of the city, some of the factories kept up production, even after dark. The Battersea Power Company's coal-powered generators provided an uninterrupted supply of electricity until eight o'clock at night. After that, the factories closed and then re-opened the following morning. This was to allow for maintenance of the large generators.

Deke Dunberry, a former member of the prison guard, who had been kicked out the service when he was caught drunk on duty, patrolled the streets among the factories of the south bank, and was a familiar face to many of the factory workers. He mainly worked the night shift, but since the area was quiet at night, he frequently had the time to shelter from the cold in the small guard's office, and even to keep a pot of tea brewing on the small coal stove.

At least three times a night, he walked the streets carrying a small lantern and armed with his trusty Webley & Scott revolver, which he carried in a leather holster on his left hip. That night he again noticed that the building at 10 Whistler Street still had its lights on at nearly midnight. He had noticed this several times before, and was puzzled as to how the lights could be on when the electricity was unavailable to the area.

Deke had previously knocked on the doors at number ten, but received no reply. And since there was no complaint about it, and no suspicious activity, he had let it go. But that night was different. Deke had allowed himself a sip or two from the small hip flask that he kept in the pocket of his greatcoat. The liquor emboldened him, and he decided to investigate this peculiarity.

Without further hesitation, he walked up to the large oak doors of the premises, and banged loudly with his fist on the door. Similarly to his previous visit, there was no reply. He waited for a few moments, then banged again, harder. He waited and listened. Then he heard something, or somebody, inside. Was it his imagination? He banged on the door for a third time, his gloved hand smarting from the blows.

"My oath," he mumbled to himself, "If you're in there, you had better…"

There it was again. A shuffling sound of sorts coming from the inside. Someone was moving around. Someone who knew he was there. Deke shone his lantern on the ground near his feet, to look for a stone, or a piece of metal—anything that could be used to bang loudly on the door.

He found a small stack of bricks a few metres from the door, and bent over to pick one up. Behind him, the door opened slowly. Light – electric light from inside, illuminated part of the footpath, and a slim, dark figure appeared at the door. Deke turned sharply, reaching instinctively for the revolver in its holster.

"May I help you?" said a voice. Female. Young.

Deke was slightly surprised. "Are you here alone, miss?"

"No."

As he stepped closer, Deke could make out the woman's face. She had short, straight black hair with a slight curl at the bottom, which helped to frame her face symmetrically. She wore a white blouse, buttoned to the top, a silver pendant around her neck, and a black, narrow-fitting waistcoat. The thick black mascara on her eyelashes, and long, curving eyebrows didn't escape his notice.

"May I ask your name, Miss?"

"May I ask yours?" she replied almost immediately.

"I'm the night watch," he said sounding apologetic. "I check on the area here. The name's Deke Dunberry."

Deke allowed his eyes to wander downward and noticed she wore riding breeches instead of a dress, and black leather boots instead of women's shoes. He had heard that city women were abandoning prudent fashion and dressing much like men, but never before had he seen it with his own eyes.

"Nadia," she said. "My name is Nadia Barossa. I work here, and I assure you there is nothing here that needs to worry you."

"Now you see Miss ... er, Barossa. I was noticing you had a light on upstairs. Electric light and all. And the thing is, there is no electric light in the whole area at this hour."

Nadia grinned briefly at the confused-looking man. "We store our own electric light here, sir."

Deke looked more confused than ever. "But, how would you do that, Miss?"

She leaned closer to him, as if she didn't want to be overheard, and said in a near-whisper, "It's my boss, you see. He's an inventor. A very clever man."

"I beg your pardon, Miss. Clever enough to make his own electricity?"

"To be accurate, not so much making electricity, as storing it," she explained.

"Isn't that the damndest thing, Miss, if you'll pardon my language."

"Quite," she said. "Mister... Dunberry is it? Would you like to come inside and have a look?"

"Well, Madam... Miss, I don't want to place a burden upon yourself or on your inventor boss. He must be busy, if he finds it necessary to work at this hour..."

"If I'm not mistaken, we may even have a bottle of sherry upstairs, to help you stave off this frightful cold," she said.

Deke's face shone with delight. "Well, I will promise you I shall not interrupt an important man's work, Miss. I make you that solemn promise. If I could just, for a minute or so, step inside..."

"Of course you can," she said, and opened the door much wider, allowing Deke to see the interior of the reception foyer, with its fading wallpaper and dusty furniture. "I must apologise," she said immediately, "There is no housekeeper here."

"And your function, Miss? If I may ask, of course."

11

She leaned closer to his ear and said in a low voice, "The inventor's assistant."

"Well, of course," said Deke. "I should have thought of that immediately. Do forgive me."

"Why don't I show the way?" she said and walked on ahead, while Deke closed the door behind him and then followed her like a large, clumsy-looking puppy.

She led Deke Dunberry up a flight of stairs to the next level, with dim, wall-mounted lights illuminating the way. Deke noticed that his host was as quick as a fox, effortlessly climbing the stairs, while Deke himself breathed heavily and began to sweat as he approached the top of the stairs.

Stopping to catch his breath, Deke noticed two swords mounted against the wall; one of them looked like a military sword, the other a rapier.

"The gentleman's a collector, then?" he said, still battling to control his breathing.

Nadia paused to allow Deke Dunberry his break. "The swords are mine," she said, smiling at his surprise. "An inheritance."

"I see," said Deke. He wanted to ask other questions, but Nadia had started walking on, and he had no choice but to follow.

They walked through what looked like a boiler room, and Deke noticed the glow of brighter electric lights at the end of the passage. The door was ajar, and a strange noise was coming from the room. Deke patted the holster of his revolver, an act that often helped to give him the courage to push on.

When they finally reached the room at the end of the passage, Deke stopped before entering, his neck craning to get a glimpse of the interior. It was not what he expected.

Rather than a factory-style layout, the room was divided into different sections. One section was used for some kind of chemical work, with test tubes, large thermometers, beakers and an array of petri dishes arranged around two large microscopes – or at least, that's what Deke supposed they were, even though the instruments looked odd and weirdly shaped. Another part of the room was home to an array of copper wires, thin tubing, solenoids, and round-topped glass enclosures that stood about a metre high and had an intricate array of tiny wires and metal connectors within them, some with filament giving off a yellowish glow. In a third part, near the window, Deke saw pot plants connected up with wires to a strange machine, and the corpse of an animal, perhaps a monkey, on a dissection table—its skin completely removed, muscles and sinews laid bare.

There was a gentle hum in the background, and Deke noticed a large fan mounted on the ceiling, extracting air into what appeared to be a metal funnel. Then he noticed movement at the far end of the room. A man in a starched white shirt, plain black trousers, and wearing a small leather apron, moved into the light. He appeared no older than thirty, yet his black hair was peppered grey. He wore small, round metal-rimmed glasses, and as he approached, Deke noticed he was wearing white gloves.

Nadia Barossa turned towards Deke and announced, "Jack Lightfoot." She pointed to the man in the gloves, and then added, "Inventor."

Jack Lightfoot stopped, looked Deke up and down, and said, "A man of the law?"

Deke shook his head and removed his cap. "The night watch, sir. And I humbly apologise for the intrusion."

Jack removed his gloves and discarded them into a bin, which appeared to hold several other pairs. Then he turned to Deke with interest and said, "So have you ever worked for the police?"

"I would imagine the prison service," said Nadia.

"Right you are, miss. I was a guard in the prisons. But how did you know?"

Nadia shrugged. "Deduction. Your coat appears to be prison issue, and the boots possibly, too."

Deke was impressed. "Well you certainly have a sharp eye…"

Jack interrupted. "That's our Nadia. A bit of a sleuth. Eagle-eyed, you know? She probably knows half your family history by now."

"I've only just met the lady, sir. I would think it unlikely that—"

"Why don't you try her?" Jack interrupted again.

"I beg your pardon, sir?"

"Ask her what she knows about you," said Jack conspiratorially.

Deke was taken aback, and he hesitated.

"Perhaps dismissed? From the prison service?" Nadia volunteered.

Deke's eyes widened. "If you are clairvoyant, Miss, or a witch, then I'd rather not—"

"Be calm, Mister Dunberry. I am neither. And you do yourself a disservice by worrying so much about people who claim to have such special powers."

"Then how?"

"You're not a youngster anymore, Mister Dunberry, but not yet of an age where you can afford to retire. So, I'm assuming leaving the prison service was not a choice, at least, not your choice. Put that together with the fact that you smell faintly of alcohol and that the bulge in your pocket appears to be a flask of some kind – and that you looked particularly keen when I mentioned the prospect of sherry – and I begin to suspect that you were dismissed because you were caught drinking while working."

"Tending prisoners is a hard life, Miss. I merely did what many others did."

"I have no doubt of that, Mister Dunberry. Tell me; did you divorce your wife at that same time?"

"But how did you—"

"That mark of the wedding band you removed is faded, but still visible on your finger, Mister Dunberry. I would have guessed one year, or even a year and a half?"

"Almost fourteen months to the day that I divorced the missus in a court of law," said Deke, a veil of sadness over his face. "And we could have been together still, if it wasn't for my drinking."

"I'm sorry, Mister Dunberry. Truly."

Jack touched Deke lightly on the shoulder. "Why don't we show you around the laboratory? That is why you are here, is it not?"

"Sir, my only concern was for your safety, and for the security of your premises," said Deke.

"And we thank you for that," said Nadia, and then she turned to Jack. "Mister Dunberry was intrigued that we were able to use electricity after the cut-off hour…"

"Ah, yes. Well there is no mystery there, I'm afraid Mister… er, Dunberry. Come, let me show you." Jack walked into the next room, with Deke following on his heels and Nadia trailing behind.

Jack stopped in front of a wall of black boxes, some with wires protruding from them: "Lead-acid cells," he announced. "Useful if you want to store the energy for later use – but, well, rather unremarkable. Invented years ago… by someone else."

He turned to a bulky waistcoat that hung over the back of an empty chair, and ran his hand gently over it. "This, however, is something new; new and exciting."

He picked up the waistcoat, and put it on. The material covered what appeared to be thin tubes running down the length of the waistcoat. Small wires were visible, looping across from one tube to another. The wires were covered with resin, so that they would not come into direct contact with one another. Another, longer wire connected up with a metal object that was attached to a thick leather strap. Jack fastened the strap around his wrist, and then turned a small dial on the chest of the waistcoat.

"Observe," Jack said finally, as he reached out to touch a metal goblet on a nearby table. Suddenly, a bright flash lit up the room as electricity arced across to the goblet, crackling across its surface like a miniature electric storm.

Deke stood back, aghast. His mouth hung open from surprise and sheer disbelief. "Dear God, be merciful," he muttered.

"Just imagine the possibilities," said Jack excitedly, completely ignoring the older man's distress. "Power that you can carry with you. You could power a bicycle with this. Perhaps even a rotor, which could carry you into the air. This is the stuff that Leonardo Da Vinci dreamed of, Mister Dunberry. He only lacked a source of power."

"Who?" asked Deke softly. It sounded almost like a whimper.

"Which brings me to a recent product of my own design," Jack went on without pause. On the far side of the room stood a large wooden table, with a machine on it that looked somehow like a typewriter – which Deke recognised from the prison offices

– but in this case the typewriter had several rubber-encased wires connected to a central column, which was in turn, mounted on a flat base that had a scroll of paper attached to the back of it.

"The age of modern communication, Mister Dunberry," announced Jack Lightfoot.

"I beg your pardon, sir. It's getting late and I do not wish to burden you with questions, or take up any more of your valuable time..."

Jack smiled: "Nonsense, my good man. It's simply a pleasure to show you my inventions."

"Does this machine make any large flashes of light, sir? Or perhaps loud noises?" asked Deke fearfully.

"Nothing of the sort, I assure you. Well, that wouldn't appeal much to my customers, would it?"

"Customers, sir?"

"Well of course, man," said Jack impatiently. "I create these things so that people can use them. What would be the point, otherwise?"

When he noticed that Deke was still confused, Jack added. "This one, for example, is destined for the very prison services for which you worked."

"I beg your pardon, sir?"

"A telegraph printing machine," said Jack. "Highly advanced, I assure you."

Deke took a closer look at the machine, fascinated by the gleaming wooden panels that covered its sides, and impressed by the elegant brass keys of the keyboard.

"Imagine. A hundred miles away, someone types a message into a machine, just like this one. "Then, moments later, our machine here begins to print the very words of the message on this sheet of paper, as if by means of a ghost inside it," said Jack in a dramatic voice.

Deke appeared repelled by the word 'ghost' and, for his own safety, shuffled two small paces backwards. "A marvel, sir. That is for sure."

"Problem is, Mister Dunberry, that we lack buyers. Unless we find them, this fine machine will stand here and gather dust, never living up to its vast potential," said Jack.

"I am sure such a thing will never happen, sir. Such a

machine will impress anyone who lays eyes on her."

"I wish to sell a hundred machines just like this one, Mister Dunberry, so that every government office... every prison, no less, can communicate freely across the entire country. Regrettably, the response so far has been... lukewarm. But perhaps I have not been in conversation with the right people, Mister Dunberry. Perhaps all I need are the right names."

Deke was silent. He still didn't realise that Jack Lightfoot was asking, indirectly, for his assistance. Then it slowly dawned on him.

"I was a lowly prison guard, sir. Not someone involved in the business of the prison, or in managing the office and such," Deke said, trying to distance himself.

At that moment, Nadia stepped closer and touched Deke on the arm. "You underestimate yourself, Mister Dunberry," she said with a warm smile. "But why don't we have a discussion in more comfortable surroundings? We have some good Portuguese sherry in the library. Would you care for some?"

Deke's worried face brightened into a smile.

3

The dog growled savagely, inches away from Fryman's face. It was straining at its collar, eager to attack. Fryman's sense of self-preservation gave him renewed energy. He crawled, wormed, away from the dog, clawing at the soil to help him along. But moments later, he came up against two black, polished leather boots blocking his path. He stopped, and looked up at the man who stood in front of him – a tall figure, dressed in a dark overcoat and wearing a top hat. He could barely make out the man's face, but after a few moments the tall man bent down to have a closer look at him, and that's when Fryman suddenly recognised the gaunt look and the piercing grey eyes.

"It is him," he heard the man say. "Bring him to the house." The man's voice was calm, but had an air of unquestionable authority.

Rough hands grabbed Fryman by his arms and his collar, and lifted him to his feet. Two men half-dragged, half-carried Fryman to a waiting Landau carriage. They opened the door and pushed him inside. Fryman fell limply onto the floor of the cab and heard the door slam shut behind him. The coachman cried a loud 'Hoy!', and Fryman heard the sharp snap of a whip. The Landau lurched forward and then quickly gathered speed, racing towards the city.

A bone-rattling twenty-minute ride took them to a large estate with expansive lawns. The carriage passed through columned gates and followed a raked gravel road to the impressive manor house with its tall gleaming windows and black-tiled roof. The horses were lathered and tired, and the coachman found it difficult to calm them down once the carriage had come to a stop.

A nervous-looking doorman opened the coach door and then watched as two men grabbed Fryman and dragged him out of the cab. The two men walked on either side of Fryman, propping him up while at the same time steering him towards a side entrance.

They opened a large sliding bolt, and then opened the heavy twin doors. In the dimly-lit room, they led Fryman to a stairwell and then downstairs into the basement. As they descended the stairs, Fryman noticed an unfamiliar, sharp smell – a chemical odour.

The basement was a large, square room, with a door at the far end, and with brighter lights mounted on the walls and ceiling. Anatomical charts against the wall showed the human form in various poses; sitting, standing, bent over. Near the centre of the room was a narrow table, half of which was covered with a white sheet. The uncovered half revealed that the table top was padded and covered in leather. Fryman noticed that restraining straps were attached to the sides of the table, and that its legs were anchored to the floor with screws. His feeling of unease grew rapidly.

Then he noticed four large cages on the opposite side of the room, against the wall. Fryman could see that at least one of the cages was occupied. A large ape sat in a corner of the cage, a linen bandage covering what appeared to be a wound on its abdomen.

Fryman was led to a chair and forced to sit. One of the men put his hand on Fryman's shoulder, and pressed down. The message was clear – *don't attempt to get up.*

"The Professor told me…" began Fryman, but his voice sounded so hoarse and faint that he cleared his throat and started again. "The professor said…"

"Sit quiet," said a voice. It was the man who had a hand on his shoulder.

"He said I'd get money," Fryman said.

There was no reply.

"You ask him. He said…"

"Hold your tongue. The professor will be here soon," the man replied. He appeared to be a man of little patience, so Fryman resolved to keep quiet.

After a few minutes, the door at the far end of the room opened. The tall gaunt man, without his top hat this time, entered. He appeared casual, as if he had plenty of time to spare, and paused at the ape's cage before strolling to where Fryman was sitting.

"Thank you, Riley, for escorting Mister Sellers here," the tall man said to Fryman's guard.

"Professor, I'm… thank you for getting me out, sir," said Fryman, relieved at the opportunity to speak freely.

The professor nodded, and then approached Fryman with a look of curiosity.

"If you'll be kind enough to pay me the money we agreed, sir… then I'll be on my way," Fryman blurted out.

"Hmm," said the professor thoughtfully. "Tell me, are you still in good condition? In good health? After your escape, I mean?"

Fryman nodded, somewhat confused. "Yes, sir."

"And all went according to plan? The escape plan worked? You weren't spotted by anyone outside your accomplices?"

"No, sir," Fryman said again. "We put the other guard in my place, just like the plan said. And then I put on his uniform and walked on to the barge… it all worked out perfect."

"Excellent. And you weren't… spotted – when you swam ashore?"

"No, sir. Mind you, the water near froze me to death. That's why it took me awhile, to get my legs back and everything." In the back of his mind, Fryman was wondering if he was a little too familiar with the professor – perhaps not respectful enough to the man who had saved him from the garrotte.

"But you're fine now? You are feeling… healthy?" the professor said, his grey eyes studying Fryman with interest.

"Oh yes, sir. And I owe you my thanks."

"Excellent. Now if you don't mind, I'd like to ask you a small favour in return."

"Of course, sir. If I can, I will surely be eager to help you," said Fryman. So, the professor wanted a favour, thought Fryman. Just as he suspected all along. Probably a dirty little job that needed doing. Fryman was happy to oblige, to repay his debt.

"I'm a medical man, Mister Sellers," said the professor. "My interest is in health – how our bodies function. That's why we did those... procedures at the prison. Now if you'll allow me, I would like to examine you, to check your person for signs of illness or disease."

"But I'm quite healthy, sir, I assure you," said Fryman, now more confused than ever.

"Even so, Mister Sellers. My interest is in examining the healthy, so that I can help the ill and the frail. Besides, I should take a look at the patch on your shoulder to ensure it will cause you no discomfort. Now I wonder if you'll do me this small favour..."

Fryman hesitated, then said, "What would you like me to do?"

"If you'll be so kind as to remove your boots, as well as your jacket and shirt, and recline on the examination table over there," said the professor. He pointed towards the padded table at the centre of the room.

"And then, afterwards, could I have the money we agreed, and take my leave?" It may have sounded disrespectful, but Fryman wanted to be sure that their arrangement was still in place.

"That is what we agreed, is it not?" The professor smiled, but the smile was so ghastly that Fryman thought it better if the professor didn't smile at all. The professor's teeth were yellowed from tobacco smoke, and when he smiled, the skin wrinkled over his sunken cheeks. His eyes didn't join the smile, but instead were fixed on Fryman like the eyes of a lizard.

"If that's what you would like me to do, sir, then I shall comply," said Fryman. He felt the release of the guard's grip on his shoulder, which, to Fryman, was a signal to do as he was asked. Fryman stood up, removed the dead guard's jacket and hung it on the back of the chair. He also stripped off his shirt, which was still damp and smelling of sweat. Finally, he sat down again and took of his boots. They were prisoner's boots, with soles worn thin, and the leather surfaces badly scuffed. The boots were water-logged, and made sucking noises as Fryman pulled them off his feet. Fryman finally stood up. He felt slightly awkward without his shirt on at first, but then shrugged and walked over to the examination table.

As he lay down on the table, a movement in one of the cages caught Fryman's attention. Something large, and quite dark, was slowly moving around inside the cage. As he peered into the dimly lit environment of the cage, Fryman began to make out a shape. It was an ape, but much larger than the one he had seen earlier. Its fur was completely black and, as the ape turned its head, Fryman saw its amber eyes looking directly at him. Fryman was unprepared for the intensity of the animal's stare. It was as if there was anger and resentment in those eyes, and Fryman found it difficult to look away.

"Hmm," he heard the professor say. "The patch of skin healed beautifully. You were indeed one of our best patients, Mister Sellers."

The professor's fingers touched the small patch of skin that appeared slightly lighter than the rest of Fryman's skin. The patch was exactly square, and the skin appeared to be of a slightly different texture, yet it blended in well with the rest.

Fryman glanced towards the ape in the cage, and saw that it was still staring at him. When he looked back at the professor, he noticed that one of the henchmen had appeared, and was standing next to the examination table.

"For the next part of this examination, Mister Sellers, I would appreciate your assistance," said the professor. He opened a small glass bottle and poured some of its contents on to a white cloth, and then held the cloth up to Fryman's face.

"I would like you to breathe, Mister Sellers. Breathe in deeply."

4

The warden was a large man with diminutive spectacles, which perched precariously on the tip of his nose. He wore a black waistcoat that appeared to be ready to burst open, and was sweating profusely, rings of sweat spreading around his armpits.

"Dear, dear," he muttered, his chubby cheeks trembling slightly as he shook his head.

"It seems we have picked a bad time, Warden," said Jack Lightfoot. Next to him stood Nadia Barossa, dressed in a prim, although not unattractive, grey dress; her neck suitably covered by a high collar frilled with lace.

The warden's office was in disarray, with papers stacked in untidy piles, and a tray with breakfast tea and biscuits abandoned in one corner of the large desk. He was fussing with the papers, clumsily trying to reorganise the piles, while breathing noisily through his teeth.

"Terrible," the warden said. "Dreadful business."

"What happened, sir? And may we offer our help?" Nadia asked.

The warden paused and glanced at the elegant young woman standing near the open door of his office: "I'm sorry?" he said, sounding perplexed.

She smiled at him: "We have, in the past, assisted the police in their investigations. Mister Jack Lightfoot has a formidable reputation for finding clues, to solve even the most vexing of problems," she said.

"Well madam, while I appreciate your offer, I assure you that in this case it is much, much more complicated. It is an internal matter of the most urgent kind, and something that you'll need to leave to me..." He paused as another figure appeared at the door. It was a tall man with short-cropped, dark hair and a pencil-thin, waxed moustache. He wore a polished red leather jacket with silver buttons, and carried a white pith helmet under one arm. He nodded briefly, acknowledging Nadia's presence, and then looked sharply at the warden.

"Sheriff... what a surprise," the warden said. "I didn't expect—"

"I have been told one of your prison guards has disappeared," the sheriff said with a scowl.

"Er, yes. And I was about to notify—"

"Well, I'm here now," said the sheriff. He stepped forward and gave the warden's untidy desk a look of disdain.

"—I was about to notify the Governor's office," the Warden finished. He avoided the sheriff's intense stare, and fidgeted with some of the papers. Tiny sweat drops accumulated on his forehead.

"Are you sure this man turned up for duty? Have you searched the grounds?" the sheriff asked. He appeared impatient and annoyed. "Why would you bother the Governor's office with something like this?"

The warden swallowed deeply, and tried to gather his wits about him before speaking: "The guard reported for duty, at the right time, yesterday. We have an entry in the book. I also looked at his past record, and it appears he was mostly on time for his daily duties. He was last seen, last night."

"Who reported him missing?" asked the sheriff brusquely, his patience already wearing thin.

"His wife... asked after him," the warden responded. "Since he never came home after his shift at the prison."

"Who saw the man last?"

"Actually, Sheriff, one of the last persons to see the guard before his... unfortunate disappearance may have been... you."

"What the devil are you talking about, man?"

"The guard was… in attendance… at the execution yesterday. That's where he was last seen."

The sheriff appeared to miss the subtle tone of accusation in the warden's voice. He looked puzzled for a moment, and mildly irritated by the news, but he quickly composed himself and tried to recollect the scene: "I remember accompanying the Lady Margaret Lafroste to her carriage, which means the prison guards, and the garrotter, must have remained in the room after our departure," he said, deep in thought. Finally he looked up and said to the warden, "There's hardly any reason to suspect foul play, Warden. My estimation is that you'll find the man in a back room somewhere, with a bottle of liquor in the near vicinity."

The warden shook his head. "There are strict rules here against drinking on duty, Sheriff."

"Are you saying he'll be the first to be caught drinking while working?" The sheriff grinned. He already knew the answer to his own question.

"Nevertheless, if we don't find the man—"

"Well, who do you have working on it?" the sheriff responded sharply.

The warden paused uncomfortably, his gaze drifting from one person to the next until it settled on Jack. "Actually, Sheriff, I'm interviewing Mister… er… Lightfoot and his assistant, here, as he may be able to assist in this case." He pointed a shaky finger at Jack.

The sheriff turned to Jack and examined him curiously, as one might examine an insect under a magnifying glass. His gaze rested briefly on Jack's metal-rimmed glasses, before travelling down to his starched white shirt, polished black shoes and grey spats.

"And what, pray, is your function, Mister Lightfoot?" he finally asked.

"I'm an investigator, Sheriff, and, I should add, an inventor. This is my associate, Miss Nadia Barossa."

The Sheriff nodded stiffly in Nadia's direction, and appeared to be uneasy about having a woman in the room.

The warden filled the moment of awkward silence with a mumbled introduction: "Sheriff Emilio Ducanti was a high-ranking officer in the Queen's Guard, and is now the head of our local police force," he explained.

"Delighted to meet you, sir," said Jack. He extended a hand in greeting, but the sheriff ignored it.

"And what does an inventor hope to achieve in a prison, Mister Lightfoot?"

Nadia interjected. "It sounded like an intriguing case to us, Sheriff. A vanished prison guard, last seen in the company of the garrotter. Could it be foul play? Whatever information we find, we will report to you in the strictest confidence, if that pleases you."

The sheriff's thin moustache quivered. "I shall have you know that I have not only provided personal protection to the Royal family, I have also defended the British flag in Africa, against the Zulu. What makes you think that you will be able to uncover any information that my men cannot?"

"We are in awe of your high achievements, sir," said Nadia gently. "Which is why we thought we may help, while leaving you at liberty to pursue more important work... as commissioner, perhaps?"

Sheriff Ducanti cleared his throat and straightened his jacket: "Well, yes, newspaper speculation on my appointment as commissioner has been... premature," he said. Was there a hint of a smile under the moustache? "However there are a number of demands on my time, so I daresay your service may be of some value after all. Of course I shall expect a full report."

"Of course," Jack agreed enthusiastically, and thought it better not to say anything else.

"Of course," the warden echoed, but when he noticed the sheriff's poisoned glance in his direction, he withdrew and remained quiet.

Ducanti nodded his head once more in Nadia's direction and, with that, excused himself from the room. The warden, who was sweating profusely, removed a large handkerchief from his top pocket and rubbed the moisture from his spectacles.

"Well, that went well," said Jack buoyantly. "Now, about our fee..."

The warden stared at him incredulously.

———•—•———

The room of execution was narrower than Jack had imagined it to be. It had the chair at one end, and several rows of seats facing it. There were two exits, one of them towards the back of the room, which was the one used by officials who were witnesses to the execution.

The garrotter wore a faded, scarred leather apron, which made him look like a blacksmith. He was a large man, with sharp and unwavering black eyes. His hands were rough and large and it looked as if he hardly needed the help of the garrotte to kill a man.

"You called for me," he said gruffly. It wasn't a question.

"Mister... eh, Raskovic, I believe?" Jack waited for a response but received none. "Mister Raskovic, I'm sure you know that a man from this very place, a prison guard, is... missing." Jack faltered under Raskovic's vicious stare. "We believe you were the last person to see him alive."

Raskovic's black eyes stared blankly at him.

Jack quickly scanned the note in his hand and continued. "Seamus Prenter. That was his name. Where did you last see this man?"

Raskovic shrugged lightly. "In this room, here."

"And how did you come to see him, Mister Raskovic? What was he doing?"

"His job," Raskovic replied. "He's a guard."

"And what did he do – the last time that you saw him?"

"He helped," said Raskovic.

"With the execution? Whose execution?" prodded Jack.

"That fella. The thief."

"Very well, can you tell me the circumstance... can you describe to me what Seamus Prenter was doing here. What was his function, exactly?"

"To get the body mucked up," Raskovic replied.

"Mucked up?"

Raskovic tilted his head towards the room where the clay is

applied, and then led them to it. He stopped in front of the metal framework, and pointed at the funnel-like object that deposited the hot clay. "We put the mud on," he said.

Nadia leant closer to Jack's ear and said, "They cover the dead in mud."

This was news to Jack. "What happens to the man, once you get him covered with the mud?" he asked, genuinely curious.

Raskovic nodded in the direction of the oven. "He goes in there."

"They— bake him?" Jack sounded surprised.

"It's to harden the mud shell," Nadia whispered, "before they dump them in the river."

"You know about this?" Jack looked at her strangely. "Where do they dump the bodies?"

Nadia shrugged, and looked at the garrotter for the answer.

"They take 'em, on the barge," he said.

"Where do they take them?" asked Jack. He was still processing this new, horrific information.

Raskovic shrugged.

"Mister Raskovic," asked Nadia gently, "which door did you use?"

"Huh?" Raskovic looked at her, puzzled.

"Which door did you use, to take the body outside?" Nadia asked.

Raskovic pointed at the door closest to the wharf.

"Was Seamus Prenter your friend?"

Raskovic shook his head, now looking slightly suspicious.

"What is your job here, Mister Raskovic?"

Raskovic merely looked at Nadia. He was in no mood to explain his job to a woman.

Nadia sensed his antagonism. "Perhaps you can explain to Mister Lightfoot here how you go about... killing a man," she said.

Jack nodded. "If you'd be so kind."

Raskovic shrugged and then moved to the garrotting chair, his one large hand gently stroking the top of the backrest. Jack thought he saw a fleeting grin on the large man's face.

Raskovic began the demonstration, showing Jack the restraining straps: "We strap 'em," he explained, "tight."

Next, he placed the garrotting wire over the top of the backrest, then placed his hand on the release lever, which was topped by a wooden handle, smoothed by years of use.

Without warning, he tugged at the lever. A loud 'twang' was followed by a loud 'crack' as the mechanism released a large ratcheted wheel, and snapped the wire tight over the back of the chair.

The edges of the backrest were lined with metal, and Jack watched with surprise as the wire bit into the back of the chair, leaving scars in the metal. For a moment, Jack imagined what the device could do to a man's throat.

For a few moments, there was a deathly hush in the room. Then Jack's curiosity got the better of him. He stepped gingerly closer to the chair, and took a better look at the mechanism that connected the garrotting wire to the wheel. "Does this... ever fail?"

Raskovic shook his head. But then he looked around the room slowly, as he noticed that Nadia was no longer with them.

Jack looked around in surprise. He hadn't noticed that Nadia had left, either.

Raskovic bore an angry scowl as he stepped towards the open door. At that precise moment, Nadia entered from outside.

She saw the two men staring at her, noticed Raskovic's angry expression, and said, "Clearly no ladies' lavatory here. Did I miss anything?"

There was a moment's silence before Jack responded. "Mister Raskovic was kind enough to demonstrate to me how the garrotting chair works."

Nadia smiled. "Good, then we can go?"

"I can't see why not," said Jack.

Raskovic was still glowering at Nadia. She smiled sweetly back at him. "Thank you so much for your assistance, Mister Raskovic." Then she led the way out of the garrotting room, and Jack followed in her footsteps.

Once they were walking down the passage, away from the garrotting room, he looked curiously at Nadia: "So? Where did you disappear to?"

She smiled mysteriously, then glanced over her shoulder to ensure they weren't followed, before replying. "There is more to this than meets the eye."

5

Phyllis Secombe awoke from a delicious nap, and found her client still lying next to her, fast asleep and snoring lightly. He was a younger man than most of her clients, a dockyard worker in his twenties, and Phyllis was flattered that he preferred her over the younger prostitutes who had set up their lodgings in Dorset Street.

"Hey, mister," she said, and playfully tickled his ribs. "It's getting late. Unless you fancy paying for an all-nighter, that is."

It was still early evening, but time was money, and Phyllis knew that her regulars were likely to call soon after dark. Her young client groaned and sat up in the bed. "What's the hurry, luv?" he said.

"Time's long expired, lover, and you best be out of here before me next client gets impatient."

He stood up, and gathered bits of his clothing from the floor. She marvelled at his well-muscled naked body, and smiled with quiet contentment: "Was it good for you, my sweet?"

"Uh-huh," he replied absently, sitting back down on the bed to put his pants and boots on.

In the meantime, Phyllis slipped on her bloomers, and slid her corset over her head. She wormed the corset down over her ample breasts, and once it was positioned around her waist, she pulled the satin cords to tighten it.

"Need a hand there?" he said with a chuckle, his hand

stroking her buttocks, while his other arm snaked around her waist.

"Cheeky bugger," she said, giggling. "You better go out and earn some more money first. Come on. Move it. Go on." She pushed him towards the door while he clumsily tried to button his grey dockworker's shirt.

"Play your cards right, and I may ask you to be my girl," he said.

"I'll be your girl – by the hour," she replied.

At the door, he turned and kissed her on the lips. She opened the door and pushed him firmly outside, even though she felt the temptation to pull him back in. She resisted it, though, and instead smiled sweetly. "Come back soon, lover."

He grinned at her and then walked lightly down the stairs, whistling a cheerful tune.

Phyllis closed the door and smiled, enjoying the moment. Sometimes, she felt her job wasn't half bad. She straightened the bed, picked clothing items off the floor, and closed the small wardrobe, in which she stored her most precious belongings.

After a few minutes, as Phyllis was looking at herself in the mirror and pinching her cheeks to make them appear rosier, there was a knock at the door. Phyllis could tell that it was a man's knock. It was forceful and without hesitation.

She opened the door a crack and saw a man she had never seen before. He had a scar across his left cheek, and wore a grey top hat, which appeared to be too small for his large head. When he attempted to smile, she could see that his teeth were discoloured by years of smoking and neglect. She caught the dull glint of metal between his two front teeth.

Phyllis didn't smile back, but waited for the man to speak. When he did speak, his voice was coarse, and she noticed that his eyes were bloodshot and his nose and cheeks covered by a network of red veins, obviously exacerbated by regular bouts of heavy drinking. Phyllis knew the signs. She had seen them before, many times. This was not the kind of client she wanted to attract.

"Excuse me if I'm interrupting at an inconvenient time," the man said with a grin. "I'm here on behalf of a more refined gentleman than meself – a professor, no less. He wishes for the company of a lady such as yourself."

"A what? A professor?" said Phyllis, confused.

"That's correct, dear lady, a learned man of science. He wishes to make your acquaintance."

"But how does he... know me?" Phyllis asked, still puzzled.

"He was looking for a lady of good outlook, who could provide... certain services. The man, not wanting to ruin his public reputation, sent me in his stead – to meet with a lady such as yourself, and to invite you to his house. His carriage is downstairs in this very street."

"I trust this... gentleman knows there is a cost for my services, and perhaps a bonus... if he believes it is warranted."

The man leant in closer, and Phyllis could smell whiskey on his breath when he spoke. "I assure you, young madam, that he is a man of means. A big house, he has, with grounds the size of this whole neighbourhood here."

Phyllis was impressed, and she managed a smile, despite her misgivings about the strange offer.

"You'll need to give me some time to get... suitably attired," she said.

The man nodded: "I'll be waiting for you in my employer's carriage, outside."

Phyllis nodded, feeling slightly nervous. She shut the door and stood motionless, listening to the man's footsteps disappearing down the stairs. Then she rushed to the wardrobe, and picked her finest dress off its hanger. It was dove-grey, with a narrow blue collar that had a lacy fringe around it.

Phyllis realised that the nervousness she felt was probably due to her feeling of anticipation, and the excitement of meeting a wealthy client. Wealthy clients were rare in Dorset Street. And here she was, being invited out by one of them – to his house. As she dressed, the young dockworker she had been with earlier was all but forgotten.

The professor shook the clinging raindrops off his umbrella as he entered the Canterbury Club in lower Oxford Street. The light rain gave the air a grey, misty appearance, and the interior of the club looked warm and welcoming in comparison.

The man in the entrance hall, known simply as 'Lincoln' among the members, dutifully took the professor's coat and umbrella, and swiftly brushed off a few stray droplets that clung stubbornly to the professor's lapels.

"Rather unfortunate weather, sir," said Lincoln, in an unhurried voice.

"Quite," said the professor. "Tell me, Lincoln; has Mister Lucian Baker arrived?"

Lincoln nodded, his white-gloved hands pausing in mid-air with the professor's coat: "Indeed sir. Mister Baker arrived thirty minutes ago. He is presently in the smoking room."

"Good man," the professor said. He appeared pleased.

The professor took to the plush-carpeted stairs, and made his way down an oak-panelled passage to the first floor, where an arched doorway led to the smoking room. Even though it was relatively early, a few of the regulars were already there.

Lucian Baker sat at the far end of the room, at one of the more private tables. He was accompanied by a young man in a suit that looked unseasonally light in colour. The two appeared to be in deep conversation, their heads leaning close together. When Lucian Baker noticed the professor's arrival, he rose to his feet, smiling.

"My dear professor," said Lucian, extending a hand in greeting, "Punctual as always." His voice was subdued, to keep within the club rules, yet light and friendly.

The professor squeezed the offered hand, his bony fingers testing the softness of Lucian's more fleshy hand. His attention was almost immediately diverted to the young man in Lucian's company. As the young man stood up, he appeared tall and muscular. But it was his piercing black eyes that held the professor's attention.

"Mister Alexander Crowley, I presume," the professor said, his wrinkled face transforming itself into a smile, exposing the yellowed, tobacco-stained teeth. "What a pleasure to meet you." His voice was so soft, it was merely above a whisper.

"He prefers to go by the name Aleister," Lucian explained. "Aleister Crowley."

"A prodigious name," the professor commented, his fingers clasping the younger man's hand.

"Lucian has told me a lot about you, Professor Strasberg," Aleister said, withdrawing his hand from the professor's grasp.

"When we met in Switzerland, young Aleister here showed a keen interest in the arts of alchemy," Lucian explained. "The curiosity of youth," he added with a chuckle.

"Are you an alchemist, professor?" asked Aleister, his eyes bright and inquisitive.

"Sadly, no," the professor replied, sitting down in one of the large leather chairs. "However the alchemy of the human body does hold a particular interest for me."

"The professor is a medical man of great repute," Lucian explained to his young companion. "A giant among his peers."

"And I should not neglect to say that without the masterful wisdom of a chemist like Lucian Baker, I would still be stumbling along in the dark," the professor remarked with a dry chuckle. For a moment, he stared deep into the eyes of the young man, before adding, "And I believe he has taught you well."

Aleister leaned forward towards both the other men, and said in a whisper, "Lucian's knowledge of the great magic rites far surpasses my own. I have learned so much."

"You flatter me," Lucian said with a smile, then looked around the room to ensure they were not overheard before explaining to the professor. "Aleister was initiated at the Mark Masons Hall."

Aleister nodded eagerly in agreement. "My magical name is *Frater Perdurabo*," he said.

The professor, too, appeared excited. He spoke urgently, his lizard-like eyes gleaming: "And the chemistry? I believe you— put some of Lucian's experiments to the test."

"Indeed," Aleister replied, "and even added some experiments of my own. Some in ritual and some because..." He paused before going on. "I believe I have achieved a level of transcendence hitherto unknown among the human race."

"This young man is a thoroughbred, Simeon," Lucian said to the professor. "We met while mucking about in the *Weisshorn*. I decided he was either a wealthy layabout, or gifted visionary. It turned out he was both." Lucian chuckled aloud.

The professor placed a bony hand on Aleister's leg: "You simply must tell me about your experiments."

"Tell you? I intend to show you," Aleister said with a laugh, drawing disapproving glances from elsewhere in the room.

"Gentlemen," said Lucian, in a more subdued voice. "Perhaps we should retire to a more private venue for our discussion. Might I suggest brandy and cigars?"

6

An hour later, in Jack Lightfoot's laboratory on the south bank, a low-hanging ceiling light illuminated a polished wooden table. There was a single item on the table – a simple leather strap, marked by small grooves on its flat surface.

Jack picked it up again and examined it closely with his powerful magnifying glass.

"And you found this where?" he mumbled, peering at the grooves in detail.

Nadia sat down in the chair next to Jack's: "Raskovic's little room of horrors," she said. "You should have seen the place. Metal clamps – heaven knows what he used those for – and strips of leather, handcuffs, even one of those tongue screws, straight out of the Inquisition's torture chamber."

"Hmmm, maybe it's a collection," said Jack absently.

"Or a hobby," Nadia said.

"I think you're right; these grooves match the garrotting wire exactly," Jack said.

Nadia picked it up and wrapped the broad leather strap around her throat: "It would be enough to stop the garrotting wire from strangling you," she said.

"You mean for testing the garrotting machine?"

She shrugged: "Or for pretending to execute someone, without actually killing him."

"And by 'him' you mean...?"

"Fryman Sellers," said Nadia, patiently waiting for Jack to catch up.

"So how does that connect to..." said Jack, but then he paused. The penny had dropped.

"A switch," said Nadia. "For some reason, he decides not to execute Fryman Sellers, but they still need a body, so he kills one of the guards instead."

"Of course. But why him?" said Jack.

"He probably picked Seamus Prenter out of convenience – simply because he was there. But why did he let Fryman Sellers go free? That is the question," said Nadia.

"So Seamus Prenter is..."

"At the bottom of the Thames," she said. "Or wherever they dispose of the bodies of executed prisoners."

"And Fryman Sellers is..."

"...presumably a free man," Nadia said thoughtfully.

＊

Fryman Sellers awoke with his head encased in a leather mask. The mask had two eye holes with glass lenses, which allowed him to peer out, although the lenses were foggy from his own breathing. He could make out the light on the ceiling, and when he lifted his head slightly, he saw that he was lying on his back on a flat surface that was raised off the ground – a bed or a padded table.

Fryman was immediately aware of the searing pain in his groin. It felt as if his scrotum was on fire, but when he tried to shift his body to alleviate the pain, he found that he was strapped down. His arms too, were tied to the examination table with leather straps, and his legs were strapped into stirrups that held his knees up and bent – which put him in a helpless position with his crotch exposed. He could feel that he was naked from the waist down.

He attempted to lift his head higher, but found that a strap around his throat restricted this movement. Out of the corner of his eye, he noticed movement. Even though he could not see clearly, he recognised the professor approaching.

Fryman tried to speak, but his tongue was dry and swollen, and he could only manage hissing noises.

"Welcome to my operating room, Mister Sellers," he heard the professor's voice. "You'll be glad to know that the operation appears to have been successful. You should be right as rain, soon."

"Operation?" Fryman tried to ask, but the question came out as a strange gurgle.

"You will find it difficult to speak. Don't worry, in a few minutes I shall give you some water, and it will gradually improve."

Fryman attempted to shake his head, but the mask and neck straps restricted his every movement.

"Do not concern yourself, Mister Sellers," said the professor. "I have attempted many operations of this kind, and have managed to build up considerable expertise. Practice makes perfect." The professor grinned, and Fryman could make out his yellowed teeth through the lenses.

Fryman fought anew against his restraints, his muscles straining against the leather straps.

"You must conserve your energy, Mister Sellers. You'll need it for the recovery process," said the professor. He placed himself between Fryman's legs and muttered, "Now all we need to do is bandage you up."

The professor opened a small glass bottle containing white, almost translucent fine crystals, and poured some of its contents into a small ceramic bowl. He crushed the fine crystals with the back of a spoon and then dipped a shaving brush into the powdery substance.

He leaned forward, examining Fryman's grotesquely swollen scrotum closely, before brushing some of the powder on the area. Fryman stiffened, and then tugged violently at his restraints, uttering garbled cries of pain. Tears flowed freely down his cheeks.

"A great invention, carbolic acid," the professor said, ignoring Fryman's cries. "Without it, your wounds will putrefy, and you'll be of no use to me at all."

In the meantime, the professor opened the valve of a gas canister placed near the operating table. The gas was fed through a small tube to the leather mask that covered Fryman's head. Inside the mask, Fryman was vaguely aware of a soft hissing noise.

Fryman's convulsions began to subside. His face was red and his cheeks puffed out, from utter exhaustion and pain. The professor, in the meantime, dusted strips of cotton with the same powder, and then applied them as bandages to Fryman's groin. Once again, Fryman's face contorted with pain, and his body trembled as he slowly lost command of his own muscles. His arms twitched and then lay still at his sides.

He heard the professor's voice saying: "Time to sleep, Mister Sellers."

7

Reginald Henry Lafroste's vision was blurry, but he could still make out the patterns on the pressed ceiling of his bedroom. He recognised the footsteps of his wife, Margaret, as she ascended the steps to bring him his daily bowl of broth.

Once an active sportsman and successful entrepreneur, Reginald was now bedridden, struck down by a mysterious, debilitating disease. Some days were better than others. On good days, he could reach out to the magnifying glass on his bedside table and scan the newspaper. On the bad days, he couldn't even feed himself, and suffered the humiliation of having to be carried to the toilet by his manservant.

The Lafroste residence was an elegant home at the top end of Gloucester Street. The Lafroste family, once members of the lower middle class, had distinguished themselves by successfully investing in the railroad industry and then acquiring a small linen factory, which grew into a profitable business. Margaret Lafroste's biggest fear was that her husband would die, leaving her to make investment decisions, and dealing with bankers and clients.

Reginald's condition had deteriorated at first, then improved, and then steadily declined until he was no longer able to help himself out of bed. Margaret placed the bowl of broth next to his bed and straightened the crisp white sheets. She stared at her husband's face and saw the pain and the frustration in his eyes.

He appeared unfocused and confused.

"Bad morning?" she said gently.

He nodded slowly. Tears welled up in his eyes.

She pressed her fingertips against her mouth, willing herself to remain strong.

He opened his mouth to speak, but the words died in his throat. Instead, he sighed, and his hand twitched weakly. He held on to the sheet to steady it.

"You are still thinking of her, aren't you?" Margaret said with an edge in her voice.

Reginald stared at her and frowned, his blue eyes watery and impotent.

"It was unfortunate," Margaret said. "She tried to help you. We all did."

She sat down next to him on the bed, and lifted his head, propping it up with a small pillow.

"Eat a little something," she said finally. "It will make you feel better."

She picked up the bowl of broth and dipped a spoon into it, then placed a white napkin under his chin, like a bib, and offered the spoon to his lips.

Reginald didn't respond immediately, but then reluctantly opened his lips and tasted the warm broth.

"We must find someone else," Margaret said.

Reginald pressed his lips firmly closed, and then shook his head.

"We... killed Justine," he said finally. His voice came out as a faint whisper.

Margaret look at him sharply, the next spoon of broth hovering inches from his mouth.

"We tried to save your life," she said.

Reginald turned his face away and stared blankly at the opposite wall.

"You are precious to me," Margaret said. "I'll do anything... I did what I could..." Her voice trembled. Fighting back the tears, she again said: "Eat a little something."

Reginald shook his head resolutely. Margaret stood up and took the bowl with her, but she paused at the door, looking back angrily at her husband in the bed.

"I have always known," she said with tearful eyes. "I've known about your... special relationship with Justine. I was always the outsider."

She wiped away her tears, and then added in a more sober voice, "Now it's over. Justine is dead."

———◆———

"He is dead. I know he is," the woman said, her nervous hands tugging at the ragged scarf around her neck. Her hair looked stringy and unwashed, and her ill-fitting dress had several stains on it. She sat on a small chair near the stove, to keep warm. Still she shivered, and she gripped the seam of her apron with one hand, pressing so hard that her knuckles showed white.

Nadia Barossa extended a sympathetic hand towards the woman's shoulder, but she pulled away, unwilling to trust the strangers who had arrived unannounced at her home.

"We want to help you," said Nadia gently. "We want to help you find out what happened to your husband." She glanced briefly at Jack, who was sitting opposite the woman on a three-legged stool.

"I knew something was wrong when Seamus left for work that morning," the woman said, her eyes fearful. "Six crows," she said. "I could see six crows sitting near the front door of our house. They were sitting there, watching us – not even bothering to move, until Seamus shooed them away. They are nasty things, crows. My grandmother told me it's a bad omen when crows turn up at your doorstep. There were six of them. The devil's number," she said, shuddering anew at the thought.

"Was that the last time you saw your husband – that morning?" Nadia said.

The woman nodded, and dabbed at her tears.

"Can you tell us if your husband had a favourite place? Somewhere that he loved to go?"

The woman gave Nadia a confused look: "You mean like the Olde Cock Tavern?"

"Did he go there often?"

"Sometimes, in the early evening. Why?" the woman asked.

"We are trying to think of places he might have gone – by himself. Can you think of any?" Nadia prodded.

"By himself? He wouldn't go by himself, would he?" the woman said, with tears flowing anew. "He would come here – here is where he'd go," she said, and began sobbing.

They waited as the woman sobbed, a handkerchief pressed against her nose, and tears flowing freely.

"They never explained where he's gone," she said finally, sniffling loudly. "They couldn't even find his... body." She began crying anew. Nadia and Jack looked at one another, reluctantly coming to the conclusion that asking further questions was pointless.

"Madam," said Jack, "Would you say that your husband was a... strong man?"

The woman interrupted her sniffling and looked at him with curiosity. "Now why would you ask me a thing like that, sir? He was strong, yes, I suppose he was."

"Tall? Muscular, would you say?" Jack asked.

"Nay, not tall. My Seamus wasn't tall so much, but he was strong. Built strong, you know? Why do you ask?"

"Perhaps he was, in my thinking anyway, attacked – on the street, on his way home," said Jack.

She seemed annoyed by his suggestion: "Mister... Lightfoot, is it? If my husband was attacked on the street, they would have found him on the street. People don't just go disappearing now, do they?"

8

Phyllis Secombe awoke on a small bed, naked, but covered with a white sheet and woollen blanket. For a few moments, she had trouble recalling the events of the night before. She had a raging thirst and was relieved to find a jug of water and a glass at her bedside table. She rose shakily to her feet, poured water into the glass with trembling hands and gulped it down eagerly, then poured another.

Suddenly realising that she was standing naked next to the bed, Phyllis pulled the white sheet off the bed and wrapped it tightly around her body. She noticed that her small clutch bag was on the bedside table and checked its contents. It was all there.

She had no idea what time it was, and the room was completely unfamiliar to her. A dressing table with a mirror stood against the wall, along with a single chair, and she discovered a chamber pot placed discreetly under the bed. Daylight shone through the crack in the shutters, and Phyllis realised that it was late morning. Could she have been asleep all this time?

She recalled being driven up to the large house in the carriage, and then being invited into the parlour, where she was offered a generous glass of wine. She remembered drinking the wine rather eagerly, being especially nervous at meeting her first rich client. She also remembered eating some of the delicate pastries that were brought to her on a small tray. But the memories were fuzzy from there on.

She had suffered a headache, Phyllis remembered, and had felt slightly faint after drinking more of the wine. And then, nothing. Somehow, she had lost all memory of what happened next.

An electric light on the ceiling gave off a warm glow and, as Phyllis explored the room, she found the door locked and the window shutters stuck, or latched, so they could not be opened from the inside. She felt a flurry of panic, and again tried the door, without success. She knocked, and then smacked the door with the flat of her hand, feeling the sting on her palm.

"Hello!" cried Phyllis in a thin, frightened voice. "Can anyone hear me?"

She heard footsteps in the passage and listened intently as the footsteps moved to the door. She could hear voices; male voices.

"Excuse me!" Phyllis shouted, and banged with the flat of her hand against the door. "This door is locked... sir!" She added the 'sir' as an afterthought.

A key rattled in the lock, and Phyllis felt relieved. They hadn't forgotten about her, after all.

When the door finally opened, two men stepped into the room – one of them a silver-haired gentleman, tall but scrawny and wrinkled, with skin that appeared almost translucent. He smiled at her, showing his yellowed teeth, but the smile didn't spread to his eyes. His grey eyes remained cold and without emotion.

"I must apologise, madam, that we have inconvenienced you so," he said, his eyes locking on to her and watching her reaction thoughtfully.

"Well, sir, I have been here for some hours," she said. Phyllis's voice was strong, but inside she felt fearful and unsure. She sensed that the man in front of her had full power over her situation. Was he eccentric, perhaps, or a villain, plain and simple?

"I am the owner of this house, madam, and I apologise if it has not been to your liking," he said.

"The house... the room is just fine, thank you sir," said Phyllis.

"May I ask for your name, madam?"

"My name is Phyllis," she said, and then added reluctantly, "Phyllis Secombe." She was not sure that it was wise to tell the man her full name, but she did it anyway. Perhaps it would help him to trust her, she thought. "What is your name, sir?" she asked boldly, "if I may ask, that is."

The man examined her face closely for a moment before answering: "My name is Simeon Strasberg, madam," he said, leaning slightly closer to her as if to examine the detail of her face. "I am a professor of learning."

"Are you aware of my fee... sir?" Phyllis asked. She was uncomfortable with bringing up the matter of a fee, especially with her first rich client, but thought that it needed to be said. Being held in a room for hours was not only uncomfortable for her, but restricted her ability to make money elsewhere, and Phyllis felt it was only fair to receive compensation for it. She was ready to pad her fee to make up for the lost time.

"Your fee?" he asked blankly, still examining the details of her face. "Well, of course. Your fee will not be an impediment, madam. I assure you."

Phyllis was proud of herself for mentioning it. At least now she was free to charge him that little extra that she had in mind.

"Might I ask you one or two questions?" the professor said. The smile returned to his face, but it didn't cause Phyllis to feel any more relaxed or reassured.

"Questions?" she said. "Of course."

He smiled approvingly. "Might I ask if you practice... some form of contraception?"

Phyllis puzzled over the word, before replying. "I'm sorry, sir. I don't know what you mean."

The professor smiled again: "My apologies, madam. What I meant was; how do you prevent pregnancy... stop yourself from having babies?"

Phyllis smiled, feeling a slight sense of relief: "Oh, you don't have to worry yourself over that, sir. I use a rubber... a whatchamacallit," she said. She opened her small clutch handbag and with her fingers explored the contents until she found a small, oval, rubber device. She held it up to show it to the professor.

He nodded, smiling: "I understand, and I hope you don't mind me asking."

"Of course not, sir," she said, almost cheerfully. The old man was merely worried about making her pregnant, she thought. It was almost sweet, in a way.

"And have you ever been pregnant before?" he asked.

Phyllis paused. It was a strange and unexpected question indeed. Why would the old man want to know that?

"No sir, I haven't," she said. "I've been very careful."

"Excellent," he said, still smiling, and then added matter-of-factly: "Now, if you don't mind removing the sheet..."

"The sheet? Here?" Phyllis said. She was not uncomfortable about taking her clothes off in front of clients, but this request seemed strange, especially in these circumstances. Phyllis felt a sudden chill run down her spine.

Upon noticing her hesitation, the professor spoke. "I should very much like to examine you." His expressionless eyes watched her intently. He grinned again: "Of course I do not wish to alarm you. If this makes you uncomfortable in any way..."

Phyllis shook her head. "Not at all, sir. However, this room... there is only a small bed here, that's all, and I thought you'd prefer something more... spacious... with such a large house and all."

The professor appeared momentarily confused, before he responded. "I see what you mean. No, my intention is not to have sexual relations with you, madam. Merely to taking a closer look at your sexual parts, if you'll permit me."

To Phyllis, the old man's candour was both surprising and unsettling. "I'm sure I do not understand what you mean sir," she said. "You want to look closely at my... woman parts?"

"Precisely," the professor said with a grin. "I am a man of medicine, and have a special interest... in the human body. Would you consider such a request?"

"Well, I..." Phyllis began cautiously. "I have just never had such a request before."

The professor waited for her to think it through. He appeared quietly amused at her response.

"What would you have me do, sir?" she asked finally, her mouth dry from the nervousness that gripped her entire body.

"Merely remove the sheet, madam – and then lie back on the bed, if you don't mind."

Phyllis nodded timidly. She glanced back at the bed and then retreated towards it, still clutching the sheet around her body. She could feel the old man's presence behind her. He was staring at her partially exposed back – she could feel it.

Phyllis allowed the sheet to slip away, exposing her naked back and buttocks to the professor. She draped the sheet over the bed and lay down on top of it, facing the ceiling, and waiting for her client to do his inspection. She felt embarrassed and ashamed. Is that what the man wanted? He was certainly more eccentric than most.

The professor picked up the chair and placed it near the bed, and then sat down, positioning himself within touching distance of Phyllis's legs.

Her body looked uncomfortably stiff, and Phyllis was staring resolutely at the ceiling.

"Would you mind?" the professor said, gently prying her legs apart. Phyllis parted her legs, and felt the coolness of the air against her exposed pubis. She shivered slightly.

The next moment, she felt his finger probing inside her. She felt it venture deeper, exploring the most private part of her. "Hmm," she heard the professor's voice. "Your sexual parts look healthy. Good circulation of the blood. Can you tell me when last you had your menses… when last you bled?" he said.

Phyllis felt tears well up in her eyes. She had heard about the strange demands of deviants from some of the other girls in Dorset Street. And now she was in the hands of the strangest deviant of all.

"About two weeks ago," she said in a trembling voice.

"Hmm," the professor said again. "Can you remember the date?"

Phyllis suddenly propped herself up on her elbows, tears rolling down her cheeks: "Sir, might I ask what the meaning is of this? Why do you ask me such questions?"

"I thought it was obvious," the professor said with a grin. "I am looking for a young lady such as yourself – young, healthy, and fertile."

9

The woman wore her hair in a neat bun, with tiny curls escaping the arrangement and hanging softly over her dainty ears. Her hair was such a dark colour of brown that it appeared almost black. Her skin was flawless and appeared silky in the soft light.

She looked excitedly at Jack Lightfoot. "I came prepared for the experiment, Mister Lightfoot."

Jack Lightfoot noticed that Helen Gartner's eyes were light-brown, with specks of a darker colour embedded in them. He stared at her in awe. She was beautiful enough to steal his breath away.

"I beg your pardon?" he said, as if in a slight daze.

"Prepared," she repeated. "Undergarments are sometimes so unnecessary, don't you think?"

Jack swallowed heavily. "Quite," he muttered, with a grin that failed to hide his embarrassment.

"My father was an engineer, you know. He took me to Africa once or twice; showed me how the natives lived. Naked mostly, and without a moment's regret, I might add. Here in England, people have such... narrow minds."

"I couldn't agree more, Miss Gartner. May I show you the... device?"

"That is why I'm here, Mister Lightfoot," Helen said, with a hint of impatience.

"Very well, it's through here." He slid open a tall green curtain and revealed a doorway that led to a smaller room, adjacent to the study. A large contraption stood in the middle of the room. It consisted of a wooden chair attached to a metal framework. The back of the chair was padded and covered in leather, while the seat was attached to two footrests, which resembled stirrups. Below the chair was a complicated-looking assembly, built of wires and a set of interlocking gears.

"I named it The Little Dilly," said Jack with a smile as he presented his contraption with a brief wave of the hand.

"Charming," said Helen, peering curiously at the odd-looking machine. Looking closer, she saw that there was a perfectly round hole in the seat, and she felt strongly drawn to putting her finger in it.

Jack noticed that Helen was staring fixedly at the hole and so, to demonstrate, he lifted up the seat. Positioned underneath the seat was a mechanical arm, pointed upwards. At its tip was a rubber cap, about twelve inches in length.

"I see," said Helen quietly, looking at the machine with renewed respect.

"Yes, this is the massager – in-built with an inertia action so that the movements are rather more fluid," Jack explained, his awkwardness already forgotten in the excitement of being able to show off his work.

Helen was quietly impressed. "This may well assist with my condition," she said.

Jack nodded in agreement: "I had lengthy discussions with your physician, madam – and even showed him my rough drawings. Of course, there were a number of refinements since then. He felt it may be rather well suited to sufferers of hysteria..." Jack was not certain if it was wise to go into any detail about the lady's personal medical conditions.

"In fact," Jack added, "the good doctor felt an invention such as this might be beneficial to other... sufferers."

"You are a clever man, Mister Lightfoot, to devise such a machine," said Helen Gartner. She touched, with one hand, the rubberised section of the mechanical arm, and discovered it was rigid and, at the same time, cushioned by the soft rubber cap.

A quiet knock on the door interrupted the thoughts that were whirling through Helen's mind.

It was Nadia. She pushed the door gently ajar and peeked into the room.

"I hate to interrupt, Mister Lightfoot" she said, smiling pleasantly at his client. "Deke Dunberry arrived and I knew you were rather keen to have a word with him. He brought a guest."

"Um, quite. Quite so," Jack said, straightening himself into a more formal posture. "Um, have you met Lady Helen Gartner?" Jack was slightly flustered, despite the formalities, and turned to Helen: "My assistant, Nadia Barossa."

"Delighted to meet you, Miss Gartner. But I don't want to interrupt. I can see you are busy," said Nadia, a wicked smile playing at the corners of her lips.

Helen Gartner smiled back. "What a lovely assistant you have," she said to Jack. "Please don't interrupt your affairs on my account."

Jack's nervous hands fluttered over the desk, until he pressed his fingertips on to the desktop to keep them still.

"Would you mind showing Mister Dunberry to the library, Miss Barossa?" he said. "I shall join you momentarily."

"But of course," Nadia said, with a gracious smile and just a hint of mirth in her voice. She left the room and closed the door behind her. Once she was out of earshot, she leaned against the wall and muffled a fit of giggles.

———◆———

"I clean. I clean room," Pu Wang confirmed. He was a diminutive, elderly Chinese man dressed in a simple brown tunic and wearing a round cap. His withered hands gently stroked the seam of his tunic, and his glance darted from Deke Dunberry to Jack Lightfoot and back again.

"Mister Wang, can you tell us if you cleaned the room, the garrotting room, on the day that Mister Seamus Prenter disappeared?" Jack asked.

The old man looked briefly around the room, his gaze pausing fleetingly on Nadia, before he turned his attention back to Jack. He appeared uneasy, even slightly panicky, in the unfamiliar environment.

"You ask Mister Warden," he blurted out suddenly. "I clean. I clean room."

"I tried to explain to him…" said Deke Dunberry with a sigh. He looked frustrated.

"Mister Wang…" Jack started, but he stopped when he felt Nadia's hand on his shoulder.

Nadia stepped forward, carrying a short stool with her. She placed the stool next to the old man and sat down. The stool was so small that it appeared as if Nadia was on her knees. She smiled disarmingly at the old man, and placed her hand on his rough, veined hand.

"What happened?" she asked gently. "What did you see?"

The old man gazed at her intently before replying. When he finally spoke, he did so softly, and he focused on Nadia, ignoring the two men in the room.

"Me, I always clean the room after," he said slowly. "Sometime, the man in chair – he make a mess. On the floor. So, I clean. Every time."

Nadia nodded, and pressed his hand in encouragement.

"Sometime, I clean blood. Sometime, the man make a piss, or shit," the old man said. "And I clean, after."

"What happened that day?" Nadia asked gently.

The old man paused for a moment, and appeared deep in thought. Then he shook his head, as if he didn't quite understand. "That day, I don't clean," he said finally. "That day, already clean."

Nadia nodded again. "Who cleaned it?"

The old man shook his head again, summoning up his memory of the day – then he shrugged. "Don't know. Me, I clean the room."

"You cleaned the room anyway?"

The old man slowly nodded. "I clean the room."

Nadia turned her attention to Deke Dunberry. "Mister Dunberry, is there anyone else, to your knowledge, who may have been given the task for cleaning the garrotting room after the execution?"

Dunberry shrugged at first, then responded. "Pu Wang always cleans it. That's his job. Has been for years."

Pu Wang nodded. "I clean room."

"Well, it appears someone else did, on that day," Nadia said. She again touched the old man's hand. "Can you remember the name of the other man? The other guard who was working there that night? What is his name?"

Pu Wang looked at Nadia for a brief moment, then cast his eyes down to the floor. "Name…" he repeated absently.

"Can you remember his name, Mister Wang?" she asked again, her voice a mere whisper.

The other two men watched in silence.

"Name…" Pu Wang said again, and shook his head. Then he suddenly looked up, his dark eyes fixed on the opposite wall, and said, "Ab-bott".

Deke Dunberry recognised the name. "Abbott," he said. "That's Jerome Abbott. I remember him from my time there."

"Ab-bott," Pu Wang repeated softly. Nadia smiled at him and nodded approvingly.

10

The basement of the professor's large house was damp and dimly lit. Simeon Strasberg's heavy shoes created tiny echoes in the narrow passage and on the stone stairs that led down to the cellar. He walked slowly and deliberately, to avoid slipping on the smooth floors.

Upon entering the cellar, he saw Duddo sitting, as usual, at his desk and scribbling notes in a large, leather-bound book. Duddo, who was the gatekeeper at the manor house, always tried to look busy when the professor was around – he found it was better for his own health and wellbeing to keep to his duties and to avoid asking questions.

The professor was a little more cheerful than usual that day. "How is our patient doing, Duddo?"

Duddo sighed and shook his head slowly: "He's none too happy, Mister Professor," Duddo said, watching the professor's expression closely.

The professor stopped. His grin disappeared, and his eyes locked on to Duddo. The metal-rimmed spectacles framed the Professor's inquisitive grey eyes. "How so?"

"He's been getting his food regular-like. Just like you ordered, Mister Professor," Duddo said defensively.

"What ails him?" the professor said, slowing his words. The nervous Duddo could see the old man's pale tongue flick out as he spoke, and an involuntary shiver ran down his spine.

"He's unhappy. Says we're keeping him prisoner, Mister Professor," Duddo replied quickly.

"And you have been feeding him the mushrooms?"

Duddo nodded furiously. "Just like you said, Mister Professor."

"Open up," the professor said sharply, nodding his head towards the door. Duddo obeyed almost instantly, his porky fingers fumbling with the key before managing to guide it into the lock.

Moments later, the heavy door swung open. Fryman Sellers lay motionless on the stone floor.

"Get him up!" the professor commanded, and this time he sounded angry.

Duddo almost stumbled in his haste to get to the man on the floor. He grabbed Fryman by the arm and attempted to lift him off the floor, but the man proved to be heavier than he anticipated. Duddo renewed his grip, and grabbed Fryman's collar with his other hand.

As he bent forward, Fryman suddenly appeared very alive. His hand shot out and he grabbed Duddo by the throat. His other hand grabbed one of Duddo's lapels, and Fryman quickly pulled himself to his feet – his eyes wild and foamy spittle flying out of his mouth.

The grip on Duddo's throat was like steel. Duddo's face turned red and his mouth opened, but the only sounds that came out were groans and a gasp for air. But then Duddo pushed back. He drove Fryman up against the opposite wall. Fryman's head hit the wall with a dull thud and he seemed disorientated for a moment. Duddo head moved forward, and his forehead connected with the bridge of Fryman's nose with such violence that blood sprayed across the wall, and Fryman crumbled into a heap at Duddo's feet.

"Well, there it is, Mister Professor," said Duddo apologetically.

"I did not doubt you for a moment, Duddo," the professor said. "Now if you'd be so kind – I would very much like to examine him in the laboratory. From the looks of it, an anaesthetic won't be necessary."

Duddo nodded and, grunting under the weight, lifted

Fryman's limp body and carried it out of the room.

When Fryman opened his eyes a few minutes later, he was strapped to the examination table. Blood was still dripping from his nose and congealed blood stained the front of his shirt. His arms were strapped down individually, and his feet bound to a metal bar at the foot end of the examination table. He looked up and saw the professor standing over him, the lizard-like eyes staring at him and watching the detail of every movement.

Fryman opened his mouth and tried to speak. His mouth was dry and his voice indistinct.

"Pardon?" the professor said.

Fryman tried again, and this time the words were audible: "Kill me," he said. "Kill me now."

The professor didn't reply immediately, but instead watched Fryman curiously for a few moments, before responding. "Don't be silly. I need you very much alive."

"Why are you doing this?" Fryman said, his voice hoarse and sounding as if he was nearly at breaking point.

"It's a small price to pay, Mister Sellers," the professor said. "If this experiment works – as I know it will – you will be famous. You will usher in a whole new world, Mister Sellers. No longer will humans merely survive. We will rise up like giants, like gods." He grinned broadly, and a light of triumph shone in his eyes.

"You are completely mad!" Fryman shouted, straining against the straps that held him down. "You are a madman!"

The professor looked up towards the open door, and called out to Duddo in the adjoining room: "Duddo, I shall need your help!"

Moments later, the dutiful Duddo entered the room and took his place beside the examination table. He looked down at the writhing Fryman and shook his head almost sorrowfully.

"Now Duddo, I shall need you to hold his head. Hold it very still," said the professor.

Upon hearing this, Fryman let out a deep guttural noise; a growl. He arched his back and pulled and tugged violently against his restraints. Then he screamed. "Why? What do you want from me?"

"Want from you?" said the professor, looking curiously at his patient. "Why, all I want from you, Mister Sellers, is your compliance."

Fryman sobbed as Duddo grabbed his head in his meaty hands and then applied pressure to keep it in place.

The professor lifted a glass jar containing a clear liquid up to Fryman's face: "This, Mister Sellers, is what men have been dreaming about. In the past, men have felt its effects, but they have paid the supreme price. You, on the other hand, will survive. You are indeed fortunate..."

The professor attached a narrow rubber tube to a small, cylindrical glass instrument, in which he created a tiny vacuum to suck up a miniscule amount of the contents of the glass jar. He brought the instrument, with the tube attached, up to Fryman's face. Then he began to feed the tube into Fryman's nostril, and pushed it deep into his nasal cavity.

"What is that? Take it away!" Fryman groaned, but he found himself unable to move, with Duddo's powerful hands keeping his head still.

With the insertion of the tube complete, the professor tapped with his fingernail against the cylindrical instrument: "This substance is much feared in the world, Mister Sellers, but I have managed to tame it. I have brought it under my command." He grinned at his patient, and added, "Just as men of medicine have tamed poisons and turned them into medicines, I have tamed a terrible disease and made it useful..."

"What? What!" Fryman shouted.

"You are about to be infected with rabies."

Fryman's scream echoed around the room.

11

Sheriff Emilio Ducanti arrived in a hansom cab in a busy area of the East End. Jack and Nadia were waiting for him at the entrance to Flower Street; a name that appeared to have been added as a joke, to an area that was anything but fragrant. The squalid street led to run-down tenements at its top end. Jobless men smoked on their doorsteps, and unwashed children poked sticks at lumps of rubbish in the street, while a scrawny dog, its ribs clearly showing, tried to nap on the broken, grey pavestones that led to a dilapidated building on the corner.

Ducanti stepped out of the cab, his nose twitching in response to the smell of putrefaction that hung in the air. He nodded briefly in Nadia's direction, and then said to Jack, "I sincerely hope your suspicions about Mister Abbott are not misplaced, Mister Lightfoot. The police have better things to do than chase ghosts."

"It's a process of elimination, Sheriff," explained Jack as they walked. "My associate and I believe there was considerable collusion within the prison that set the unfortunate events in motion."

"It is easy to make accusations, Mister Lightfoot, but quite another matter to provide proof," said Ducanti, as he quickened his step. He clearly wanted to make his visit to the area a short one.

Jack too, walked faster to keep pace, while Nadia trailed slightly behind.

"We believe, sir, that internal collaboration was a necessary factor in securing the escape of the prisoner—"

"Which building is it?" Ducanti cut him short.

"This one..." Jack said, pointing at an utterly charmless grey building, with narrow windows and a dark interior. Its plasterwork had been eaten away by years of neglect, and the building stood cheek-by-jowl with other, similarly neglected structures.

Jack pushed open a heavy wooden door, which was scarred and splintered in places. The door's timber was raw, unvarnished. One of its hinges hung slack, and the bottom of the door scraped against the floor as it slowly opened.

Creaking, wooden steps led to a mezzanine, out of which flowed a dark passage illuminated by a sliver of sunlight on the far wall. They found three closed doors, the last one marked with the number four, in scrawled paint.

Jack stopped in front of the door. "According to our sources," he said in a hushed voice, "Mister Abbott is a lodger here, or at least, has been in the last month. He has been seen in this vicinity two days ago."

Ducanti stepped up close to the door, and banged loudly on it with his fist. When there was no immediate response, he called out in a loud authoritative voice. "Mister Abbott! Open this door at once. This is the Metropolitan Police!"

There was a small noise at the end of the passage – a door closing quietly, so as not to attract unwanted attention – but there was no response at number four, and no hint that anyone was living there. Ducanti shot an accusing look at Jack, and began to beat the door with his fist: "Mister Abbott, I advise you to step out of your quarters forthwith!" he shouted. The door creaked under the impact, but there was still no response.

"Very well," Ducanti said in a tight, determined voice. He twisted the door handle, and to everyone's surprise, it opened, creaking softly as it did.

"Mister Abbott," Ducanti said, much louder this time. "I must insist..." He wandered into a small entrance hall with dirty grey walls and pressed on, walking slowly and carefully, towards the door at the far end. Jack followed in his footsteps and Nadia trailed behind. She appeared to take careful note of her surroundings – a crooked nail hammered into the wall by an angry person, brown smears, and scratch marks – none of it fresh.

The next doorway led them into a small lounge, and that's where they found Abbott, hanging by his neck from a ceiling beam. His body was completely still and had, by the looks of things, been hanging in that position for some time. The dead man was barefoot, and was wearing the pants belonging to his prison uniform, and a threadbare shirt.

A lazy fly buzzed around in the room, breaking the uncomfortable silence. The rope around Abbot's neck appeared well used and grimy. The other end of the rope was firmly tied around a pipe, which fed water to the kitchen. A wooden dining chair, its seat sunken from years of use, lay on its side on the floor near the dead man.

"Well, it appears guilt got the better of our friend," Ducanti finally said. He turned towards Jack. "You were right, Mister Lightfoot. There was indeed a plan hatched inside the prison to kill Seamus Prenter, and one presumes, to dispose of the body. I expect this suicide is sufficient evidence that our deceased friend here is guilty as charged."

Nadia stepped closer to the hung man, and then turned her attention to the chair on the floor. Ducanti looked at her curiously. "Anything the matter, madam?"

"I doubt this man committed suicide, sir," Nadia said quietly, and glanced briefly at Ducanti.

"I beg your pardon?" Ducanti said, and he appeared mildly irritated.

Nadia pointed at the section of rope that extended to the ceiling beam. "Look how high he's hanging," she said.

"What nonsense," said Ducanti. He snapped the chair up from the floor and moved it into the position where it would have been at the time of the suicide: "He would have used this chair to stand on when—" Ducanti stopped. There was a gap between the soles of the man's feet and the seat of the chair.

"He was strung up..." Jack said slowly.

Without a word, Ducanti picked up a kitchen knife and cut through the rope that held Abbott's body aloft, then he slowly lowered it to the floor. The body lay awkwardly on its side, until Jack Lightfoot pushed it into a face-up position, unseeing eyes staring at the ceiling. Abbott's body was already beginning to give off an unpleasant odour, and Jack pulled himself back, unwilling to touch the dead man.

Nadia bent down to take a closer look at the body, particularly the dead man's hands and throat. "Scratch marks," she said absently. "He was trying to get the rope off his neck."

She gently pushed the face to one side, revealing a bruise on the man's left cheekbone. Ducanti spotted it and did some sleuthing of his own: "He was fighting someone off. That was a powerful blow to the face," he said.

"Sheriff," said Nadia after carefully watching the reaction on Ducanti's face. "We have reason to believe the garrotter had a part in this…"

Her words hung in the silent air for a few moments, before Ducanti responded with a nod.

"We will need to carry on this investigation," he said.

———•———

It took another half hour for the other members of Ducanti's police unit to arrive at the murder scene. He left instructions for the body to be taken to the morgue, and to be locked away securely, and then invited Jack and Nadia to share his cab back to the Metropolitan Police headquarters.

Once they were on their way, he leaned forward and spoke above the rattling noise of the hansom cab. "I should like to hear more about your theories, Mister Lightfoot. It appears you and your associate have uncovered a few surprising clues during your investigation. Perhaps the warden was right about you, after all."

"Why, thank you Sheriff," Jack replied with a relieved smile.

"Perhaps Mister Lightfoot has mentioned to you already, Sheriff – that we believe it is unlikely the trail will end with the garrotter," said Nadia.

"Whatever do you mean, madam?" said Ducanti, sounding slightly surprised.

Nadia carefully opened a small chamois bag and withdrew the thick strip of raw leather that was marked by the garrotting machine's wires. She handed it to Ducanti, who peered at it curiously.

"I found this in the garrotter's room," she said, watching for a response from Ducanti. "The marks on it match the thickness of the wire on the garrotting machine. Mister Lightfoot and I suspect that it may have been used to... garrotte a man, without killing him."

Ducanti was still puzzled. "And what would be the point of that?"

"If one wanted a condemned man to walk free... then it would make sense," said Nadia.

"So the garrotter saves one man from the garrotte but then comes back to kill Jerome Abbott afterwards?"

"We believe Jerome Abbott was his accomplice, sir, and we can only assume that Abbott was not a trusted person, and so he was killed to ensure he would not speak about the crime to others."

"You are implying, Miss Barossa, that the execution that I attended – that I had witnessed with my own eyes – was a ruse. And that the condemned prisoner, Fryman Sellers, was aided in his escape?"

Nadia and Jack nodded simultaneously.

Ducanti was putting the pieces together: "...And that the missing man, Seamus Prenter, was a substitute."

"Exactly, sir," Jack said.

Ducanti mulled it over in silence, before he spoke to Nadia. "You have either entirely lost your mind, or this is the most extraordinary circumstances I have ever encountered. We shall need to question the garrotter at once."

"We fear he may not be... entirely cooperative, Sheriff," said Jack hesitantly.

"By God, I'll have him tell us what we need to know and more," said Ducanti angrily. "The utter brazenness – putting on a fake execution – in my presence."

"Sir," said Nadia quietly, "It seems to us the garrotter would not have had the... capacity for planning such a crime."

"Well, he's—" Ducanti paused for a moment. "Are you suggesting someone else was behind this?"

"It seems logical," Jack said.

"But who? Who would contemplate such evil?"

"That is unknown, sir," said Nadia, "however, if you'll permit this, we would welcome the opportunity to ask some questions," Nadia said.

"Investigate it further," Jack added.

"So you suspect someone?" Ducanti said, almost hopefully.

"No, sir," Nadia said. "However, there are one or two unanswered questions."

"Which are?"

"According to the list we obtained from the Warden, Dame Lafroste was present at the execution – and she was also Fryman Sellers's accuser," said Nadia.

Ducanti grinned. "Come now Miss Barossa. Surely you don't—" He straightened up and spoke sternly. "Dame Lafroste had every right to witness the execution of the man who had done her wrong."

"She had the right, sir, but why would she?" said Nadia.

"The Lafroste family has contributed much to this city; to the poor. I will not allow an honourable family's name to be tainted, simply because you have run out of ideas," said Ducanti sharply.

"Our intention is not to accuse anyone, sir – merely to ask one or two questions."

"Don't you see?" said Ducanti. "Don't you see what it implies?"

"It might provide a valuable lead, and—" Jack began.

But Ducanti cut him short. "I will not allow this – not any of it. If you wish to remain in the temporary employ of the Metropolitan Police, then I suggest you discard your misplaced ideas and come up with a worthy suspect. And if you dare approach Dame Lafroste about this, I shall make it my personal business to see to it that you will not investigate as much as petty theft in this city in future."

The hansom cab slowed as it approached the Metropolitan Police headquarters. Ducanti impatiently slid the window down and shouted at the driver. "Stop here!"

The carriage stopped near the street corner, and Ducanti turned to Jack and Nadia. "I shall expect results from your investigation – results, mind you, not speculation – in exactly one week. If not, I shall have to terminate our little arrangement."

He opened the door of the cab to let them out.

"Good day, detectives."

12

When Professor Simeon Strasberg reached the front door of the large, Gothic-styled house at the north-east end of the city, he was met at the door by an unusually excited Lucian Baker.

"My dear Simeon. Come in, come in," said Lucian, his eyes shining. "A most auspicious occasion. Exciting. Invigorating, by god..." He hurriedly ushered Simeon inside, and closed the large, black door behind them.

Inside the house, the lighting was dim. A chandelier shone beautifully in the foyer, reflecting soft, diamond-like spots of light throughout the room.

"Let me take your coat," said Lucian, and clumsily assisted the ageing Simeon as he shrugged off his heavy black overcoat. "I sent the servants home," Lucian mumbled. "We should keep this to ourselves, especially now."

"Has Aleister arrived?" the professor asked eagerly.

"I expect him presently," Lucian replied. He seemed slightly out of breath. "I have prepared everything in the drawing room. Right this way."

He led Simeon down the passageway, and then opened an oak-panelled door, which allowed access into a spacious room with a large fireplace and ornate mantelpiece. The room had a table in the centre, which was draped in a black cloth that hung almost to the floor. The paintings on the walls depicted ancient Greek and Roman scenarios, many of them rituals of one sort or another.

A number of ritual objects were arranged on a smaller table, adjacent to the large table in the centre of the room. Some were small, metal figurines, while other objects included bunches of herbs in glass bottles and vials, bone fragments, plumed feathers, an incense burner, and two thick, leather-bound, hand-printed volumes with magical symbols stencilled on to them.

"On loan from the temple," Lucian explained briefly, as they both looked at the array of items on the table.

"Willingly?" Simeon asked with a grin.

Lucian smiled too. "Authorised by an ordained priest named Lucian Baker," he said with a chuckle. "I felt it unnecessary to burden the others with the knowledge of our project."

"Excellent thought," said Simeon, smiling.

"Sherry?" Lucian asked, indicating a decanter with several glasses on a tray near the fireplace.

"Should we?"

"The young magician does not mind," said Lucian, "in fact, he encourages it." He poured two glasses and handed one to Simeon.

"Might I ask... about your relationship with the young Aleister?" asked Simeon. He lifted his glass briefly in the gesture of a toast, and watched Lucian's expression with interest.

"Ah, Simeon, you always were... cautious about my associations," said Lucian, smiling. "Aleister is an ambitious young man. He knew about my... talents, as a chemist, and heard about my association with the *Ordo Templi Orientis*. He is seeking an initiation, you know."

"I have no doubt," Simeon replied.

"So we corresponded for a while, and then met in the Mattertal," Lucian went on. "He's a keen climber. Made an attempt on the *Weisshorn*. I'm not much of a climber anymore; it's more of a common interest, you know."

Simeon nodded and sipped his sherry.

"One thing led to another. I offered him accommodation while he was in Switzerland," said Lucian. "A passionate young man," he added, smiling. "I taught him a thing or two about the rituals. Eventually told him I'd put in a good word for him at the temple – if he was a good student, which he was. Very good."

Simeon smiled at Lucian's comment. "What's this business about being a beast?" he said.

"Little more than a joke," Lucian said, still smiling. "Aleister claims he is devoted to evil. He seeks it out. Learns from it."

"Curious."

"There is a bit of history there," said Lucian. "He attended a preparatory school in Cambridge, run by a certain Reverend Henry d'Arcy Champney. Aleister learned to hate him. Hate him so much that it... elevated him. It made him strong; powerful even. That's how he described it. To him, it followed that hate comes from our dark side, and so that evil must be powerful. That's how he reasoned."

"I understand," said Simeon.

A loud knock on the front door reverberated down the passage, and Lucian excused himself to attend to his new guest, while Simeon remained in the room and waited. He walked around the room and studied the paintings on the wall, which, he noticed on closer inspection, depicted either bloodthirsty or sexual scenes in the background.

Simeon heard voices approaching and the two other men entered the room moments later, Aleister Crowley dressed in a long, flowing garment; a robe as far as Simeon could make out. He greeted Simeon warmly, taking the old man's bony hand into both his hands and holding it there for a few moments.

"Professor Strasberg, I am indeed honoured that you chose me for this, the highest of tasks," said Aleister. He appeared comfortable, even confident in his surroundings, and his smile was casual. An attractive young man, the professor thought.

"Aleister, we are friends here, and colleagues. Please call me Simeon," the professor said.

Lucian placed a medium-sized leather bag on the table, and unhooked the clasp, which allowed the top of the bag to spring open. A white silk cloth covered the rest of the bag's contents.

"Aleister has agreed to bring us some of the ritual items he has acquired," said Lucian, his cheeks pink from the effect of the sherry.

"Egyptian," Aleister said, nodding. "Treasures I have uncovered, and acquired at great cost, on my travels. The thing with the Egyptians is that they are so damned secretive," he said.

"In some cases, it has taken me months to negotiate to buy some of these most rare artefacts."

"We are well aware, Aleister," said Lucian. "Simeon and I have been seeking a rather rare and unusual item, without success. Years of fruitless searching..." Lucian paused when he noticed the professor's expression, which cautioned him to silence.

"Well, I am intrigued," Aleister said. "If I can be of service in any way—"

"I appreciate the sentiment, Aleister," Simeon said, "however, even your vast knowledge, and your... secretive network, may not be able to assist us in this."

Lucian nodded slowly in agreement.

Aleister smiled mysteriously and removed the silk cloth which covered the contents of the leather bag. He then dipped his hand into the bag and a moment later, extracted a thin wooden box with ink markings on it. The box had darkened with age and had a tiny golden clasp that kept the lid securely shut. Aleister snapped the clasp open and slowly, reverently, revealed the contents – an oblong, black stone amulet with rounded edges. It glimmered in the yellowed light of the room.

"Gentlemen, you are looking at the private, and most intimate, property of the most famous member of the Ptolemaic dynasty, the ruler of Egypt; Cleopatra." He paused for dramatic effect, and then continued. "It has been revealed that the queen of Egypt used this item for her most intimate pleasure. It is not only a rare object of ritual, but carries within it the power of the gods of Egypt."

Aleister lifted the wooden box and held it closer, so that Simeon and Lucian could inspect it more closely. They were awestruck and Lucian, in particular, was unable to avert his gaze.

"Cleopatra used it to—?" Lucian began to say.

Aleister nodded: "A lady of notable passion, so I am told."

"She would have been diagnosed as suffering an extreme form of hysteria today, and confined in an asylum," Simeon said matter-of-factly.

"Gentlemen, the point is that if my... associates can obtain an item so rare, then surely they stand a better-than-average chance of locating other rare items, such as the one you seek."

"It's called the *Book of Transmutation*," Lucian blurted out.

"Lucian," Simeon said sternly, "we agreed—"

"We may finally have an opportunity to locate it. Years of searching, and we have absolutely nothing," Lucian said, his voice urgent, almost pleading.

"I promise to treat this with the utmost discretion," said Aleister, "Permit me to help. Please."

The professor shook his head. "Too risky. I feel it is too risky. We have leads... and this may destroy our only chance."

"My associates know the value of discretion. A whisper into the right ear can bring surprising results. All it takes is patience, gentlemen."

"And money," Simeon added. "One whiff that we are looking, will send prices skywards."

"So you were expecting to obtain this artefact... gratis?" Aleister said, his eyebrows raised.

"Of course not," said the professor, "but not at a vastly inflated figure, either."

Aleister passed for a moment before speaking. "All I can offer is to help you locate the *Book of Transmutation*. If I am successful, the negotiation to arrive at a suitable price will be up to you."

"What about your price, Mister Crowley?" said Simeon, a suspicious tone lingering in his voice.

"I can safely predict what Aleister may expect in return," said Lucian, and smiled when he noticed that Aleister was nodding lightly. "He has been rather enthused about being initiated into the *Ordo Templi Orientis*..."

A quiet knock on the door interrupted the conversation. Lucian glanced at Simeon, who nodded a confirmation, and then he moved briskly to the door to open it.

"Your... assistant," Lucian announced flatly, and opened the door wider.

The professor's henchman, Riley, stood large in the doorway and smiled awkwardly, a metal glint showing between his front teeth. "I wish you gentlemen a good evening," he said. "I brought the lady to the backstairs hall, just like you said, professor."

"Well done, Riley," said Simeon. "Why don't you bring her upstairs? Do we have your permission, Lucian?"

Lucian, who appeared to snap out of a daydream, responded. "Of course, my good man. By all means."

Riley nodded and, with one last look at the three men before him, turned and again took to the stairs. A few minutes later, he reappeared, carrying an unconscious woman wrapped in a large sheet of linen. He laid her limp body gently down on the table, and then stepped back, awaiting further instructions from the professor.

The professor lifted the sheet off the woman's face. It was Phyllis Secombe. She moaned lightly and moved her head, but seemed in a state of trance. The professor prised open her left eye. The pupil appeared dilated.

"Not long now. She will slowly gain awareness," Simeon said. He removed the sheet, gradually exposing more of Phyllis's sleeping form. She was naked, and her cleavage was moist with sweat.

Aleister took a closer look at the sleeping woman, and nodded approvingly.

"Light the candles," he instructed Lucian. "We must prepare the altar."

Lucian acted without hesitation, and lit two large candles on either side of the table, then placed ritualistic objects on the corners of the table; an Egyptian ankh symbol, a curled snake made of an unidentifiable dull metal, and two tiny figurines, symbolising the male and female sexes.

"I shall request all people not directly involved in the ritual to leave the room," he said, looking directly at Riley.

Riley didn't respond until the professor nodded at him. Then he left the room wordlessly, and closed the door behind him.

Aleister removed his jacket and draped it over one of the chairs, and then casually sat down and took off his shoes and socks. His trousers soon followed, and then his white cotton shirt. When he stood up, he was dressed only in his drawers and undervest. He ignored the professor's stare, rummaged in the leather bag, and moments later produced a neatly folded, brightly-coloured tunic. Parts of the tunic were made of silk, and were richly embroidered.

He revealed the elaborate designs as he unfolded the tunic – a detailed image of a peacock, a black cat, a animal that appeared wolf-like, and several strangely-shaped symbols.

"My god, Aleister. It's wondrous," said Lucian.

"It's from India. The man who made this is now dead. His fingers cut off because thieves found it too troublesome to remove his rings in the usual way," said Aleister.

"Dear god," Lucian whispered.

Without ceremony, Aleister removed his undershirt and drawers and, for a moment, stood naked in front of the other two men. He then slipped on the tunic, which was so long that the hem almost reached the floor. He reached into the leather bag once more, and took out a hat, triangular in shape but folded flat, which he unfolded and then carefully positioned on his head. On the front of it the image of an eye was embossed and below it the image of a snake; a cobra, which appeared ready to strike.

Phyllis, still motionless on the table, groaned lightly. The professor glanced at her, and then back at Aleister, awaiting his response.

"The hour is upon us," said Aleister, his voice carrying a dramatic tone. "Prepare the subject."

"The sub... her?" Lucian said, pointing at Phyllis. Aleister nodded.

Lucian fussed over the naked woman, positioning her arms across her chest, with the flat of her palms over her breasts, so that her nipples were covered by them. He straightened her legs, to align them with her body, then tried to move her feet so they appeared to be pointing upwards in the same direction. He stopped fussing when Aleister approached.

Aleister gently moved the hair out of her face, and then placed his hand on her belly, which moved rhythmically as she breathed. Phyllis still appeared to be in a deep sleep.

"Part her legs," said Aleister, beginning a rubbing motion on Phyllis's belly.

"Part... legs?" Lucian repeated stupidly, and then hastily moved Phyllis's legs apart, exposing the dark-pinkish labia, which half-opened like the petals of a rose.

Aleister cupped Phyllis's pubis, his middle finger probing. "Let us begin," he said finally, and looked at the other two men. "I shall need at least one assistant for this ritual. An assistant clad only in the air that is around us."

Lucian looked at the professor.

"What will you have me do?" asked Simeon.

"I shall help you where I can, Simeon," said Lucian, and he awkwardly began to remove items of his clothing.

Aleister, in the meantime, moved to the head of the table on which Phyllis lay. He placed a flat hand on her face, feeling her breath against his fingers.

"She is ready," he said in a soft voice. "We must not waste time."

13

Bow-tied, top-hatted gentlemen and elegantly attired ladies alighted from their carriages and automobiles, and were greeted at the door by a dark-suited doorman, who smiled generously while ushering them inside. In the entrance hall, another staff member of the manor house awaited them, and recorded their names in a visitor's book. This information, copied on to a separate sheet, was given to a footman, whose task it was to keep the host informed about newly arriving guests.

Jack and Nadia arrived late, and greeted the doorman with a subdued nod. It was not wise for uninvited guests to appear too eager, as Nadia explained to Jack moments before their arrival. There was a small throng in the entrance hall, with some of the guests having their names taken down. Nadia nudged Jack, then grabbed his arm and steered him towards the far wall. There, they slipped through an unlocked side door, and made their way through what appeared to be a servants' passageway to the main reception room.

They were met by the buzzing conversation of a large group in the reception room, and took a moment to gaze at the elaborate chandelier and huge flower arrangements.

"Hat," whispered Nadia urgently as she realised that they had passed by the coat room. When Jack gave her a puzzled look, she said, "Take your hat off." Only then did Jack realise that everyone else in the room had already shed their coats and hats, and he quickly removed his.

"Perhaps I could be of service," a voice behind them said. The tone was menacing, rather than welcoming.

When Jack and Nadia turned around, they saw a man in an ill-fitting black suit. He appeared out of place in the elegant surroundings. His upper body looked large and powerful, much like that of a wrestler, but his shoulders were hunched over, as if they were carrying a heavy weight. It was Riley.

"Well that's very kind of you," said Nadia. "We seemed to have missed the cloakroom."

Riley grinned, showing his yellowed teeth. "Right this way."

He turned and nonchalantly walked on, and Jack and Nadia meekly followed him.

"Here we are, then," Riley announced as they reached the cloakroom counter, where a young girl with blonde hair smiled pleasantly at them. "The boss... the host likes to be informed about all new guests arriving," said Riley, with a less-pleasant smile. "He don't like to miss out on meeting important people personally."

"There is really no need to worry... the host," Nadia started, feeling awkward that she couldn't recall the host's name.

"I'm Jack Lightfoot," announced Jack jovially, "and this is my valued assistant, Nadia Barossa."

Riley watched them suspiciously for a moment, and then slowly nodded. "I'll be sure to inform Professor Strasberg," he said.

"Jolly good," said Jack, and then paused: "Say, is that Professor Simeon Strasberg?"

"Of course it is, Jack... Mister Lightfoot. It was printed on the invitation, remember?" said Nadia quickly, hoping that the strange man would not ask them to produce an invitation.

"It is him," said Riley. He now appeared less suspicious and more confused.

"I read much of his work," said Jack, unperturbed. "Fascinating theories—" He stopped abruptly, when he noticed Nadia's glare.

"I'll be sure to inform—" Riley began, but Jack cut him short.

"My card," said Jack, and handed Riley an embossed card with the words 'Jack Lightfoot, Inventor, 10 Whistler Street, South End' printed in bold font. Nadia wanted to stop him, but it was too late. Riley stared at the card for a few moments, reading it slowly. Then he simply nodded and walked off.

"Jack, we were meant to be incognito," Nadia reminded him.

"But it is Professor Simeon Strasberg. I met him, briefly, in Vienna. The man's a genius of science," said Jack.

Nadia leaned in closer, and spoke close to Jack's ear: "We are here to investigate Dame Lafroste, and for the moment we don't know the association between her and—"

"Surely you are not suggesting that Professor Strasberg... Do you really?"

"We don't know, Jack," Nadia said impatiently. "And we won't find out by drawing attention to ourselves..." Nadia suddenly stopped, and then said, "There he is."

"Professor Strasberg?"

Nadia flinched at Jack's loud question. "No," she said. "Lord Faderley. Word is that Dame Lafroste and her husband have a close and cordial relationship with him."

Jack turned and saw an elderly man, dressed formally, with his white-grey hair exquisitely parted and his large moustache waxed to fine points. On his chest he bore a family medallion, encrusted with fine jewels.

Lord Faderley excused himself from a small group and casually insinuated himself into another conversation, this time with a woman whom Nadia recognised instantly; Dame Lafroste. She saw Dame Lafroste smile and touch Lord Faderley's hand warmly as the two met.

"Well, if Lord Faderley is—" Jack began to say, but he stopped when he noticed Nadia was no longer at his side. She was already moving in Margaret Lafroste's direction, lightly apologising as she deftly squeezed past two men who were reminiscing about their service in the Crimean War.

Once she was within earshot, Nadia could overhear snippets of the conversation between Margaret Lafroste and Edmund Faderley.

"...A mere shadow of his former self," Margaret Lafroste was saying. "I fear that he may no longer..." she paused, her voice faltering.

"Dear Lady," she heard Lord Faderley's sympathetic voice. "We have no choice but to submit to sound medical advice. Allow me to speak to Reginald. The man's very life is at stake."

Margaret Lafroste nodded, and dabbed her nose with a small lace handkerchief.

"He is stubborn," she said finally, "...in the extreme. But perhaps I could ask you to..."

Nadia strained her ears, but Margaret Lafroste's words were suddenly interrupted by a louder female voice. "Mister Lightfoot! How delightful," the voice chirped. "I simply had no idea you would be here!"

Nadia recognised the voice. It was Helen Gartner, Jack's private client.

Nadia turned and noticed that Helen was moving closer, until she was nearly within reach of him. She wore an elegant gown, and proudly displayed a jewelled tiara, and silver necklace set with diamonds. She was strikingly beautiful.

Jack put on his most charming smile. "Lady Gartner," he said. "A surprise indeed." He dipped his head, lifted her gloved hand and brushed it against his lips.

Helen Gartner was, however, eyeing Nadia instead. "You saw it fit to bring your assistant to this event, Mister Lightfoot. Is that common practice in your profession? I find it a bit unusual; irregular even." Helen was clearly seldom at a loss for words.

"I... my assistant and I were hoping to speak to Professor Strasberg on matters of scientific inquiry, my lady," said Jack.

"Poor thing," Helen Gartner replied with a good dose of scepticism in her voice. "Work, work. You do nothing but work."

Margaret Lafroste had turned around when she overheard the mention of Professor Strasberg's name. She looked at Jack curiously, and said, "Pardon me for being so rude, sir, but are you a friend of Professor Strasberg?"

"Jack Lightfoot at your service, madam," said Jack with a smile, but then he added awkwardly: "I saw the Professor in Vienna, once. That's where we met."

"A doctor of medicine, then?" she inquired.

"Regrettably not, madam," replied Jack. "But science, yes. I am an inventor."

"How charming," said Margaret Lafroste, although she appeared less than charmed. It was clear she did not hold inventors in the same high regard as men of medicine.

"A particularly... inventive inventor," Helen Gartner chipped in. "I can vouch for it." She smiled fondly at Jack and touched his sleeve, shooting a brusque glance in Nadia's direction.

Nadia studied Margaret Lafroste's face for a few moments, and found it difficult to look away. The older woman had stern lines around her lips, and she squinted, so Nadia guessed that she was probably short-sighted. Her dress was immaculate; dove-grey with a frilled collar, and conservatively cut, but made of the finest materials. She was clearly flaunting her wealth and influence.

"And this must be your charming wife," said Margaret Lafroste suddenly, and smiled coldly at Nadia.

"My associate, Nadia Barossa," said Jack, his lip developing a strange twitch.

"How odd that Professor Strasberg has never made mention of you," said Dame Lafroste with a glint of suspicion in her eyes.

Jack shifted uncomfortably on his feet.

"Thanks for your gracious welcome, Dame Lafroste," said Nadia, trying her most charming smile. She received a lukewarm nod of the head in return, and felt Margaret's eyes fixing on her as a snake might eye its prey.

At that same moment, a door opened at the far end of the room, and Simeon Strasberg entered, with Riley close at his side. Riley whispered something, and pointed at Jack and Nadia. The professor gave the briefest of nods, and moved through the assembled crowd, stopping here and there to exchange pleasantries with guests.

"We should probably be on our way," said Jack, who was feeling more uncomfortable by the minute, especially when Helen Gartner clutched his arm, and insisted on holding on to it.

"Nonsense," said Dame Lafroste, sensing his dread. "We must have champagne."

As if he was acting on a command, a servant appeared moments later, carrying a tray of champagne glasses. Dame Lafroste relinquished her half-empty glass and picked a fresh one off the tray, then waited for the others to follow her example. Jack reluctantly took a glass, and felt the strong urge to drink it down in one gulp. Nadia too, stepped forward and gently picked a glass of champagne off the tray.

"Oh, look," Margaret Lafroste said in musical tones. "Our host."

Simeon Strasberg slowly made his way through the chattering group of people. As he approached, his polite smile widened into a grin. Nadia noticed that the old man's hair was almost pure white and very fine, like single strands of silk that shimmered in the light. His sunken cheeks gave his face a skull-like appearance, and the grin made him look forbidding, rather than friendly.

When he finally joined their small group, Margaret Lafroste spoke loudly. "I take it you know Mister Lightfoot? He seemed eager to meet you, Simeon."

Strasberg nodded slowly. "Mister Lightfoot." His voice was soft, almost too soft, and Jack barely recognised his own name.

"It's an honour, Professor," said Jack, extending his hand towards the old man.

The professor didn't shake his hand, but instead, stopped with his face mere inches away from Jack's. Jack caught the odour of chemicals on the professor's coat, and his nose wrinkled involuntarily.

"Jack Lightfoot. I know that name," the professor said. "I shall have to include it on my guest list in future," he added with a sly smile. "Tell me, Jack, what do you know about alchemy?"

At first, Jack didn't know if he heard the professor correctly. "Alchemy? Nothing but myth and legend, professor."

"Alchemy is transmutation, Jack. And I will soon possess the keys to transmutate life itself," Simeon said, and looked meaningfully at Margaret Lafroste. "Why trifle with machines, when we can change flesh and blood, eh?"

"I am... not sure I understand, sir," said Jack.

"Ah, you will," said Simeon. "You will."

14

Rose Blassington made her way from Thrawl Street, where she lived, along a dirty and cluttered footpath to Chesterton Lane, where many of the area's prostitutes plied their trade. It was later than usual for her, but Rose was feeling feverish and light-headed, and unsteady on her feet at times. She had been feeling ill for two days. Still, if there was any chance of finding a client, it was worth her while venturing out in the cold.

Sounds of a drunken brawl came from a nearby building, and yet the street was quieter than usual, with most of Rose's typical clients having already found what they were looking for. Rose walked to the corner of a narrow laneway, one that led to a rat-infested tenement, and paused when she heard someone approaching. Even in the dim light, she could tell that it was a man. He walked slowly, and had a heavy footfall. Perhaps a drunkard, Rose thought, but maybe a client.

He wore a cap that was pulled down over his eyes, and he slowed further when he spotted her. Rose thought it strange that his arms appeared to hang loosely at his sides, and she noticed that the man had an unusual gait, and that he swayed slightly from side to side.

"Evenin' lover," Rose said boldly. There was no time for shyness when looking for a client. "Looks like you could do with a bit o' cheering up." She tried to smile, but was overtaken by a coughing fit.

The man stepped closer, and Rose heard the wheezing noises that he made, as if he had trouble breathing. She was about to unbutton the top of her blouse, when a sudden chill down her spine caused her to pause. Perhaps it was not worth the risk, she thought.

Before she could retreat, the man lunged forward, grabbed her neck and thrust her sideways and up against the nearest wall. Rose's head bumped hard against the brickwork, and she felt the dizziness of the blow clouding her mind. A large, calloused hand squeezed her throat and she was unable to breathe or to cry out.

His other hand ripped the front of her blouse and bodice wide open, and his claw-like nails left deep scratches on her skin. The man grunted like an animal, and his grip continued to tighten around her throat. A moment later, his face was near hers, and she could smell his fetid breath.

Rose felt weak but fought back, scratching at the man's arms, and trying to reach his eyes. Again her head banged against the brick wall, and for a moment it felt as if her lights were going out. Rose resisted, and tried to kick out at her assailant, but it had no effect on him.

She heard the material of her dress stretch and break as a demented hand ripped it wide open. He let go of her throat and forced her to the ground. Rose sunk to her knees and then fell over, landing on her back on the fractured pavestones that lined the laneway. A moment later, the man was on top of her. Her lacy undergarments were ripped apart, exposing her defenceless body to the onslaught.

Rose briefly lifted her head and, in hazy vision, saw that the man was half-naked, his male organ an angry red, and engorged with so much blood that it seemed grotesquely enlarged; more animal-like than human. His grunting and salivating too, made her think of a large animal – an angry bear or wolf – ready to devour its prey.

He entered her with a force that she had never imagined possible. Rose tried to scream but her voice disappeared in the night air, drowned out by the man's growling noises and the incoherent words that he loudly mumbled.

His nails clawed at her breasts, and left a deep gash just below her rib cage. He thrust into her, again and again, with such frenzy that her entire body slid backwards, towards the wall. As the man's frenzy reached a peak, his fingers pressed into her side, and dug into her flesh, widening the gash. His fingers reached inside her, touching her innards as if he was searching for something. He clawed and pulled, viscous matter clinging to his fingers.

As the man's orgasm overtook him, he wailed and his back arched, pulling his head backwards. Spit flew from his mouth as he howled at the top of his voice. Beneath him, Rose lay quite still. She had lost consciousness, and the wound in her side was bleeding profusely.

The man pulled out of her and crawled away clumsily, deep growling sounds still audible.

A man carrying a lantern appeared at the street corner, and ran to the spot where Rose lay bleeding. He lifted the lantern and caught sight of the crawling rapist, who had lost some of his momentum and was slowing down.

Riley carried his lantern towards the crawling man. "You've been a very naughty boy."

He heard footsteps behind him and turned. It was Duddo, the gatekeeper at the manor house.

"I found him," said Riley. "Looks like he killed a whore."

But Rose was not dead. She groaned and tried to lift her head, but lacked the strength. Her head sagged back, and her vision turned misty grey.

Duddo carried with him a chain, which had what looked like a dog collar at one end. He stepped closer to the man who was still on all fours. As Riley held the lantern close, he saw the man's feverish eyes, and the foaminess around his lips. It was Fryman Sellers, but he appeared to be transformed from a man into a half-beast.

Fryman's hair was sparse, most of it plucked out with his own hands. His breathing was deep and rasping, and his face ravaged by pain. His eyes were wild, like a cornered animal.

Riley took a small club out of his coat pocket. He held it up in the lantern light, so that Fryman could see it.

"Bite me again and you'll wish you was dead," said Riley. He then slipped the collar around Fryman's throat and tightened it. Fryman did not resist. He looked exhausted, defeated.

"We're taking you home," said Riley.

Rose too, heard those words, but a moment later her consciousness shut down, and her world faded into blackness.

She didn't see the arrival of another figure, a tall gaunt man wearing a top hat. Simeon Strasberg bent down near Rose's motionless body. He noticed the scratch marks on her, and studied the wound in her side, where Fryman's hand had clawed its way inside her.

He gently prised Rose's legs apart, and saw a surprisingly large quantity of semen, mixed with her own blood, oozing from her vagina. Simeon studied every detail intently, filing the information away.

Then he took a small glass jar from his coat pocket and placed it on the footpath. He carefully withdrew a surgical knife from an inner pocket and, after pausing to consider where to make the first cut, he went to work.

15

A line of burly, unwashed men stood quietly in the anteroom, their faces emotionless and lined from years of disappointment and regret. Some wore prison garb – roughly-stitched, dull grey uniforms with black-numbered labels sewn on the front – others were simply dressed in whatever rags were available.

A prison guard opened the door and shouted, "Next!" The shouting was unnecessary, as the room was not large, but it was a prison method, a tradition almost, to shout commands, especially since some of the older prisoners tended to be hard of hearing.

The next man entered through the door into the adjoining room, which had a large timber table positioned near the centre. Behind it sat Jack Lightfoot and Nadia Barossa, both with papers and writing implements in front of them.

"Say your name, and sit!" the guard commanded.

The prisoner removed a ragged cap, and revealed a straggly mop of greasy, grey hair. He moved forward two paces, then stopped and said, "Thomas Phillip McGrady, that's me name." He shuffled further forward and sat down in the low-backed wooden chair at the table, opposite Jack and Nadia.

McGrady was a scrawny man, in what looked to be his late-sixties. He looked tough and wiry, and peered suspiciously at Nadia, unused to seeing a woman within the prison walls.

"What is your term, Mister McGrady?" asked Jack, his pen poised, ready to write down the details.

When she saw the confusion on the man's face, Nadia elaborated. "How long are you in for?"

"Gave me twenty years, they did," said McGrady and spat on the floor.

"No spitting!" the guard called out.

"On what charge?" Jack asked.

"What did you do?" translated Nadia.

"Me? I hit the missus. Took her head off with a spade," McGrady replied. He sat back in the chair, watching their reactions. Jack and Nadia didn't flinch. The warden had warned them in advance of the 'unpalatable' tales they could expect to hear from the prisoners.

"Show some respect!" the guard barked, but Jack held out his hand to quiet him.

"How old are you now?" asked Nadia.

"Fifty seven years, me lady," the man said with a grin.

"Mister McGrady, is it correct to say you assisted... volunteered to help a man of medicine to do some... experiments here in the prison?" Jack asked.

"You mean this?" said McGrady gruffly. He pulled up a tattered sleeve and exposed a patch of skin on his inner arm, which appeared discoloured and slightly inflamed.

"How did it happen?" asked Nadia.

"The professor, that's what they called him. He came in here. Said there was a good meal in it for us, and even a good word with the Warden," McGrady said and glanced at the guard. Then he spat again and said, "Horse shit!"

The guard stepped forward and struck McGrady with a short baton. It caught him above the left ear, knocking his head sideways. But McGrady didn't fall out of his chair. Instead, he casually straightened himself up. Blood began flowing from a small wound on his scalp.

"Stop that please," Nadia told the guard sharply. Then she turned to McGrady. "What did they do? What did the professor do to you?"

McGrady again showed her his inner arm. "He cut me flesh," he said. "Then he patched me with some other piece of skin.

Didn't work though. Got infected and all, they said. Looked like a chunk of lard. I ripped it off."

Jack was feeling nauseous, and could not hide his expression of disgust.

"The professor, he didn't like it none," McGrady went on. "Said his... exper-miments didn't work on me."

"Experiments," Jack corrected, before he could stop himself.

"Did it work on some of the others?" Nadia asked.

McGrady paused in thought for a moment, and shrugged. "Some, I reckon."

"Did you know a man called Fryman Sellers?"

McGrady grinned. "Got his comeuppance, that one," he said. "Came in here and said he didn't kill that girl. Everybody knew different."

"What about the experiment?" asked Nadia. "Did it work on him?"

McGrady nodded. "He been lucky. Been the blue-eyed boy, that one," he said.

"So the professor spent more time with him?" asked Nadia.

"He spend all his time, the professor," said McGrady. "Me thought they be married," he added, with a dry chuckle.

The guard edged closer, but Jack held up his hand, stopping him.

"Did you see his arm? The skin on his arm?" Nadia asked.

"Sure," said McGrady. "Smooth as a babe's."

"You didn't like him much, then," said Nadia. It wasn't a question.

"Thought he was better 'n other people," McGrady said. "He 'ad a funny smile – like this." McGrady parodied Fryman, by jutting out his jaw and pulling his mouth into a bizarre grin. "Even when they led him off, he smiled."

"Did he talk about anything? Before he was executed?"

McGrady thought again for a long moment, before he responded. "Said he was goin' to be rich."

"Rich? When he was heading for the garrotting chair?" said Nadia, frowning.

McGrady shrugged, then tapped a dirty finger against his forehead. "Mad as a rat on rum," he said.

Nadia took a muslin cloth parcel from the satchel that hung from her chair, opened it and took out a small pork pie, which she handed to McGrady.

"Thank you, Mister McGrady. You've been most helpful," she said.

McGrady eyed the pie greedily, and snatched it from her hand before the guard had a chance to take a step forward.

"Let him eat it," Jack said to the guard, who looked as if he was about to grab McGrady by the scruff.

McGrady took a large bite of pie and stood up.

"Mister McGrady," said Nadia in afterthought, and McGrady stopped in his tracks. "Why did Fryman Sellers kill that girl? Do you know?"

McGrady cocked his head. "Maybe she just don't listen," he said and grinned.

The guard grabbed his arm and pushed him out of the room, while McGrady hastily finished the rest of his pie.

16

Reginald Lafroste sat up in his bed, propped up by a number of duck-down pillows. His face was pale, and his breathing laboured. Outside his window, the morning fog was slowly dissipating, allowing the sun's rays to break through and to add a little colour to the room. The dark-haired, Hungarian servant girl, Masja, had opened the shutters early, at the insistence of Margaret Lafroste, and then went about her usual duties, which included preparing Reginald's breakfast, a broth that appeared lifeless and insipid in the bowl.

When she brought it to him, Reginald merely shook his head and looked away.

"Mister Lafroste..." the girl implored, but Reginald Lafroste was adamant. He pressed his lips together, refusing even a mouthful.

Masja was flustered, and uncertain about what to do about her employer's refusal to eat. She blushed deeply, and put the bowl down on the bedside table, then fussed with the bed sheets until she could think of nothing else to do. She dreaded having to report her failure to Dame Lafroste, who was frequently in an unhappy mood.

She was about to leave the room when Margaret Lafroste appeared at the door. Masja froze when she saw the look of displeasure on the woman's face. She shook her head in reply to Margaret's unspoken question.

"Leave us now, Masja," the older woman said, and waited until the servant was out of the room before she approached her husband's bed.

Her face was stern, but tired, when she spoke. "This cannot continue."

Reginald Lafroste shook his head slowly. Tears moistened his eyes. His mouth felt dry, and he found it hard to swallow.

"I spoke to Professor Strasberg," said Margaret. "He is willing to help."

Reginald looked up at his wife, pain clearly visible in his eyes.

"If we do nothing, you will die," said Margaret, her voice unsteady despite her resoluteness.

Reginald opened his mouth, but his words came out as a low murmur, hardly audible at all: "We must not..." he started saying.

"I have prayed over this," said Margaret. "We must make the sacrifice so you can live. That is the only way."

Reginald looked away, towards the window.

"You have withered in front of my eyes. This cannot continue. But I shall expect your consent... your blessing," she said.

Reginald lowered his head, as if he was ashamed.

"There is a boy. The butcher's delivery boy," she continued. "He is fine... healthy. Simeon has made a test – and found him suitable." Her eyes grey misty, sorrowful: "It is not easy for me. But what needs to be done, needs to be done."

Reginald shook his head almost imperceptibly. He looked like a beaten man, unable even to lift his arm without assistance.

"Without the boy, your life will be over. You will suffer great pain, greater even than now. And then it will be too late. You will slip away."

When Reginald still did not respond, she urged him. "I shall need your agreement..."

Silence hung heavily in the room as Reginald finally nodded. Tears rolled down his cheeks.

———————

Sheriff Emilio Ducanti bent down to take a closer look at the remains of Rose Blassington. The body lay face-down on the dirty footpath in Chesterton Lane, where it had remained unseen, or ignored, for several hours before someone alerted the police.

When he turned the body over, it revealed a more grisly picture. Rose's clothes were torn open and her lower abdomen had been sliced open with a very sharp knife. Her intestines protruded from a lengthy cut, which extended from one side of her pelvic area to the other. The cut was deliberate and precise, as if it had been done with forethought. The cut also extended downwards, towards her pubic area, and Ducanti's first thought was that it might have been a crime of sexual revenge – but his theory faltered when he noticed that the cuts were not made in anger, but rather with skill.

The black-suited Constable Jacob Wensley stood close by, making a conscious effort to avoid looking directly at the open wound. He was a man in his thirties, with a wife and two children, and he felt queasy to see a woman so flagrantly and brutally violated.

"The urchins would have seen something, surely," mumbled Ducanti as he examined the body. "Ask around..."

"Yes, sir," the constable replied, relieved to get away from the murder scene. Street children, many of them homeless, inhabited the area in great numbers, but they were notoriously difficult to speak to if you were a policeman. Constable Wensley knew this, but he much preferred this task, to tending to a corpse.

Ducanti looked at the murder as an opportunity. For about two years, he had campaigned for a new criminal investigation unit to be set up, headed by him, of course. The commissioner had been reluctant to take up the matter with the ministry, especially since the Metropolitan Police Force was still in its formation phase and was badly in need of additional government funds. A gruesome murder was perhaps just what he needed, to convince the commissioner to change his mind.

When the paddy wagon arrived, Ducanti gave instructions for the corpse to be wrapped in a sheet of canvas, and transferred to St Thomas's Hospital in Southwark, where he wanted a doctor to look at it.

"I shall expect a report from a medical doctor as to the circumstances of the woman's death," he explained to the driver. "Instruct the hospital to keep this matter in the strictest of confidence, and to report back to me directly," he said.

Ducanti knew that a body carried into a hospital in a bloody sheet would alert the attentions of both hospital staff and nosy passers-by. He expected the story to be told to the press in a matter of hours. As such, the commissioner was sure to hear of it.

His thoughts were interrupted by the approaching Constable Wensley, who held a street urchin by the arm and dragged the reluctant boy towards Ducanti.

"I done nothin'!" the boy shouted, pulling violently to try to get away.

"We'll be the judge of that," said Wensley, his grip on the boy's arm tightening. Then he turned his attention to Ducanti: "Found this one snooping about, sir. Taking a keen interest in what was going on here."

Ducanti sighed. The chances that the boy knew anything were slim at best.

"Bring him closer," Ducanti said.

The boy was about eleven, unwashed with caked dirt on his face.

"What were you looking for, boy?" Ducanti asked.

The boy shook his head vehemently, and gave Ducanti a defiant look. Ducanti had seen that look before among the street children of the area. They grew up rough, and it didn't take long for them to become callous.

Ducanti knew that threatening the boy would produce no result, so instead he took a coin out of his pocket and said: "Tuppence if you tell me exactly what you saw. If you lie to me, I'll spread the word around here that you're a snitch." For the first time, he noticed a hint of fear in the boy's eyes.

"It was nothin'," the boy said. He shifted uncomfortably in his oversized shoes.

There was something about him – something about his demeanour – that piqued Ducanti's interest. He turned to the constable. "Constable, this boy is lying. Lock him up... with the murderers. They'll know what to do with him."

Constable Wensley appeared shocked for a moment, but then he stammered, "Yes sir. At once, sir."

"No!" shouted the boy. "I did nothin' wrong!"

"Come with me, grub," the constable growled, struggling to retain his grip on the squirming boy.

Before he could be led away, the boy shouted. "I found something! That's all!"

The constable stopped, allowing Ducanti to step closer. Ducanti saw tears in the boy's eyes. "Found what?" he said sternly.

With a trembling hand, the boy dug into one of his pockets and produced a small lump of clay.

"If you're mocking the police..." Constable Wensley began angrily.

The boy pressed the lump of damp clay with his fingers, breaking it apart. It revealed something shiny inside; a tiny metal pin. He slowly took the pin out, careful not to let it slip out of his fingers, and handed it to Ducanti.

"Where did you find this?" Ducanti asked. He briefly examined the delicate pin.

The boy pointed at the spot where Rose Blassington's body was found.

"Show me exactly where you found it," Ducanti said, and he motioned for Wensley to take the boy closer to where the body lay.

The boy moved forward slowly, reluctant to revisit the scene, and then stopped and pointed at a collection of four cobblestones in the lane. "It was here," he said softly. It was directly next to where the body was found.

"What time?" asked Ducanti.

"I don't know sir, I swear. I can't tell the time," the boy said in a panicky voice.

"Did you see anyone else?"

The boy shook his head: "No-one sir. I swear by God."

Ducanti paused in thought for a moment. "You're coming to the station with us."

The boy protested loudly, until Ducanti spoke. "Quiet! You won't be locked up." Then he turned to Wensley and said, "Get the boy's name. And give him some food."

As Wensley led the boy away, Ducanti took another look at the design on the tiny golden pin. The head of the pin was in the shape of an egg.

17

Few members of the Canterbury Club knew about the existence of the Skull Society, and only those in the inner circle were awarded an invitation. The Skull Society met irregularly, and its exclusive membership comprised lawyers, architects, medical doctors and explorers. Their rather unusual meeting place was in the basement of the Canterbury Club.

The room, a converted wine cellar, fitted out with oak-panelled walls and rich carpeting, had a number of tables and chairs, and some lounge furniture, as well as display cabinets and even a small stage in one corner. No servants were allowed at the meetings, and members had to help themselves at the bar – something they did with enthusiasm.

Discussions, generally held over liberal doses of brandy and through the fog of cigar smoke, centred on controversial aspects of archaeology, fringe anthropology, experimental science and, frequently, the sexual habits of humans and animals. As the meetings were secret, the discussion was free of any rules. The members felt suffocated by the narrow views of society and if there was a binding principle, it was the utter rejection of the primness of Victorian London.

General La Fey, a former military commander and renowned hunter of tigers, loudly shared an anecdote from his days in southern Egypt. "...so before I could gather my wits, the boy had lifted the donkey's tail and was penetrating it with extreme gusto, before my tired eyes," he said, to guffawing laughter from a few men who had been intently following the story.

"Gentlemen! Gentlemen!" A voice interrupted. It was Lucian Baker, and he called for silence by holding up both hands, and waving them at the assembled group. "It is time to welcome our speaker for tonight!" The din in the room died down somewhat. "A man we all know and love," he said, still speaking loudly.

"Let him bend over first!" shouted someone from the audience, again to raucous laughter.

"A rare treat tonight! Please welcome... Professor Simeon Strasberg!" Applause erupted, and Lucian waited for it to subside before he added, "And his topic tonight..." He glanced at a scribbled note on a piece of paper before continuing. "Beast or superior warrior?"

None of the audience members knew what the title meant, but they liked the sound of it. Strasberg took to the small stage under loud applause.

"Gentlemen," he began. "I believe we find ourselves at the frontier of science, and I suspect you shall hear my words, spoken to you here today, echoed around the country, and eventually the world." He paused dramatically, studying the faces of the men assembled in the room, before continuing. "What I am about to tell you is not idle speculation and, no, I have not finally succumbed to senility or frailty of mind. But first, I feel it my duty to introduce you to a former friend and colleague – unfortunately, not in person, as he has been dead for about three years now. His name is Vladimir Kuchinev – a scientist, a pioneer, a fearless researcher and, some would have you believe; a madman."

Here and there, an eyebrow lifted, and smiles appeared on the faces of the audience. They anticipated an entertaining talk.

Simeon Strasberg uncurled a large sheet of paper and affixed it to the nearest wall panel. It was a charcoal-drawn picture of a naked African woman, her figure shaded to accentuate her voluptuous curves, broad hips and full lips. She was the very image of a fertile young woman, ready for childbirth.

"This is a drawing of one of the women used in Vladimir's experiments in Africa. What was the experiment? To make the woman conceive a child – an easy enough task many of you may think..."

Guffaws went up from the audience, but subsided when Simeon continued. "The difference was, that this woman was to be impregnated not by a man – but by an ape."

"To give birth to... what?" A voice in the audience responded, among other sceptical voices.

"That is exactly what my friend Vladimir wanted to ascertain," said Simeon Strasberg. "What if we could get an ape to impregnate a woman, so that the woman could carry an ape baby to full term, and deliver it, just as a human baby would be delivered?"

"At least she'd have a dutiful husband!" bellowed the somewhat drunk General La Fey, attracting a mixture of laughter and further comments.

"What, dear friends, if the baby turned out as strong as an ape, but with the understanding... and obedience of a person of the Negro race?" continued Simeon. "Could we produce a labourer that seldom tires, or perhaps a soldier with the strength of five men? Think of the possibilities, gentlemen!"

"And?" shouted a voice in return. "How many ape babies did she produce?"

"Regrettably, none," said Simeon, his expression turning more serious. "But that does not mean it cannot be done. Just as the flesh of one person is often not accommodated in the body of another, so the seed of one species may not be accommodated in another. However, some persons tend to be more... compatible... or they can be made so, by applying treatments. Vladimir Kuchinev did years of research on the topic."

"What happened to Vladimir whats 'is name?" asked General La Fey drunkenly. "Was he attacked by an enraged baboon?" He laughed loudly at his own joke.

Simeon Strasberg shook his head slowly, and responded in a serious tone. "I expect he died of... disappointment."

There were a few murmurs in the crowd, and then the room settled into relative silence.

"I would like you to know," said Simeon, "that Kuchinev's ideas did not die with him. At this very time, in fact, I am conducting experiments that aim to prove that the impossible is indeed possible. However, I shall not attempt to mate a human with an ape, but rather transplant some of an ape's sexual organs into a human male. Is it possible to combine the characteristics of a human with that of an ape? Is it possible to create a super human being? We shall soon know the truth…"

Simeon was distracted by an excited-looking Lucian, standing at the back of the audience, waving a scrap of paper above his head. When Simeon frowned and hesitated, Lucian beckoned wildly, urging him to leave the stage.

"Excuse me," said Simeon at last. He stepped down from the small stage and pushed his way through the group of assembled men. When he reached the back of the room, he could see that Lucian was not only excited, but elated.

"I've just had word," said Lucian. "The most wonderful news!"

18

The Earl of Whittlecast, Lord Edmund Faderley, kept a fashionable townhouse near Kensington Palace, and agreed to receive Margaret Lafroste for tea at ten o'clock that morning.

A stiff-looking house steward met her at the door and ushered her to the library, where she was served with a small tray of tea and decorative cakes. The Earl arrived a full seven minutes later, hinting that she was a lower priority in his busy schedule. Margaret understood the not-so-subtle language of titled persons, only too well.

"Forgive me, madam," Lord Faderley said upon entering. "Urgent business matters, left unattended, can become such a burden, don't you agree?"

Margaret Lafroste smiled sweetly, and set her cup aside, ready to rise to her feet, but Lord Faderley stopped her with a motion of his hand. "Please madam; there is no need to stand up. Are we not friends?"

"Thank you for seeing me at such short notice, Lord Faderley. I'm aware of the important decisions resting on your shoulders…" Margaret LaFroste said graciously, but leaving the sentence hanging in the air. She extended her hand and he showed her the brief courtesy of touching it, with a nod of his head.

The earl settled into a large leather armchair, looking as if he had enjoyed a good night's sleep. His eyes were bright, and his plump cheeks rosy. His small, feminine hands fluttered briefly, before he spoke. "I find our talks utterly charming, Dame Lafroste. It's been so long."

"I regret such an imposition on your precious time," Margaret Lafroste said, "And I must express my appreciation. You are a gracious, generous man."

The house steward appeared at the door, and wordlessly stood there until Lord Faderley waved him away with a gesture of the hand. "We will require some privacy."

The house steward nodded deeply and left the room, closing the heavy doors behind him.

"And so on to important matters," Faderley said with a smile, and leaned slightly forward. He sensed that Margaret Lafroste did not want to dally.

"Professor Strasberg and I have had discussions and have mutually agreed that to approach you would be a prudent thing to do, given the recent developments," Margaret said.

Lord Faderley's brow wrinkled. "My dear lady, I am entirely at a loss."

"It is about the professor's most recent social engagement – the one to which he invited both of us," she said.

"Ah yes, the dinner party," said Faderley, his face lighting up with the memory. "Utterly charming."

"Unfortunately, the fine event was spoilt by the arrival of uninvited guests," Margaret continued gravely, "A shocking state of affairs, really, as the professor's staff was in attendance to verify that each attendee did indeed have a proper invitation."

"How annoying for the host," Faderley said, nodding his head in empathy. "How did they slip in?"

"The most likely explanation, is that they pretended to be part of the larger group," said Margaret. "Fortunately, their arrival did not go entirely unnoticed. A sharp-eyed member of the professor's staff noticed two persons who seemed... somewhat out of place in the elegant surroundings."

"Really? Terrific!" said Faderley, looking relieved that the matter was resolved.

"But not before they had a chance to indulge in conversations with some of the assembled guests," she said.

"Dear, oh dear," said Faderley. Then he leaned forward with a puzzled frown. "What on earth did these people want?"

"It appears they were looking for information to slander our gracious host or, indeed, his guests," she said with a pained expression. "For all we know, they were also attempting to gather information about some of the most prominent guests – figures that may even have included your Lordship." She did not usually address him as 'Lordship', but felt it necessary under the circumstances.

"What?" Faderley was instantly angered. "This is an outrage."

Margaret nodded: "Most certainly, and something that cannot be tolerated under any circumstances."

"I shall alert the police at once," said Faderley. "Who are these..." For a moment, he searched for the appropriate words, before exploding with "imposters?"

"Why you have seen them. Remember the young man and his female... associate?" said Margaret Lafroste, suddenly less formal. "The woman took a keen interest and..." Margaret glanced over her shoulder for dramatic effect, "...and I think she may have deliberately listened in on our conversation."

"Good Lord," said Faderley, his cheeks turning pale. "Did we say anything... inappropriate?"

"Don't worry Edmund," Margaret replied. "Our conversation was completely... innocuous."

"Thank God," he said, relieved. "But how dare they! I shall get the sheriff to investigate this at once!"

"There is another matter... something troubling that has been uncovered in the meantime," she said.

"But... what can it possibly be?"

"I've made some discreet inquiries. It seems as if the Sheriff himself may be behind this."

Faderley was dumbstruck. He opened his mouth, but any words died in his throat.

Margaret Lafroste relished his reaction. She was ready with the rest of the story: "I hear it has something to do with a purported *mystery* at the prison. Apparently, no crime has actually been recorded. So far it has only been conjecture and innuendo, and I'm rather afraid that the Sheriff may have been taken in by a couple of wholly unscrupulous people – in my mind, people who may want to fleece the Crown by way of the Metropolitan Police."

Faderley straightened up in his chair. "Dame Lafroste, let me assure you that I will personally look into this matter. By God, we cannot tolerate the likes of these people when we are trying to advance the cause of safety and security in the police. It is unthinkable. Preposterous!" Faderley's plump pink cheeks jiggled with indignation as he said the words.

"I bow to your superior knowledge, Lord Faderley," said Margaret LaFroste, appearing concerned, but inwardly enjoying the moment.

"These imposters..." said Faderley. "What did you say their names were?"

"Jack Lightfoot, and Nadia Barossa," she replied.

19

Lucian had swapped his usual snappy business suit for a dowdy grey jacket and worker's cap, and he had a knapsack slung over one shoulder. He met Simeon Strasberg on the platform at Earl's Court station. The professor, too, was dressed in simple clothes; a cotton shirt, brown trousers, and a pair of scarred and dusty boots.

They greeted one another with a perfunctory handshake and Lucian handed Simeon a crumpled note, which read: *Mile End*, and then *Gosling Street*.

It was mid-afternoon and the station was bustling. A steam locomotive pulled in about three minutes ahead of schedule, and Lucian and Simeon pressed through the crowd to get on board. The smoke emitted from the steam engine swirled about on the platform and a sulphurous smell stung their nostrils.

Once inside, they found a seat and sat down together. Lucian found himself sitting snugly against an old man who reeked of rum, while Simeon managed to claim the window seat, closely flanked by a man in a ragged coat who muttered continually to himself.

Lucian and Simeon watched their fellow passengers in silence as the wooden carriages creaked and moaned. Most of the passengers were workers, some of them travelling to do their shifts at factories, butcheries, tanneries or markets. Some looked tired, their faces drawn by constant fatigue.

The train journey took the pair past Victoria Station, and on to Charing Cross, then past Whitechapel to Mile End. When they alighted at Mile End Station, it was impossible to tell the difference between night and day. The underground station was poorly lit, and the light was further diffused by locomotive smoke and steam.

Simeon followed closely behind Lucian, who ascended the steep stairs to the streets. They kept near to the wall, to avoid the push and jostle of the large group of people moving in the same direction.

"I should have brought Riley," Simeon mumbled as they finally reached the street.

Lucian, who could barely make out Simeon's voice above the street noises, responded loudly. "Pardon?"

"It might have been useful to have Riley follow along with us," said Simeon.

But Lucian shook his head. "Not the protocol, old chap. Aleister gave strict instructions against that sort of thing."

"Yes, but Aleister does not have the answer to everything, does he?" said Simeon. He peered up the street: "God knows what insidious trap awaits us."

Lucian leaned closer to Simeon's ear. "I've always been a man of caution." He opened the flap of his coat and revealed a revolver to Simeon, tucked away in a leather holster.

Simeon nodded. "Do we know where Gosling Street is?"

Lucian adjusted his coat to conceal the revolver. "I've consulted the maps. Follow me."

They allowed two carriages and a steam-driven car to pass, before crossing over the congested road. Lucian seemed confident in his stride, and Simeon followed behind him.

They soon reached a quieter road, and Lucian nudged Simeon and pointed at a smaller alleyway, and a roughly drawn symbol on the broken wall. "That's it. That symbol..." It was an oval, with an indistinguishable squiggle attached to it.

Simeon peered at it curiously but didn't comment. Instead, he simply continued to follow Lucian.

At the southern end of the alley, workmen who had been employed on the Underground had left a pile of debris, bricks, sandbags, timber off-cuts and gravelly stone. Lucian was about to turn around, when he spotted a broken doorway. The door had been split open and left hanging on its hinges. The same strangely-shaped symbol was carved into one side of the door.

"This must be it," Lucian muttered, and walked towards the broken door. "But how—"

He noticed a quick movement at the door, saw a bit of ragged clothing and an arm or a leg visible only for a moment, before it disappeared into the darkness.

Lucian unclipped the top of the holster and placed his hand on top of the revolver. A shiver rippled through his body, but there was a hint of bravado in his voice when he spoke. "Follow me."

Once they made it through the broken door, it was so dark inside, Lucian stopped and reached into his knapsack. Moments later, he produced a small kerosene lamp, wrapped in oil cloth. He handed the knapsack to Simeon, unwrapped the lamp, and spent several matches in an attempt to light it.

"Confounded thing," he mumbled, moments before the lamp finally lit up.

Simeon remained silent, but he peered into the darkness that surrounded them. As the lamp began to glow, he saw a small movement. "There!" he said to Lucian.

Lucian, who was still nursing the lamp, looked up in confusion. "What?"

"I saw something. There. Something moved," said Simeon. He pointed at the far wall.

Lucian lifted the lamp up above his head, allowing the light to spill into the darkest corners, and they caught sight of a small boy, no older than eight, slipping away to hide behind a large, battered wooden crate.

"Stand or I'll shoot!" said Lucian loudly, advancing towards the spot with the lamp held high, and his revolver firmly clutched in one hand.

A young, panicky voice replied almost instantly. "You no shoot! You no shoot!" The boy lifted his hands in surrender, with most of his body remaining hidden behind the wooden crate.

"Show yourself! Stand where I can see you," said Lucian, his voice stern and at the same time trembling with excitement. "Who are you?" he demanded.

"Me Yusuf," the boy said, his dark eyes fearful in the gaslight.

"An Arab. Now we're getting somewhere," Lucian muttered to Simeon. "Where is Massood?" he asked the boy.

"I show you," said the frightened boy, his eyes locked on the revolver in Lucian's hand. "I show you Massood."

"Any trickery and you'll know all about it," Lucian said. But the boy looked confused, puzzled. It was clear he didn't understand much of what was being said.

"Are you ready Simeon?" said Lucian. "Onwards and upwards, eh?"

Simeon nodded, but grabbed hold of Lucian's sleeve. "How do we know this is not a trap?"

"He seems to know this Massood. What else do we have, Simeon?"

Simeon nodded again. He looked worried.

"Well? Come on, boy. Show us to Massood," said Lucian impatiently. He waved his revolver and the boy hurriedly nodded, and then pointed towards a pathway leading towards a partially demolished wall.

"Here. Here. You come," the boy said, gesturing with his hand while cautiously leading the way.

They stepped through the broken section of wall, stepping carefully over loose bricks and plaster, and followed the boy down a narrow passage that was dark, except for a burning torch at the far end of it. As they approached the light, Lucian noticed the torch was roughly made; a wooden stick with a cloth and frayed rope wrapped around one end. It smelled of oil.

The passage changed direction in a southerly bearing, and widened slightly, until they came across stone steps that descended underground. The boy hesitated before taking the first step, and Lucian swiftly grabbed his arm, squeezing it tightly. "You take us straight to Massood," he said in a menacing tone. "If you try to escape, you will pay dearly. Do you understand?" Lucian pointed the revolver at the boy's face.

The boy pulled away, his eyes wide with fear. He nodded frantically.

"Carry on," Lucian said, and then followed the boy down the stone steps. Simeon trailed closely behind.

Within minutes, they became aware of a stench wafting up from the depths; the strong smell of sewage, mixed with a cocktail of chemicals. Lucian covered his nose with a handkerchief, and noticed that the lantern glowed hotter than usual.

They followed the boy through a labyrinth of tunnels, deeper underground, down to the network of sewers beneath the city.

"By Zeus, how much further, boy?" said Lucian, his face turning an angry red.

"You come," the boy said again, beckoning. Then he disappeared into another tunnel, and Lucian and Simeon had little choice but to follow.

As the tunnel widened, they passed by a small, ragged mob. Two men, a woman, and three boys, all of them dark-skinned, dirty and hungry-looking, stared at Lucian and Simeon as they walked past. Lucian noticed that the woman carried a basket, half-filled with frayed rope, cloth and other bits of sewer-borne detritus. He again covered his nose with the handkerchief, while edging past the small group, taking care not to touch any of them.

The tunnel soon narrowed again, and they noticed images of distorted faces and grotesque human-animal hybrids carved into the brickwork, or chiselled into rock where no bricks existed. Lucian noticed something that looked like a bird with a human head, coloured in ochre and with a fan tail etched in black. It was difficult to make out the detail in the half-light, but the images looked as if they were part of someone's nightmare. Some of the half-human creatures appeared to be devouring bits of flesh and, when he paused to take a closer look, Lucian noticed that smaller creatures, childlike in their size and shape, looked as if they were being cannibalised by the larger monster-like creatures.

As they progressed down yet another dark tunnel, Lucian and Simeon saw a flickering light up ahead. They were ushered into a narrow, darkened room that looked more like a cave. It smelled musty and felt cold.

There was a movement in the lantern light. A man, dressed in a dirty loincloth, his upper body and legs completely bare, shifted slowly and groaned as he adjusted his weight on a makeshift bed. He struggled to sit upright, and needed the boy's help to steady himself.

The boy brought him a small bowl of water, and the man scooped up a palm-full of the liquid and splashed it on his face, and then rubbed the wetness over his bald head. His dark skin glistened in the half-light.

"Are you Massood?" asked Lucian, his voice reverberating in the hollow room.

The man stared at him, his eyes reddened by lack of sleep, exhaustion and illness.

"You have come... for the book," Massood said, his speech slightly slurred, and his voice so weak that Lucian and Simeon had to strain to hear him.

"Yes," said Lucian. When he received no reply, he added, "Are you ill? Do you need a doctor?"

Simeon stared at Massood. "He is dying," he announced flatly.

Massood stared back at Simeon. His eyes appeared strangely enlarged and the pupils were very dark. "Medicine man," Massood said slowly, his lips curling into something like a smile. Small drops of blood formed on his cracked lips. "You cannot help."

"We were told you have the Book of—" Lucian began, but he stopped when he noticed that Massood was holding up his hand.

"A curse," said Massood. He looked tired and barely able to sit up.

"What curse? What are you saying?" Lucian asked impatiently.

"If you give us the book, we can help you," said Simeon.

"The book will curse you..." said Massood. He lifted his hand as if he was about to point at them, but then let it fall limply by his side. "The Englishman..." he said. "He bring the curse... to me."

"What Englishman?" Lucian asked.

"Perhaps your friend," Simeon replied dryly.

"Aleister? Why would he—" Lucian began indignantly. He turned to Massood and said: "Where is the book? Where are you keeping it?"

The man didn't reply, but instead raised his hand and put it out towards them, showing them his empty palm.

"He wants to be paid," mumbled Lucian.

Simeon put his hand into his inner coat pocket and produced a fat envelope held together with twine.

Massood's hand twitched slightly, and he stretched his hand out further, waiting for the envelope to be placed in it. But Simeon hesitated. "How can we be sure?" he said to Lucian in a quiet voice.

"For God's sake, man," said Lucian, as Massood slowly retracted his hand. Then he turned to Massood: "May we... look at it first?"

Massood shook his tired head, and said something to the boy. It was a strange language, and neither of the white men recognised it.

The boy looked dumbstruck at first, staring at the two men. Then he said, "You must go."

Lucian was immediately angry: "Do you think, after coming this far—" he said, in an exasperated tone. He stopped abruptly and started again. "Tell him we want to see the book."

The boy, wide-eyed, just shook his head. "You go. Now," he said. He hardly flinched when Lucian produced his revolver and waved it recklessly at Massood, and then at him.

"Very well," Lucian said finally, and turned to his companion: "Simeon. Pay the man now, or we will never see the book again. Do you understand? Aleister warned me about this."

Simeon stepped forward and thrust the envelope towards Massood, whose bony fingers grabbed it without hesitation. Simeon hung on to the envelope for a moment, but then allowed it to slip from his hand.

Massood stared at the envelope without uttering a word. He stared at it so intently, that it reminded Lucian of a stage magician he once saw, performing a disappearing trick in front of a crowd.

At last, Massood turned his head and said something else to the boy. The command was brief, and the boy reacted almost instantly. He stepped forward, grabbed the envelope, and before Lucian or Simeon could do anything to stop him, disappeared into a narrow passage towards the back of the room, the envelope firmly clutched in his hand.

Simeon moved forward involuntarily, but Lucian grabbed his arm and held him back. "We have him. We have him, as insurance..." he muttered, pointing the revolver at Massood.

"A swindler's life would be worthless," said Simeon, his wrinkled face pale and tense.

They waited in the silent, cave-like room for minutes that felt like hours, staring at Massood and trying to listen for little noises – anything that might indicate that the boy was on his way back. Massood, too, was quiet. His face began to display signs of the pain that was attacking his body. He could barely remain in an upright sitting position. He seemed weak and looked ready to faint.

"How much longer? Where is the boy?" Lucian finally blurted out.

"Be calm," Massood said, lifting his hand and making a small waving motion, as if trying to dismiss their worries. His voice was a whisper.

Lucian's lamp flickered briefly and, for a moment, it looked as if it would go out, but then the warm glow of the flame resurged, projecting alien shadows onto the walls.

To Lucian's surprise, the professor stepped forward and sat down on the edge of Massood's makeshift bed. The timber legs creaked as he sat down. Massood looked up at the old man, his dark eyes confused. He suddenly appeared frightened under Simeon's stare.

Massood tried to say something, but instead broke out in a cough that shook his body.

"You will not last long like this," said Simeon at last. "But without the book, I will make sure you suffer the agonies of hell before you die."

Massood look bewildered, but once he saw the look in Simeon's eyes, he shrunk back slightly. Lucian swallowed hard. "Simeon..." he started saying, but the professor held up a hand to silence him.

"You are... a devil – the master of devils," said Massood. Droplets of sweat ran down his chest and his hands were shaking uncontrollably.

Simeon Strasberg did not reply. He simply stared at Massood, while a heavy silence hung over the room.

Finally, they heard movements from the back of the room. The boy, breathing hard from running, entered. Under his arm, he carried a large, heavy-looking bundle wrapped in a dusty cloth. Massood nodded slowly, and the boy handed the book to Lucian.

Simeon rose to his feet and looked over Lucian's shoulder as he unwrapped the cloth and revealed a battered wooden box. Lucian carefully set the box down, and opened its lid. Inside the box was a leather-bound volume, with a symbol of a snake curled around an egg impressed on to the cover. The yellowed pages were brittle and ancient, and the inks badly faded.

Lucian opened the book on a random page and saw a drawing of a simple bean-shaped figure. Some of the detail had been obliterated, but he was still able to make out what it was – a human foetus.

"The Book of Transmutation..." whispered Lucian.

20

Rose Blassington's body was dressed in an evening dress, fringed with lace around the collar and cuffs. An attractive bonnet was affixed to her hair, and her body arranged in such a way that it appeared to sit upright in a chair. Her head was resting against a small pillow, which kept it from leaning flatly against the wall. To anyone entering the room, Rose might have appeared alive, but the lifeless eyes broke the illusion.

After a sudden, bright flash of light, the photographer looked up from behind his camera, waiting for the little cloud of magnesium smoke to clear. "It's done," he declared, and replaced a small metal cap on the camera lens, then took great care removing the bulky camera from the large wooden tripod.

Emilio Ducanti stepped forward from where he had been standing at the back of the room: "What will happen now?"

"With the photograph?" the photographer asked. "I shall complete the chemical processing first, and then produce a photograph, as requested by the family of the deceased. The plates, however, remain the property of Apsley and Company."

Ducanti nodded, and waited patiently as the photographer collapsed the camera bellows and loaded the camera into a large box-like suitcase. The photographer offered him a card with details of Apsley & Co Photographic Studio. Ducanti accepted and examined it with curiosity.

"I wish you a good day, sir," the photographer said, tipping his hat and turning to leave. His assistant was left behind to pack up the remaining items belonging to the studio.

Jack Lightfoot and Nadia Barossa brushed past the photographer on their way in. They approached Ducanti, but their attention was drawn by two morgue workers, who were tasked with disassembling the photographic diorama. Rose Blassington's corpse was removed from the chair and laid flat on a stretcher, her bonnet carefully removed, and her clothes loosened for later removal.

Jack, who had heard about the not-uncommon ritual of taking photographs of the deceased, stared at the macabre scene in front of him. Nadia stood quietly at his side.

"A moment please," said Ducanti suddenly, interrupting the morgue workers. He stepped up to the corpse and kneeled down next to it, then reached out and removed the small pin that he had placed on the lapel of Rose Blassington's dress. Then he stood up. Nadia was immediately curious and strained to catch a closer look at it.

"Did that belong to... the deceased?" she asked.

Ducanti looked at her strangely for a moment, then nodded. "I pinned it to her dress because it was found at the place where the murder occurred," Ducanti replied. "Presumably, it's hers."

"May we see it?"

Ducanti appeared reluctant, but finally handed it to Nadia.

"Do you know its function?" Ducanti asked. He was surprised at Nadia's keen interest.

Nadia shook her head. "A lapel pin, I presume. It's too small to be a hat pin. A tie pin?"

"Are you suggesting it belongs to a gentleman?" said Ducanti.

"It's within the realm of possibility," she replied.

Ducanti's frowned. He held out his hand, and Nadia placed the delicate little pin in his palm.

"Be that as it may, I did not invite you here to discuss my latest investigation," said Ducanti. "Why don't you accompany me to the office? There are matters I prefer to discuss with you in private."

Ducanti turned on his heel and Jack and Nadia followed him past a splayed cadaver and several sheet-covered corpses to the mortuary office. The office had a strange chemical smell, and anatomical drawings and charts were pinned to the walls. The desk was nearly filled with papers, many of them stamped with the Royal Hospital of Dunsbury seal.

Ducanti closed the door behind them and turned to Jack. "I've been informed that you, Mister Jack Lightfoot, and your associate, invited yourselves to a dinner party hosted by Professor Simeon Strasberg..."

Jack shuffled his feet uncomfortably under Ducanti's angry stare.

"As it happened, one of the guests at this affair was none other than Dame Lafroste," he added.

"And how delightful it was to meet her," said Jack, trying to smile.

"Now I distinctly recall forbidding any contact with Dame Lafroste!" Ducanti had worked himself up into a state of anger, and he was close to spitting the words. "So imagine my surprise when the Commissioner – the *Commissioner* – told me about your little escapade."

"We are dreadfully sorry, Sheriff. It was ill-advised," tried Jack, but the Sheriff was in no mood to soften.

"I expect you don't need me to tell you, that your services to the Metropolitan Police will no longer be required," he said.

"Sheriff, we are willing to extend our most humble apologies to Dame Lafroste—"Nadia began, but she was cut short.

"That you will most certainly do, Miss Barossa. I have drafted the letters, and I shall expect you to sign them now."

Ducanti produced two letters, addressed to Dame Lafroste and Professor Strasberg respectively, from his inner coat pocket and placed them on the office desk.

"In the meantime, I shall inform the Commissioner that your services have been terminated."

Ducanti stewed in his anger while Jack and Nadia meekly signed the letters of apology. They were in a mild state of shock at their sudden dismissal, and Jack looked a little pale. Nadia noticed his discomfort and touched him lightly on the shoulder. Jack hardly noticed. He nodded a perfunctory goodbye at Ducanti and then awkwardly found his way out of the office, with Nadia following on behind him.

As they walked towards the mortuary exit, Nadia noticed that the morgue workers were continuing their grim task of undressing the body and lifting it on to a stretcher. Nadia paused, and peered curiously at the corpse.

Jack, who realised that Nadia was no longer at his side, turned back. "Nadia," he whispered urgently. "Nadia!" They were in enough trouble already, without inviting the renewed wrath of the sheriff.

Nadia didn't reply but held up a hand, gesturing for Jack to wait for her. Then she stepped closer to the corpse on the stretcher, and bent down to have a closer look at Rose Blassington's body.

"The cut..." Nadia muttered, as she noticed Jack's nervous energy beside her.

"Nadia, we must go. Now," said Jack urgently, his eyes darting to the door of the mortuary office.

"How curious," Nadia said, ignoring him. "The cut looks like it might have been made by a blade – the kind that might be used by... a surgeon."

"We—" Jack began, but then he paused. "What on earth do you mean?"

Nadia crouched down next to the dead woman's body, touching the cold skin surrounding the wound. She also inspected the purple discoloration around the more brutal wound in the dead woman's side. The morgue worker looked at her with a mixture of surprise and curiosity but said nothing, assuming that she was working for the sheriff.

"Nadia, he's coming," said Jack suddenly, a note of panic in his voice.

Nadia looked up and saw the sheriff approaching. He was looking over the two letters that he held in his hands. Nadia quickly stood up and followed Jack to the exit. They left the building without looking back.

Behind them, Ducanti looked at the two departing figures, and shook his head.

21

Simeon Strasberg's bloodshot eye appeared grotesquely enlarged behind the magnifying glass. He had been studying the oddly-formed letters and hand-drawn shapes for hours on end. He sat back, straightening his back and letting out a deep sigh. None of the text in the book made any sense at all.

The manuscript contained nearly two hundred vellum pages, collected into eight sections. The punctuation was basic, and some of the sentences broke off halfway, as if the scribe was interrupted in his work.

Some of the pages contained astronomical diagrams, while others showed the human figure, most of the time, naked female figures, in various poses – with anatomical drawings scattered among them. There were also drawings of plants, pharmaceutical devices and what appeared to be apothecary jars. One of the larger sections contained drawings of mechanical devices, some of them connected to human figures with tubes.

The yellowed pages were roughly bound, and the spine of the book stitched with a coarse-fibred thread. Some of the page edges were ragged and browned by relentless page-turning over the ages. Much of the ink had faded, but most of it was still legible.

The professor heard a rap on the door and looked up immediately: "Yes?" He covered the open book with a cotton cloth.

The door opened and Riley's face appeared. "The gentlemen have arrived, Professor," he said.

"Let them in. Let them come here," said the Professor in response. His tone was impatient. His guests were late – and on such an important occasion. He moved to the fireplace to warm himself while waiting for his guests, and noticed the lines on his pale, ageing hands. Age was gaining on him fast, and there was so much to be done.

The door creaked slightly, and Aleister Crowley entered, followed by a short-statured man in a grey coat, which appeared two sizes too large for him. The small man removed his bowler hat and clasped it in a nervous hand, waiting to be introduced.

"Professor Strasberg," said Aleister with a wide smile. "May I present Tennison Abbywick, master of antiquities," he said.

"You are the translator?"

"Mister Abbywick is much more than that, Professor Strasberg," replied Aleister on Tennison's behalf. "He is an interpreter. We can but hope to glimpse the secrets that lie within this gentleman's brain."

Despite Aleister's introduction, Simeon Strasberg felt disappointed, cheated even. Tennison Abbywick was short – so short, that standing face to face, he barely reached as high as the professor's chest. His black, stringy hair was thinning on top, and combed over his balding scalp. His face was thin and pointy, much like that of a rodent, and his eyes a watery blue-green and inquisitive. Tennison's forehead seemed a little clammy from perspiration. He grinned nervously, showing a pair of yellowed front teeth with a wider-than-usual gap between them.

What could a man like this possibly contribute to the hidden secrets of the Book of Transmutation?

"So I take it then, Mister Abbywick, that you have studied the ancient languages? Oxford, perhaps?" said Simeon Strasberg. He didn't hide that he was sceptical about Abbywick's credentials.

"Well, sir... professor, if you mean formal studies..." Abbywick began hesitantly. "I have studied some of the ancient Greek texts, and have discussed them with Oxford scholars..."

"So you went to Oxford?"

Abbywick shrugged. "For two months."

When he noticed the professor's suspicious frown, Aleister hastily interjected: "It's more of a natural talent, Professor Strasberg. Mister Abbywick has an ability that can only be described as... uncanny."

"I hope you are right, Mister Crowley," said Strasberg sternly. "I cannot begin to explain how important this manuscript is to my work."

"Is that the book?" said Abbywick, his eyes resting on the cotton cloth that covered Strasberg's newly-acquired treasure.

The professor nodded slowly.

"May I?" asked Abbywick, and Strasberg nodded again, more reluctantly this time.

The small man crossed the room, and with trembling fingers, gently lifted the cloth. His demeanour changed when he saw the yellowed vellum pages. It was as if he became more robust – overtaken by an inner strength of mysterious origin. The small, nervous little man seemed to undergo a transformation. He looked electrified – imbued with a power that produced a glow in his face, and a forcefulness that demanded attention.

From that moment, Abbywick's hands moved with certainty and directness. He donned a pair of white cotton gloves before gently touching the pages. He leaned in close to one of the pages and sniffed, as if picking up an ancient scent, and with gleaming eyes scanned the content of page after page.

"Iron gall nut ink," he finally said, breaking the intense silence in the room.

"I beg your pardon?" said Simeon.

"Ink made from fermented vegetables," Abbywick explained, lightly touching the brown-black ink on one of the pages. "If the process is performed well, it makes the ink darker, which is fortunate for us – it keeps the text legible for so much longer." Abbywick's voice turned to a near whisper. He was obviously thrilled by what he saw. "Where did you find this work?" he said, and then added almost shyly "If I may ask..."

Aleister answered his question. "The mad Arab, Massood."

Abbywick looked disappointed. "Then we may never know its true origin," he said.

"You know this man?" Simeon asked, suddenly curious.

"Our paths have crossed," Abbywick replied. "A long time ago." He picked up Simeon's magnifying glass and closely studied the text on one of the manuscript pages. "Hmm, most certainly a quill," he mumbled.

"What can you tell us about its origin?" asked Aleister eagerly.

Abbywick shook his head. "It's curious," he said, pointing to one of the pages. "These look like western astronomical drawings. But the figures look eastern, perhaps Indian. It doesn't make sense. Then there is the script. I saw something like it in the volumes of ancient Germanic sects…"

"It could also be gibberish," said Simeon, his voice tight with frustration. "Utter gibberish."

Abbywick looked up. "Do you mean… a hoax?"

"It has occurred to me," said Simeon.

Abbywick's eyebrows lifted. "If it is a hoax, the hoaxer would have lived a very long time ago. This manuscript is certainly several hundred years old," he said.

Simeon stepped forward and began flicking through the manuscript, advancing several pages until he stopped on a page with an illustration of a bizarre-looking machine, which looked somewhat like a pot-bellied stove, but with a window built into the front of it. Presumably, this window allowed the viewer to see the contents of the stove.

"Could I impose on your superior knowledge on these matters?" said Simeon. "I would like to know the function of this… contraption."

Abbywick's fingers gently stroked the manuscript page, as if he had a personal connection to its contents. "I will need time to study it," he said. "And consult my own books."

"If anyone can translate this work…" Aleister interjected. "Professor, Tennison Abbywick has done work on some of the priceless relics of the Catholic Church. He has been consulted on, in the translation of the Egyptian hieroglyphs—"

"The work will need to be done here," said Simeon bluntly. "The manuscript cannot be allowed to leave these premises."

"Professor Strasberg—" Aleister began.

But Abbywick nodded. "If that is what you require, I shall work here."

"Excellent," said Simeon Strasberg, smiling for the first time. "Can you begin today?"

Abbywick nodded. "As soon as I fetch my books."

He turned for the door, but then paused and looked back at the other two men. "I may be mistaken, of course, but the text about the... contraption... the one you pointed out in the manuscript, translates to something like 'mother'," said Abbywick. "If I recall correctly, the word may also be interpreted as 'womb'."

22

Jack adjusted the backrest of his machine, and tightened two small screws to secure it in place. Then he stood back and admired his handiwork. The Little Dilly, as he named it, was gleaming. The leather seat was polished to a glossy finish, and the wooden outer frame varnished, which brought out a rich, golden colour in the timber.

The heart of the machine, the small electrical motor, was attached underneath the seat and a metal rail extended to the front of it, which fitted between the stirrups that were mounted on either side. The metal rail, in turn, had a piston-driven, projectile-shaped object with a rubber cap mounted on it. The metal portions of the machine cheerfully reflected the light, and the chair, which was slightly tilted back for maximum comfort, looked inviting.

A quiet knock on the door interrupted Jack's last-minute inspection of the machine. He was satisfied – no, proud – of the work he had done.

"Enter," said Jack, just loud enough for the person on the other side of the door to hear.

The door opened, and Nadia looked in. She was smiling, and said, "Your client is here, Mister Lightfoot." She had a naughty gleam in her eye.

"Very well," said Jack, in an almost-formal tone. "Please send her in."

Helen entered, looking as beautiful as she had the first time she inspected Jack's creation. Jack noticed that she was wearing looser, modern clothing. She had long abandoned corsets and tight lacing, but this was the first time that Jack had seen her wearing culottes and a shirt blouse. Her hair, usually done up in a bun, was arranged loosely around her shoulders.

Jack opened his mouth to speak, and formed the words with his lips, but seemed unable to articulate his thoughts.

"Mister Lightfoot," said Helen in a cheerful voice. She extended her hand and he bowed slightly and brushed her hand against his lips. Her hand was warm, soft and fragrant, and Jack was tempted to squeeze and hold it.

"Miss Gartner," he said, after wrestling with his memory to retrieve her last name.

"Jack, I was delighted to receive your message. Is it ready?"

"Don't hesitate to call if you need me," said a voice from the door. Nadia had an impish smile on her face as she closed the door behind her.

"Is she always here?" asked Helen.

"Nadia?" Jack sounded surprised. "Well, no. Not here... always. But, yes, we are... associates."

"It looks wonderful," said Helen. She had caught sight of the machine and walked over to it, running her hand over the framework. "How very elegant."

"I refined the mechanism," said Jack, more confidently now. "I think it will please you."

"I have no doubt it will," said Helen. A light blush spread across her cheeks.

Helen lightly touched various parts of the machine; the smooth leather seat, the gleaming timber, and the rubber-capped part which was small but stood erect at the centre, a few centimetres from the front edge of the seat.

"I hope you don't mind. I told a friend about this. An intimate friend," said Helen.

"Of course not," Jack said.

"She was delighted, and was hoping to meet you."

"Of course," Jack said again, and then suddenly blurted out nervously. "I have not had the opportunity to test it. And since it is such a... personal product, I thought the owner herself should do the honours."

"I expected nothing less, Jack," she said with a smile. "I would not have been in favour of a stranger testing this device on my behalf – your associate, for example."

"Nadia?" Jack was speechless for a moment. "I hardly think that would have... I just don't think she would have..."

"Exactly my point, Jack," Helen said.

Jack was confused, but nodded anyway.

"Shall I test the machine now?" asked Helen, her eyebrows cocked.

"Er... certainly," Jack stumbled over his words. He pointed at an upright, folding dressing screen with an intricate flowery pattern on it. "There is, behind the screen, a nightdress you may wish to put on... before attempting... before you use... um... test the equipment."

"How thoughtful," Helen said and smiled sweetly. She walked to the screen, peeked around it, and saw a chair and a hanging rail to hang up items of clothing. "I shan't be long," she said and disappeared behind the screen.

Jack felt the overwhelming need to leave the room, but realised there was no escape. Helen would expect to be given the proper operating instructions.

"I look forward to you showing me exactly how it works, Jack," she said from behind the screen, as if she could read his mind.

"It's quite simple, really," he said weakly, and looked nervously around him. Where was he supposed to look when she entered? It was simply not proper to look directly at her, he decided.

Jack heard the sounds of clothing being removed. The screen moved slightly, possibly caused by a light bump or other movement, as Helen removed items of clothing. Jack felt a sinking feeling in his stomach.

Moments later, she was beside him. How on earth did she remove her clothing so quickly? Jack felt panicky, especially when he noticed that she had removed all her underthings. She was wearing the nightdress, but he could clearly discern the outline of her breasts, and could even make out her nipples under the light fabric. He forced himself to look away towards the machine.

"If you'd dare... care... to take a seat," he said, his voice dry and croaky.

Helen sat down on the leather seat, her hands clutching the timber supports on either side. She leaned back in the seat, and smiled. "Comfortable," she said.

"The... aim is to use this part..." said Jack, pointing to projectile-shaped object. "...Once the legs are in the correct aspect... position."

"Am I making you nervous, Jack?" Helen said. A little smiled played around her lips.

"As a matter of fact, madam, I..."

"Rather simple, as you explained," she cut him short. "My feet go in here..." She lifted one foot into a stirrup, then lifted the other, and her nightdress crept up high and exposed both her bare thighs.

"I must leave now. I beg you," pleaded Jack. He spoke urgently, but in a loud whisper.

"Why don't you tell about the machine?" Helen said. "How does it work, exactly?"

"The... mechanical details?"

She nodded, and waited for him to continue.

"The new... innovation," he said, "is a tiny coil. When it moves back, the coil tightens – winds up like a clock spring, if you like. Then, when it moves forward, the coil is released, causing a vibration in the... instrument. It is likely to increase the sensation of um... the... the vibration."

"Fascinating," Helen replied. She touched the tip of the rubberised section of the object, and then enclosed it in her hand to warm it, before slowly guiding it towards her. "I'm listening, Jack. Please carry on."

"The backward and forward action has an inertia effect," he explained, while staring at the opposite end of the room. "It means there is a gradual slowing of the movement, taking away the feeling of... abruptness."

Helen lifted her nightdress, exposing her nakedness from the waist down. With one hand, she slowly stroked her mons pubis, which was as soft, smooth and hairless as her cheeks. Her fingers pressed lightly to spread open her inner softness, and she allowed that part of the machine to enter her, swallowing it slowly into her body.

Jack thought he heard a gasp, but tried to exclude it from his awareness in the room.

"Switch it on," he heard her say. "Switch it on now, Jack."

Jack was trembling violently, and his fingers fumbled as he reached for the small silver switch that was mounted on the timber frame. A moment later, there was a small hissing noise, then a release that sounded like a sigh. The moveable arm of the machine pulled back slightly, then pushed forward by a mere inch. Helen's head pushed back against the chair, and she closed her eyes as the machine repeated its motion.

Jack glanced at her face, and thought he recognised signs of pain.

"Are you hurt?" he said, his voice panicky. "Allow me to stop this at once."

But she grabbed him by his sleeve and whispered something.

"I beg your... pardon?" he said, leaning forward.

"It's a miracle, Jack," she whispered. "You created a miracle."

23

A pale, ghostly light shone from the corner of Reginald Lafroste's room. Heavy drapes cut out the sunlight as well as most of the street noises, which created an eerie quiet, broken only by occasional hollow noises from other quarters of the house.

Reginald was deathly pale, his face deeply lined and his cheeks sunken. A bloodless-white, bony hand gripped the sheet as he tried to adjust his position in the bed, without much success. He was not alone. Margaret Lafroste sat in an upright chair, positioned against the opposite wall. Her face was expressionless, but the emotional pain of her husband's struggle had clearly left its mark.

A hollow needle and tube were attached to Reginald's arm, which fed him with fresh blood from his donor; a young boy who was made to sit on a high chair, with a leather belt around his chest restraining him and holding him upright against the back of the chair. The boy, too, looked sick. His face was greyish pale, and he appeared too weak to move, his arms lying limply at his sides. A needle and tube had been attached to an artery in his neck, and the rapid blood loss caused the boy to hover between conscious and unconscious states.

Margaret Lafroste looked up as she heard footsteps in the passageway. The steps were slow but deliberate, and approached the door of the room. Moments later, the door opened and Simeon Strasberg entered. He looked inquiringly at Margaret Lafroste.

"How is our patient faring?" he asked, his hands pink from a fresh scrubbing.

Margaret Lafroste wanted to reply but stopped short. Instead, she shook her head sorrowfully.

The professor made his way to Reginald's bedside, and leaned over him, and took his jaw into his hand, tilting his face towards the light. Reginald groaned and tried to lick his lips with a dry, lethargic tongue.

"I have every confidence..." Simeon started, but he stopped when he noticed Reginald Lafroste's weak headshake.

With great effort, Reginald grabbed Simeon's sleeve and attempted to pull him closer. His mouth opened to speak, and Simeon leaned closer to listen.

"Stop," Reginald said. "You must... stop this."

"It's too early to..." Simeon began, but Reginald tugged his sleeve.

"Save the boy," Reginald whispered urgently.

Simeon looked at the boy on the chair, and then returned his gaze to Reginald.

"We must make you well again," he said.

When Reginald spoke again, Simeon could clearly make out the words.

"I'm dying."

Margaret Lafroste appeared at Simeon's side. "What have you done?" she said, eyes glossed with tears.

"He is... not responding well," said Simeon.

"You said—" Margaret began, her voice loaded with emotion. "You promised!"

Simeon gave her a cold look: "I did what I could. It is out of my hands now," he said.

Margaret Lafroste struggled to keep her emotions under control.

"I supported you," she said.

"That sounds like an accusation," said Simeon. "I cannot make miracles."

"Really?" said Margaret, a flash of anger passing over her face. "I thought miracles were your speciality."

Simeon looked down at Reginald's white, emaciated body. "There is nothing more I can do here."

Margaret turned to her husband, clutched his hand and sobbed bitterly.

"The boy…" said Reginald, his voice a weak whisper.

Simeon heard it, and looked briefly at the boy in the chair. The boy's body had slumped, and he was hanging limply in his restraints. His face was ashen grey, and his thin arms appeared colourless.

"I'll send Riley to fetch him," he said. "He's done."

———•———

Nadia Barossa drew antagonistic looks among some female passers-by as she walked through Leadenhall, eyeing the shops, as well as the bustling shoppers. Her short hair was uncovered, and was slightly upset by the gusts of wind that tugged at the skirts of more glamorously dressed shoppers. She wore a loose blouse and knickerbockers, a style of dress that still frequently drew criticism from the establishment, but made her feel comfortable and in control.

Fashion magazines described the modern woman's dress sense as 'mannish' and published shrill criticism of the new styles. This simply served for Nadia to be more daring, and more disdainful about the prudish public sentiment. She was secretly amused at the way some women still slavishly followed their families' instructions, to wear conservative dresses and be chaperoned.

Nadia paused to admire the wares of an ironmonger, who showed off an array of polished grates, fenders, and candlestick stands, then moved on to the tobacconist shop window with its elegant snuff-boxes, cigar-cases and prized Meerschaums.

It was at that moment that she saw his reflection in the window. There could be little doubt that it was Raskovic, the garrotter. He stood a head taller than the people around him and, although his face was partially obscured by a large hat, Nadia instantly recognised the man's forward-leaning gait, and the strange way he kept his shoulders rigidly straight while walking.

Nadia turned, and watched the garrotter as he progressed down the street. She began following him, keeping at a distance and taking care not to lose sight of him.

Raskovic walked reasonably fast, heading due south. Nadia followed him, keeping a cautious hundred-metre distance between them. She was grateful that she had decided to wear comfortable footwear, but slightly disappointed that she chose the knickerbockers – the wrong thing to wear if one wanted to avoid drawing attention.

She pushed past a potato salesman, who stood behind a tin box full of potatoes, sitting atop a small stove. Then she managed to gain some ground, shrinking the distance between her and the garrotter, as he progressed along Fenchurch Street towards Mark Lane Station.

Nadia followed him across the street and down the steep stairs to the station, ignoring the stares of two top-hatted men, who clearly did not approve of her choice of clothing. Feeling exposed, she tried to shield herself from the garrotter's view by hiding behind two other train passengers while he bought a ticket.

When it was her turn to buy a ticket, the black-uniformed man in the ticket office looked at Nadia with suspicion, as if she was an imposter, and then reluctantly handed her the train ticket plus change. She was relieved to catch up with the garrotter on the platform, and took up a position behind a large pillar, to keep out of his sight. When the train arrived, she pushed her way through the crowd to get in the same carriage as the garrotter. Fortunately, his large stature made him easy to spot, even at a distance.

It took half an hour, and multiple stops, for the train to reach Earl's Court, where the garrotter finally disembarked. Nadia was a bit surprised when she saw him walk in the direction of the upmarket Kensington area. The streets were quieter here, and signs of affluence were everywhere. Still, she persisted, trying to appear nonchalant as she kept up with the garrotter's brisk walking pace.

He turned into a smaller side street, and then wound his way through an alleyway at the back of a row of houses. Nadia followed, but when she reached the end of the alley, Raskovic was nowhere to be seen. It was as if he had disappeared in the afternoon air. Nadia stopped for a moment, puzzled. Where could he have gone?

She began walking again and picked up the pace, hoping that she'd catch sight of him in one of the small lanes, or in any one of the criss-crossing streets. She was breathing fast, and walked briskly on, determined to pick up the trail. But there was nothing. The garrotter had slipped from her view.

Nadia slowed down, her brisk walk turning into a more casual stroll, and then she finally came to a dead stop, standing at a street corner and weighing up her options.

The garrotter, too, had stopped. He had found an accessible staircase and raced up, taking the stairs in twos and threes. Once he was at the top, he had a clear view of the surrounding area, and he saw Nadia standing at a corner, two streets away.

He saw her hesitating and looking around. Finally, she shook her head, and walked away in the opposite direction.

24

Upon his arrival at the manor house, Tennison Abbywick was ushered in to the library, to meet with Simeon Strasberg, as they had arranged. He was surprised to find Simeon in a darkened room. A single gaslight on the far wall illuminated the room, and cast an elongated shadow for Abbywick, who approached the professor's chair with apprehension.

The *Book of Transmutation* rested on a small table at Simeon's elbow. But Abbywick was alarmed when Simeon looked up at him. The older man's face was ghostly, his cheeks sunken deeper than before, and there was a thin film of sweat on his forehead. Simeon watched him with eyes rimmed red from an intense fever.

"You appear to be... ill," said Abbywick. His face showed his concern for his client.

Simeon nodded. "Since yesterday," he said. "I've been feeling rather poorly."

"I'm not a medical man, professor, but it seems you need help."

Simeon grinned painfully. "Rather ironic, don't you think," he said. "I consider myself to be a... medical man."

"People catch the fever, sometimes without a clear cause," said Abbywick.

Simeon gestured towards the book. "The Arab – Massood – said the book was cursed."

Abbywick looked anew at the book. "He said that? In those words?'

Simeon nodded. "And he appeared to be ill, too."

"Curious indeed," said Abbywick, a deep frown creasing his forehead.

"What is your belief, Mister Abbywick? In your experience, is there such a thing?"

"In my experience, professor, curses are only effective when victims choose to believe in them."

The professor nodded tiredly. "A sensible answer, Mister Abbywick. And yet..." He lifted his hand and dropped it again.

"Is there another physician that you may be able to—"

"Yes," Simeon cut him short. "And he, too, appears at somewhat of a loss."

"If this is a... curse of some kind, the book itself may provide a clue," said Abbywick.

Simeon leaned back in the chair, and waved a hand lightly at the book. "By all means... have a look."

It was clear that Abbywick was keen to begin work on the book, despite his client's dilemma. He removed a pair of white cotton gloves from his coat pocket, and put them on. "I have found that perspiration, often found on human hands, can do damage to the delicate pages of old manuscripts," he said, by means of explanation. Then he picked up the book and placed it on the table that was strategically positioned near the centre of the room.

Abbywick's gloved hand slowly and very carefully opened the cover. His hand slid lightly over the first page, caressing it.

"Mister Abbywick, may I ask you to share your discoveries... by speaking your mind aloud?" said Simeon.

For a moment, Abbywick looked troubled by the request, but nodded his agreement anyway.

"The binding is what one may expect from a manuscript produced in the Middle Ages," he said, trying to describe his impressions. "The cover is... some sort of wood, covered in leather. Ivory inset under the title – a simple emblem that looks a bit like an eye. This decoration seems to indicate that this was regarded as an important volume of work. The leather layer has cracked and shows signs of wear. In my estimation, the book has done a considerable amount of travelling – and I wouldn't be surprised if it had changed ownership several times."

Abbywick picked up a magnifying glass and inspected the first page more closely. "The text appears to be written left to right," he said." And the pages are numbered... which allows us to confirm that they are all there..."

"I regret to rush you, Mister Abbywick, but my interest lies in your ability to translate the text. Would you be so kind? Any page will do."

Abbywick nodded and mumbled an agreement, but then his eyes fell back on the leather cover, which was cracked along the top edge, and peeling slightly away, exposing the wooden base underneath. He set aside the magnifying glass and removed a small leather pouch from his inner coat pocket. He untied the leather strap that secured the pouch, and then unfolded it, revealing a set of silver tools inside. His nimble fingers removed a small set of metal pincers and a flat, blunt knife. He used the knife to gently prise open the crack in the book's leather cover, and then used the pincers to extract a brittle, yellowed square of linen which was folded in half.

"What have you found, Mister Abbywick?" asked Simeon, but he didn't receive an immediate reply. Abbywick was engrossed in his discovery. He laid the piece of linen on the table top, and then gently unfolded it with the pincers while holding one end flat with the knife.

"This would have been added much later," said Abbywick finally. "It is a note – to the new owner of the manuscript."

"A note? Can you read it?"

"More like a warning, it would seem," said Abbywick. "Written in Germanic text, in a style more modern. Certainly added years after the manuscript was bound."

"Mister Abbywick," said Simeon, impatience rising in his voice. "What does it say?"

"Without verifying the individual words..." said Abbywick. His memory recalled snippets of the old language, and the letters began taking meaningful shape in his mind, as if they were shifting into clearer focus. "It warns the manuscript is protected against thieves and vagabonds... it mentions that the curse of death is carried within these pages."

Abbywick looked at Simeon with renewed concern. "It could mean that your current illness may be as a result of..." He did not complete his sentence, but instead refocused on the book.

"There is, in addition, a faint symbol on this page – faded over time," Abbywick continued. "The Cross of Lorraine..."

Simeon lifted his head. "I've heard of it."

"By legend, the Cross of Lorraine was used by the Knights Templar, before they adopted the Maltese-type cross. But in the old Hermetic texts, it was also described as an occult symbol," said Abbywick.

"What does it mean?"

Abbywick's expression was solemn. "This symbol was also used by chemists... originally alchemists," he said. "They put it on bottles of poison."

Simeon blinked, his pale face showing his confusion. "Poison? The book is poisoned?"

Abbywick rapidly turned a few more pages, and then looked at Simeon. "Several pages have the imprint of the Cross of Lorraine on the edge of the page. It could well be that the ink that was used to draw this symbol was mixed with poison. A mere touch of the fingers while turning the pages would have been enough—"

"What poison? What would they have used?" Simeon struggled to rise out of the chair.

"The history... Professor, I'm not an expert on poisons. I am a man of books."

"Chemists, did you say?" said Simeon, a wild look in his eyes. "We must summon Lucian at once." He stood up and stumbled towards the door, momentarily steadying himself by pressing with one hand against the wall. At the door, he turned. "You must not stop, Mister Abbywick. Your translation is more important now than ever."

Abbywick watched, dumbfounded, as Simeon left the room and shut the door behind him.

—•—

"He's breathing normally now," said Aleister Crowley, examining Simeon Strasberg's face closely.

The old man was wheezing, but at least breathing. His

sunken face was immobile, the spittle at the one corner of his mouth the only evidence of his body's fight against the poison in his blood.

"Praise all the gods and spirits," said Lucian. "Yet, we may still lose him." He paged rapidly through an old book on alchemists and their potions, its pages scarred and stained from overuse. "If the poison is medieval, the answer is most likely within the pages," he said.

"Medieval? How do we know for certain?"

Lucian looked up at Aleister. "We don't. We have only Abbywick's expertise to go by. He estimated the Book of Transmutation was written in the fifteenth or early sixteenth century. Abbywick suspects the idea of poison may have been... inspired by the Council of Ten."

"Alchemists?"

Lucian nodded. "They prepared poisons and killed for profit. And it is consistent with the period." He redirected his attention to the book, and finally found a page that he had been searching for. "Here," he said, his finger running over lines of text on the page: "Absorbed through the skin... convulsions... disorientation."

There was a loud hammering on the door, and Aleister opened the door for Riley, who entered carrying a heavy wooden chest with a large lock securing the lid. He put the chest down, causing a loud thud to reverberate in the room.

"Be careful.... You must be careful with that," said Lucian nervously. He fished a key out of his pocket and worried the lock until it sprang open. Then he lifted the lid, revealing row upon row of small bottles and jars.

Aleister peered over his shoulder, curious about the contents of the chest. "What are you looking for?"

"Naturally, one cannot be absolutely confident in these matters, but I suspect the poison may be the deadly nightshade – a favourite of the Council of Ten," said Lucian, his fingers running over the jars and then pausing over a small sub-section of the chest. "And if I'm not mistaken..." He removed a small, box-like container filled with vials and small bottles, then extracted another container below it, which fitted much like a piece of a jigsaw puzzle into the array. He removed a small jar of dried beans and held it up against the light. "Aleister, my lad. This may well be it."

"Dried beans?" said Aleister, surprised.

"Calabar beans," said Lucian. "I shall prepare a paste for the treatment. And then it will be in the hands of the spirits. May they be merciful."

25

Grey skies cast an oppressive gloom over the funeral of Reginald Lafroste. A large crowd, mostly dressed in blacks and greys, assembled at the graveyard as the coffin arrived by horse-drawn carriage. The carriage stopped near the mausoleum, where Reginald's body was to be laid to rest.

The mausoleum was small and circular and had six pillars, reminiscent of the classical Roman style, supporting a domed roof. Its two large, heavy doors were open, awaiting the casket.

Dame Margaret Lafroste arrived separately, escorted by Lord Edmund Faderley, who supported the widow's arm as they walked side by side. They were intercepted by Lucian Baker, who removed his grey gloves and took Margaret Lafroste's hand in a gesture of sympathy. "Dame Lafroste, Lord Faderley," he said. "May I express my deepest condolences at the most terrible news of your husband's passing. A great man indeed."

"Thank you, Mister Baker," said Margaret and prepared to move on, but Lucian wasn't finished. "I'm also here to pass on the condolences and sincere regrets of Professor Strasberg, who despite all efforts, is unable to attend."

Margaret paused and frowned, looking sharply at Lucian.

"I regret to tell you that Professor Strasberg has taken ill. His health concerns us all greatly," said Lucian.

"What is the nature of this... illness?" asked Margaret Lafroste. On the one hand, it sounded like an excuse, but she sensed that Lucian was sincere.

"At this time, the exact cause is unknown, Dame Lafroste. The professor was struck down by a sudden and mysterious illness yesterday. Fortunately, I was able to offer my knowledge of herbs and medicinal plants, but I fear my intervention may have come too late—"

"Dreadful news indeed, Mister Baker, especially today," said Margaret Lafroste, her eyes misty.

"I am dreadfully sorry to bring you such bad tidings, Dame Lafroste. A black day, indeed."

A priest walked up to Margaret, nodded his head at the two men by her side, and bowed his head, revealing a large bald spot. "If you are ready, Dame Lafroste, we can begin the ceremony for internment."

Margaret nodded. She followed the priest into the mausoleum, leaving Lucian Baker, Edmund Faderley and the other guests outside. Once they were alone, the priest turned towards her, and seemed to carefully choose his words. "The bishop has asked me to convey his gratitude for your most generous donation to the church... particularly generous from someone who is not a regular member of our congregation."

"My husband was a member of your congregation in the past. And I wanted to fulfil his wishes, of course," said Margaret, sensing that the priest was fishing for information.

"Of course," the priest said, looking slightly uncomfortable. "And perhaps you'll allow me to—"

"—start the service without any delay?" Margaret interjected sharply. "That is my only wish, father."

He nodded, slightly nervously. "Then we shall proceed forthwith."

The coffin, richly decorated, polished and constructed of the finest French oak, was lowered off the carriage and placed upon a four-wheeled cart, so that it could be positioned in front of the mausoleum. The priest placed a weighty Bible on a small wrought-iron stand and, with a nod from Margaret, began the service in a sing-song voice that carried over the crowd.

From a distance, Nadia watched the proceedings with a spyglass. She had a good vantage point at the top of a small hill overlooking the cemetery, and was even able to see the interior of the mausoleum.

At the end of the sermon, six black-suited men carried the coffin into the mausoleum and lowered it into its final resting place on a marble slab. The other guests – which included many of Reginald Lafroste's business partners and acquaintances – expressed their condolences to Margaret Lafroste, clustering around her in small groups. As the crowd gradually thinned out, Margaret withdrew into the mausoleum, accompanied by Edmund Faderley, Lucian Baker and a small number of guests who had remained behind.

When one of the stragglers, a middle-aged man who clutched his cap in one hand, tried to enter the mausoleum, a tall, powerfully built man blocked his way. Even from a distance, Nadia instantly recognised the figure. It was Raskovic, the garrotter, and he was clearly preventing unwanted guests from joining Dame Lafroste's select group.

A private club? Who would have guessed? Nadia kept her spyglass trained on the garrotter, and watched as the guest turned on his heels and left in a huff.

With the small group of private visitors inside, the garrotter took one last look around before closing the doors to the mausoleum. He remained standing outside, keeping a look-out.

Intrigued by the select private meeting, Nadia abandoned her cover and moved stealthily closer to the mausoleum, in the hope of overhearing what was going on inside. She had to cover a considerable distance, hiding behind a row of trees, and then moving cautiously forward until she was able to cover the final few feet by moving from one large gravestone to the next, ducking behind each one to avoid being seen by the garrotter.

She sneaked along a curved path, and approached the mausoleum from the side, treading carefully to avoid stepping on dried twigs and leaves. The garrotter was out of her view.

Inside the mausoleum, Lucian stood at the head of the coffin, his arms outstretched towards the group of twelve people assembled there. "While we bid his body farewell," he said in a loud voice, "we welcome his immortal spirit in our midst. A spirit more powerful now, than it had ever been within a weak and fragile human body."

He looked up, his eyes focused on a series of hieroglyphs engraved in the ceiling of the mausoleum.

"Masters of the cosmos," said Lucian, his face tilted heavenward, "who created all things that move in darkness or in light – and by whose authority we assemble here – may your flame blaze in brilliance and darkness unto the glory of desire."

"*Athator*," the group exclaimed in unison.

"*Nyentra kunidae athator*," said Lucian.

"*Athator*," the group replied.

Margaret Lafroste brought forward six candles and placed them on the casket, then lit the candles and took a step back, her eyes gleaming in the reflection of the light. She held up her hand, palm facing forward and said, "*Nyentra kunidae athator*."

"*Athator*," the group chanted. Again and again they repeated the word.

Outside the mausoleum, Nadia put her ear against the wall, and heard the muted sounds from inside. Pushing her body up against the stone wall, she inched forward – towards the entrance. The chances were slim that she would make it past the garrotter, but Nadia was willing to try.

The chants from within the mausoleum grew to a higher pitch and then stopped abruptly. The sudden quiet made Nadia pause. She was painfully aware of the occasional bird sounds around her, and the rustling of the wind in the leaves. Did they somehow realise she was there?

Inside the mausoleum, Margaret Lafroste had shed her coat, and revealed the plain cotton garment she wore underneath. A hieroglyph, similar to the one on the ceiling, was embroidered on the front of her garment. The two men on either side of her, Lucian Baker and Edmund Faderley, lifted the garment up and over her head, leaving Margaret Lafroste standing naked near the coffin. Her ageing, wrinkly skin was patterned with a large tattoo that flowed from her left shoulder across and down her back, all the way down to her buttocks. It was a figure of a snake, with abnormally large and inquisitive eyes.

Margaret Lafroste walked forward and took a small step up onto a small elevated platform, next to the slab on which her husband's coffin was resting.

"*Athator, Athator*," the group began chanting again in low

voices, while Lucian stepped forward and kissed her on each breast and her pubis. The others followed his example, each taking his turn to pay respects to Margaret Lafroste. The chanting grew louder.

Outside, Nadia had picked up a small stone near her feet and tossed it high over the roof of the mausoleum, to land in the grass on the other side. It hardly made a noise at all, but she felt certain the garrotter would hear it. She inched forward and heard the garrotter's boots crunching on the gravelly area near the entrance. It sounded as if he was moving away from the mausoleum entrance. She felt brave enough to peek around the corner, and as she had expected, saw the garrotter walking further away, looking into the distance. He looked hesitant – suspicious perhaps.

Nadia slipped around the wall of the mausoleum to the entrance, where she paused to listen to the sounds from within. Then she crouched down and tried to peer through a larger-than-usual keyhole, however there was a key in the lock, which blocked her view.

Nadia took a small key out of her pocket and pushed it into the larger keyhole of the mausoleum door, twisting it slightly and trying to turn the heavy key in the lock. It was not an easy task. At first, the heavy key refused to move. Then there was an almost imperceptible movement. Nadia worried the large key with her little key, until it slowly rotated into a position from where she could push it out of its position in the lock.

She heard voices inside the mausoleum and paused for a brief moment, before pushing on, inching the key out of the lock. Finally, it slipped out. She could hear it making a small clinking noise, as it fell on the stone floor inside the mausoleum.

Nadia put her eye up to the keyhole to look inside. She could barely make sense of what she saw. A man, standing with his back to the keyhole, blocked part of her view, but she still see a reasonable part of the rest of the mausoleum. She immediately recognised a face at the far end. It was Edmund Faderley, and he appeared to be completely naked. The realisation took Nadia by surprise – to such an extent, that she was not aware that the garrotter was approaching her from behind, and only heard him when it was too late.

A heavy hand landed forcefully on Nadia's shoulder, knocking her off-balance and throwing her sideways. She responded instinctively, rolling away from the garrotter and jumping back to her feet. The movement was so quick that the garrotter was unprepared for it. He reached forward with one hand to grab her, but missed. Then, as he stepped awkwardly forward, Nadia turned and ran – with the garrotter in immediate pursuit.

She jumped over a small hedge and kept running, beating aside an overhanging branch from a young willow, and jumping lightly over a small watering canal. She heard the garrotter behind her, crashing through the cemetery gardens and trying to gain on her. But she was faster. Nadia kept her lead and extended it, as the garrotter fell further and further behind. Soon she didn't hear him at all anymore, and slowed down to look behind her. The garrotter was out of sight.

Nadia breathed heavily from the exertion, but at the same time she felt elated.

Changing from a run to a brisk walking pace, she headed back to Jack's laboratory on the South Bank.

26

A silence hung over the large house, settling in to the corners of rooms and even stifling the movement of birds outside. Phyllis Secombe awoke from an afternoon nap and was immediately aware of the gooseflesh on her arms. The tiny hairs on her skin stood erect, as if her body was sensing something – something that made her feel instantly awake and alert.

She lifted the blanket and placed her bare feet on the cool floorboards. She stood up, her hand rubbing lightly over her slightly-swollen belly beneath the nightgown. Her nipples felt tingly, like the antennae of an insect, and she listened intently for even the tiniest noise.

Something was wrong in the house. No, perhaps it was right for the very first time, Phyllis thought. Perhaps this was her day. She felt a bubbling excitement within herself. So unusual, she thought. So exhilarating.

She opened the bottom drawer of the small chest in her room, which contained a towel, soap and fresh undergarments, and pulled the drawer out completely. Hidden away, at the back of the drawer cavity was a small metal item that Phyllis carefully removed, taking great care not to let it drop to the floor. It was a small silver spoon, which she had kept hidden after removing it from her supper tray. Someone had carelessly left a second spoon on her tray about a week earlier, and Phyllis immediately decided to hide it away, for whatever future use she could find for it.

She had taken it out twice before, and had rubbed the spoon handle on the rough edges of the bathroom tiles to sharpen it. At first, Phyllis had thought of sharpening the edge so she could use it as a weapon, but she later thought of a better idea; she could use it as a tool to undo the screws that held the door lock in place. Now was her opportunity, she believed. The silence in the house suggested that she may be alone, so this was an opportunity to put her plan to the test.

Phyllis tip-toed to the door, and pressed her ear up against its cool surface to listen. The house remained quiet, and there was no sound of movement in the passageway. With trembling hands, she slotted the sharpened edge of her spoon into one of the grooves of the screws that held the door lock in place. Then she began turning it anti-clockwise. The screw didn't budge, so Phyllis applied renewed pressure, putting more weight behind it and turning slowly. The next moment, there seemed to be a tiny movement. Did she imagine it, or did the screw really turn? Phyllis wasn't sure, but her heart fluttered with excitement, and she had the almost-unbearable urge to let out a yelp of excitement.

She refocused her attention on the screw, her hands slightly sweaty from the exertion. She turned the spoon again, and this time she could see that the screw turned along with it. After a couple more tries, the screw turned more freely and, once it was loose enough, Phyllis could turn it by hand. She unscrewed it completely, but then it slipped from her fingers and fell on to the floorboards and bounced, before coming to rest against the doorframe.

Phyllis was instantly panic-stricken. To her ears, it sounded as if the noise was loud enough to be heard throughout the large house. She grabbed the screw and held it tightly in the palm of her hand, slowly and silently retreating to her bed, expecting the sound of footsteps at any moment.

But the house remained as quiet as before. There was no sound; no approaching footsteps. For several minutes, Phyllis stood there, listening to the sound of her own breathing. Her heart pounded in her chest. Gradually, she managed to relax a little, and her breathing turned deeper and more regular. She stood there, rooted to the floor, for several more minutes before summoning the courage to continue.

The second screw turned more easily, and Phyllis felt a rush of excitement as it unscrewed further and further, until it dropped into the palm of her hand. Again, she paused to listen for noises, and then moved on to the last two, slightly rusted screws, applying her full strength to loosen them.

Finally, the metal cover that concealed the lock mechanism came loose, and Phyllis clutched it to her chest, hardly believing her good fortune. The next part of her task was more difficult, as only part of the lock mechanism was accessible. Phyllis wedged the sharpened edge of the spoon into the part of the mechanism she could reach, then she wiggled it up and down and sideways, all the time watching the metal parts inside the lock for signs of movement. Suddenly there was a loud click and the lock mechanism turned, but then stopped. Phyllis tried the doorknob but the door remained locked.

Her senses were heightened by the fear that bubbled inside her. Even her own breathing seemed exceptionally loud, and Phyllis was beside herself when she heard a tiny noise from the passageway outside her room. The noise didn't repeat itself. A creaking door or floor, perhaps, she told herself, and tried to return to a degree of calm.

Finally, she returned her attention to the door lock, and jammed the sharpened spoon into a different part of the mechanism. Almost effortlessly, the cogs inside turned and the door lock opened.

Phyllis's hands trembled violently. Could it be possible? Did she do it? She gently touched the door knob and with a hand that was sweaty from fear and exertion, she turned it. The door opened freely.

She stood staring at the open door for a few moments before she dared to step forward and look down the passage. It was empty, and as quiet as before. Phyllis pressed her hand over her mouth to stop herself from crying with delight.

She tip-toed out of the room and down the passage, feeling strangely guilty about her actions. She passed a large window, which had a view of the garden, and she had to resist the urge to stop stare at the beautiful green foliage. It felt like a dream to see the outside of the house for the first time in weeks – possibly months. Phyllis had lost all sense of time.

She reached the first door, but found it locked, and ventured further down the passage, until it branched off to the right. At the end of the narrower passageway, she found another door, which was latched. Phyllis lifted the heavy metal latch and opened the door. As it opened, sunlight flooded in, and bathed Phyllis in energy-giving light. She gasped with delight, and felt joy enveloping her like a cocoon.

She stepped outside, breathing the fresh air and catching the scent of the tall pine trees that were planted in the expansive garden. The sunlight on her skin made her feel elated, and Phyllis felt as if she was floating on light air. Then she heard a distant sound, and realised anew how much danger she was in.

Phyllis glanced around nervously, but there were no pursuers – no one on her trail. She headed for the gate, trying to hide her movements by walking close to a row of lush bushes, and then changed tack – aiming for a hedge closer to the property fence. Once she reached the hedge, things were easier. She managed to hide behind it as she walked, and her pace changed from a cautious walk to a frantic run.

Within a few moments, she could see the gates, and her heart lurched. What if someone saw her now? What if they stopped her at the last moment? Pushing the thought to the back of her mind, Phyllis kept running, with every breath burning in her throat, and her heart pounding wildly.

When she finally reached the gate, tired but driven on by her feelings of utter panic, Phyllis tried to pull the gate open, but a large metal latch kept it closed. Looking frantically over her shoulder, she tugged at the gate, without any success. Then she tried pulling at the latch, only to discover that it needed to be lifted up. When she finally did this, the gate swung open, and Phyllis squeezed through the opening and ran along the road, looking out for other signs of life.

The road too, was quiet. Phyllis felt so tired that she was ready to collapse in the road, but pushed herself to continue. She was free, and she was not going to let freedom slip away from her again. Looking back at the house, she realised there was no-one in pursuit. Clearly, her captors had become complacent about keeping her locked up.

She pushed on, stopping every hundred metres or so to catch her breath and to look over her shoulder to ensure that she was not being followed. Then she heard it; a bell, ringing loudly. The sound was coming from the house, and Phyllis knew at once that it was an alarm. They had discovered that she had disappeared. Gathering all her strength, she surged forward, running faster than she thought possible. She made it to the nearest turn-off, and turned into Glastonbury Street – hoping to keep out of sight of the house.

Phyllis ran blindly across the street, and only then realised that a horse and carriage was nearly upon her. The horses neighed loudly, causing her to stop abruptly – directly in the path of the oncoming carriage.

"Whoah!" shouted the coachman. The horses complained loudly, their hooves skidding on the cobbled road as the weight and momentum of the carriage pushed them forward, even while the reins were being pulled in violently. Phyllis's senses returned, adrenalin pulsing through her. At the last minute, she jumped out of the way, falling hard on the cobblestones and rolling on to her side. The horses missed her by centimetres, their hooves clattering loudly as the carriage groaned to a stop. She just lay there, in a state of shock and unable to move her limbs.

The coach door opened, and a grey-haired man stepped out, eyeing Phyllis in alarm.

"My dear lady," she heard him say with a tone of concern. "What on earth—"

The coachman too, climbed down, ready to assist. He noticed that Phyllis was wearing only a flimsy nightdress, and gave her a surprised look, uncertain of what to do next.

"My dear lady," the man said again. "Are you able to speak?"

Phyllis was trembling, but slowly felt her senses return. "I can— I'm fine," she stammered and tried to get up, but without success.

"Allow us to help you," said the man. Phyllis noticed that he was wearing a formal, double-breasted coat.

"Oh, would you?" Phyllis said, as she felt the man's strong, gloved hands grabbing her arm and supporting her back. She rose to her feet, feeling unsteady and swaying slightly from side to side.

"Bring the young lady to the carriage, General – if you'd be so kind," said a voice from the carriage door; a female voice.

"May I assist you, madam?" said the man. "Now, slowly please..."

He held Phyllis upright and gently guided her towards the carriage. The door was open, but Phyllis saw no sign of the woman whose voice she had heard. The man supported Phyllis's arm, and she grabbed hold of the door handle for additional support and stepped into the carriage's passenger cabin. Then she sunk back into the comfortable, luxuriously-cushioned seat, and for the first time saw the woman, sitting in the opposite seat.

The woman's white-grey hair was tucked under her bonnet, and she looked at Phyllis with a sympathetic smile. "How dreadful for you, dear," she said. "The coachman must have had his eyes elsewhere. I shall certainly give him a stern talking to."

The general also entered the cabin, and seated himself next to Phyllis. "Terrible business," he said. "We should have you checked out."

Phyllis self-consciously covered her belly with her arm, feeling vulnerable and exposed in her nightdress. The woman picked up a small throw from the seat beside her and handed it to Phyllis.

"This will keep you warm," she said.

The coachman appeared at the door, looking slightly sheepish. The older woman glanced at him and spoke curtly. "On your way, Gladstone. Let us proceed as planned."

"Yes m'lady," he replied. "You mean we should—"

"We must continue on our course," the woman said sharply. The coachman nodded deeply, then closed the door and took up his position at the front. Moments later, the carriage rocked as the horses started up.

Spontaneous tears welled up in Phyllis's eyes, and her trembling lips smiled. She did it. She was free. She wanted to shout for joy. She sunk back into the plush velvet-covered seat and for a few moments closed her eyes. The rocking motion of the carriage gave her comfort, and more importantly, made her feel safe. She could hardly believe her good fortune, and was amazed at her own strength and foresight in making her escape.

When she opened her eyes and glanced out the window, she saw glimpses of the stone fence of the manor house where she had been imprisoned. Just the thought of the place made the fear rise within her, and she let out a strangled cry, which she tried to suppress with her hand. The general, who was seated next to her, looked at her with alarm.

Phyllis shook her head. "'Tis nothing," she said, without further explanation.

The carriage began to slow down and then made a turn, passing through a gate. Phyllis, now alert again, sat straight up in her seat. She recognised the gate. It was unmistakable – the gate of the professor's manor house!

"What?" she said, her voice faltering. "Where are we?" She flattened her face against the carriage window. There was no mistake. They were back where she had started.

Phyllis lunged at the door, but the older woman – Dame Margaret Lafroste – grabbed her arms and held her inside the carriage. The general, who was caught by surprise, assisted her.

Phyllis screamed.

27

As soon as the carriage door opened, Riley approached with a look of grim determination on his face. Without a word, he peered into the carriage and, upon receiving a subtle nod from Margaret Lafroste, he released the step, and climbed into the cabin.

Phyllis cowered in the corner of the seat, whimpering.

"What on earth! What is the meaning of this?" said General La Fey, his indignant face glowing red in contrast to his white-grey hair.

"This young lady is a patient of Professor Strasberg's." Margaret Lafroste's voice carried no emotion.

"This is an outrage," the general protested, as Riley grabbed Phyllis's arm and pulled her towards the open carriage door.

Phyllis resisted angrily. She beat Riley with her fist, but he seemed impervious. Appearing to lose patience, he grabbed Phyllis around the waist, and half-carried, half-dragged her out of the cabin. The small throw that Margaret Lafroste had given Phyllis fell onto the floor of the carriage.

Riley worked quickly and efficiently, worming the kicking, clawing Phyllis through the open door. Once outside, he picked her up and threw her over his shoulder. She beat her fists against his back, but it made little difference.

The general too, stepped out of the carriage. "I must— I most strongly object," he said angrily, turning back to Margaret Lafroste.

"I regret that it had to be done in such a... brutal way, General, but it is quite necessary, I assure you."

"I doubt that very much, Madam," he said stiffly.

"The woman brutally murdered her own children, General. She is a danger to society. We were risking our own lives to be in such close proximity to her."

The general recoiled. "Good Lord!"

"She is under medical care here. Professor Strasberg was the only one willing to take on the burden she poses," said Margaret.

"Well, if you told me this before—"

"I couldn't, General. If that woman heard me, there's no telling what she would have done." Margaret allowed the image to settle into the general's imagination before she continued. "Let us put this terrible affair out of our minds, General."

He took a look at the front door of the manor house, which still stood ajar, and nodded thoughtfully.

"I promised Lucian I'd look in on the professor," said Margaret. "He's been rather out of sorts lately, I hear. So if you'll excuse me for a few moments..."

"Well, of course," said the general, his face still flushed.

The coachman appeared at the door, and he extended a hand to help Margaret down the steps. She stepped down slowly, carefully, but held herself upright, exhibiting her strength of purpose to the general.

Moments later, Professor Strasberg appeared at the open door, leaning on a walking stick.

"Professor!" she said, and walked to meet him.

"You have done me a great service," he said. "I must thank you for returning my... test subject to the fold. Trust me, this type of mistake won't happen again."

Margaret Lafroste accepted his thanks with a gracious nod. "I was concerned about your wellbeing," she said.

The professor walked forward in a slow and measured pace, and touched her arm. "I wanted to convey my condolences, and my apology for not attending your husband's funeral. He was a man of great stature."

Margaret nodded again. "We have all been deeply concerned about you, Professor."

"I lack the strength of youth," he said, attempting to grin. "Won't you come inside?"

Margaret supported the professor's free arm, and they both entered the manor house.

———•—•—•———

Professor Strasberg poured sherry into two glasses and handed one to Margaret Lafroste.

"My condolences," he said. "As you know, I have always counted Reginald as a friend... and I regret there was nothing I could do to save his life."

Margaret nodded acknowledgement. "He followed your career with keen interest, Simeon. He respected your knowledge; your wisdom."

Simeon took a sip of sherry and sat down in a leather armchair next to Margaret's. He was pale, and his breathing shallow.

"What happened, Simeon?" asked Margaret.

Simeon paused for a moment before he replied: "Impatience." He took another sip. "The prize I have been seeking for all these years was suddenly mine. I held it in my own hands, delirious with excitement. That was my undoing."

"The Book of Transmutation? Lucian said you finally found it."

He shifted uncomfortably in the chair, recalling his own reaction at being poisoned. "I should have recognised the clear warnings. The man who gave it to me – sold it to me – was gravely ill. But I ignored the obvious and stepped right into the trap."

"And now?" asked Margaret.

"I am on the mend, thanks to a man I met. The man I employed to translate the manuscript. He found a hidden note – with a warning."

"How extremely fortunate."

"I cheated death, Margaret. This time, I have triumphed."

"I must thank this man in person one day," said Margaret, "whoever he is."

"Tennison Abbywick, a man introduced to me by Aleister Crowley."

"Ah yes, Aleister Crowley. I hear the young Aleister wants to be a member of our circle," said Margaret.

"He has made no secret of it. He would be an asset to your... group."

"You've never attempted to join our group, Simeon," said Margaret. "I'm curious. Why not?"

Simeon smiled politely. "As you know, my priorities lie elsewhere," he said.

"What is so important about this book, Simeon? I could always rely on you to be rational – to calculate every step without error. But to risk your life?"

"The book is the key to the future, Margaret. It is the reason of my being. It is what I have searched for all these years. Looking at those pages convinced me that I was looking at the greatest treasure on earth; the secret to creating life itself."

"'Tis a pity, then, that it arrived too late for my Reginald." Margaret's face changed; anger flashed in her eyes.

"I'm dreadfully sorry," said Simeon quietly. "But it would not have helped. The book is about creating life anew, not saving lives that are already..." He didn't finish the sentence.

"What about our plans? Our vision?" The anger was gone from Margaret's eyes, replaced by disappointment.

"A grander vision will emerge, that I promise you," he said and then, after some hesitation, added: "But I need your help."

Margaret leaned forward, and kinked an eyebrow.

Simeon lowered his voice, even though there was no one else in the room. "Perhaps you remember a young man, an inventor of sorts – an imposter at the function at my house..."

"Accompanied by a young woman? Of course I remember."

"I hear he is singularly talented at making machines – delicate machines. If only I took more careful note of his name," said Simeon. He looked eagerly at Margaret, hoping she would remember.

Margaret smiled. "He produced a... delicate machine for our mutual friend, Helen Gartner," she said. "His name is Jack Lightfoot."

28

The large wooden crate positioned near the corner looked out of place in the otherwise orderly and finely-furnished room. The top of the crate was open, and Jack was doing the final checks on the machine he had built for Helen Gartner. He fussed over the machine with gloved hands.

Nadia, her hair tousled from shadow-sparring, and still holding her sword, was standing next to him. Her face was flushed with the excitement of reliving her experiences at the cemetery. "It took me quite a while to get closer to the mausoleum," she explained. "The garrotter was guarding the entrance."

Jack looked up briefly from the gleaming machine he was working on. "Be careful with that," he said, looking at the sword in Nadia's hand. "Do you mean he was standing in the way?"

"No. He was guarding the entrance, making sure that nobody could enter – no person other than those already inside."

"Hmm," said Jack sceptically, returning his attention to the machine. He had a small silver instrument in his hand, with which he tested the multitude of coil springs.

"Then I did something risky."

Jack turned to her and sighed. "Nadia, your entire excursion was risky. You should not have done any of this. You could have been... abducted."

"I threw a stone – to the far side, to draw his attention away."

Jack stared at her, waiting for Nadia to continue.

"It worked," she said at last. "He was distracted for long enough to allow me to get close to the door, and look through the keyhole."

She paused.

"Pray continue," said Jack, and he frowned.

"I saw Dame Lafroste, and I think she was standing near the casket. It appears she was surrounded by the rest of the group, but of course I couldn't be certain. The strange thing is that she was wearing absolutely nothing—"

Jack's mouth hinged open. "She was not wearing any clothes? At her husband's funeral?"

Nadia shook her head: "Not in the mausoleum. Not a stitch."

Jack paused for a moment, and conjured up an image of a naked Margaret Lafroste in his mind – then tried with difficulty to obliterate the image.

"Why?" he asked finally.

"A religion perhaps; a cult," said Nadia. "She had... markings on her body. Decorative, I think, but also probably something to do with a ritual."

"The others—" Jack questioned, and immediately regretted that he did.

Nadia nodded, and Jack understood.

"What makes you think it was a ritual?" he asked.

Nadia hesitated before answering. "They kneeled before her. And they kissed her in areas not considered normal in polite society," she said with a grin.

"Dear God."

"Jack," said Nadia, amused. "You cannot be a protected little boy forever."

Jack shook his head. "Why would they do that?"

"A ritual," said Nadia. "They paid their respects to her."

"And this is your proposition?"

"Do you have a better one?"

Jack shook his head. "We must advise the sheriff at once," he said.

"Jack, do you in all honesty think he'd listen – and if he does listen, do you think he'd believe my story?"

"Then what?" he said. "What do we do with this information?"

"Don't you see, Jack? This is a mystery. We only need to unravel the details, and then we'll get to the facts of the case."

"I think we should be best advised to leave this alone, Nadia," said Jack. "The sheriff dismissed us. This whole affair is no longer any of our concern."

But Nadia stared at the opposite wall, wrapped up in her own thoughts. "Isn't it curious that your beloved professor was not at the funeral," she said. "I would have thought that he was a member of the inner circle."

"What inner circle, Nadia? This is all in your mind."

"The group who took part in the ritual, Jack; why wasn't the professor among them?"

"Possibly because he was sensible enough to distance himself from this... pantomime."

Nadia shook her head. "I expect there is another reason altogether," she said. She laid her sword down on the floor and picked up one of Jack's small metal tools, something that looked like a set of pincers. "Let's pretend this is Margaret Lafroste." She placed the pincers on a small oak table.

"Now here is the garrotter," she said, placing a large screw next to the set of pincers. "The professor... and the jail," she said, setting down a pair of scissors to represent Simeon Strasberg, and a small metal tin to represent the jail.

"And here is the condemned prisoner, Fryman Sellers." She placed another, shorter screw on the metal tin. "And let's not forget the unfortunate Jerome Abbott – present at the execution and found dead not much later."

Nadia's finger touched the improvised placeholders, trying to put her thoughts into words. "We know that the professor and Dame Lafroste were connected—"

"Because she was invited to the professor's dinner party?" Jack interrupted.

Nadia shook her head. "She accused Fryman Sellers, who ended up in jail – the very jail at which Professor Strasberg did his research."

"Proving... nothing."

"The garrotter from the jail showed up at the funeral."

"And was the professor at the funeral?" asked Jack.

"No."

Jack smiled, self-satisfied.

"And yet we know, from the dinner party, that they were good friends. So why was he absent at the funeral?"

"Occupied elsewhere. Too busy with his important work. Travelling at the time. There could be a hundred reasons," said Jack.

"I suspect there must be a very good reason why he missed the funeral of a close friend... or the husband of a close friend." Nadia paused for a moment. "The husband, Reginald Lafroste, had friends in high places." Then Nadia remembered something that had been buried in the back of her consciousness. "Jack," she said excitedly. "Do you remember who else we saw at the professor's dinner party? None other than Lord Edmund Faderley, the Earl of Whittlecast."

"What are you implying?" said Jack. His voice sounded tired.

"There was someone at the funeral – I wasn't sure at first, but I knew it was someone I had seen before. It was Faderley. I'm convinced of it now."

"Nadia..." Jack began in a cautionary tone.

"A man powerful enough to persuade the prison authorities to do his bidding – and powerful enough to convince the sheriff to stop the investigation."

"Nadia, this is preposterous."

"I think you were right, Jack. We should indeed speak to the sheriff again."

29

A nondescript horse-drawn carriage stopped in front of the imposing Museum of Antiquities in central London, and a sole passenger disembarked. The late-evening mist was stirred up by an icy breeze, and the man drew a heavy-woven black cape tightly around his body to keep warm.

He chose a side entrance to the museum, found the door unlocked, and let himself in. However, once he was inside, he saw two men waiting at the foot of a large marble staircase: Lucian Baker and a rough-looking man, who was wearing an ill-fitting suit with a waistcoat that pulled tightly across his large belly. The man was both fat and muscular at the same time, his face adorned by a plump handlebar moustache.

Lucian looked quizzically at the newly arrived guest. Then, as he stepped forward into the light, Lucian suddenly said, "Ah, general. What a pleasure. For a moment I failed to recognise you."

"Dastardly weather," the general mumbled. "Am I late?"

"Hardly," said Lucian jovially. "Allow me to take your coat."

General La Fey handed him the cape, and glanced up the stairs – until Lucian shook his head. "We had the good fortune to find a new, and much more suitable, location for our meeting. I think you'll be most pleased."

The general moved in the direction of the staircase, but

Lucian touched his sleeve. "We're downstairs." Then he led the general past the stairs towards a darkened, almost completely hidden doorway at the rear. It was an unremarkable oak door, which looked as if it offered entry into a cleaner or caretaker's cabinet. But when Lucian opened the door, it revealed a narrow staircase leading to a basement.

They descended the dimly-lit staircase and entered through another door into what looked like a storage room for documents. Lucian led the general towards the back of the room and opened another, smaller door.

"Good grief, man," the general complained, when he saw yet another staircase leading down to a deeper level. After descending the stairs, they reached a doorway with an imposing and highly polished rosewood door, carved with ghostlike figures, ghouls and dwarves. Lucian stopped and smiled at the general.

"Welcome to one of London's best kept secrets. This place is rumoured to have been used by the monks of Medmenham Abbey," said Lucian, his eyes gleaming excitedly.

"The Hellfire Club?"

"The very same," said Lucian. He slowly opened the heavy door, and paused to allow the general to enter ahead of him.

The general stepped into the small entrance hall slowly. Thick, richly embroidered curtains blocked the view of the main room. Several coats hung on hooks against one of the walls, and Lucian added the general's cape to the collection. Then he lifted the lid of a large black box, and produced a white mask that was designed to obscure the eyes and nose. There was black shading around the mask's eye holes, giving it a skull-like appearance. Lucian held it out to the general, and smiled. "Your mask for this evening, general," he said.

The general looked vaguely irritated. He took the mask reluctantly and slipped it on so that it fitted over his eyes. Lucian was pleased with the result, but the general was in no mood for smiling.

Lucian donned his own mask – shiny-red and devilish in appearance – and then parted the curtains and ushered his guest into the main meeting room. It was much larger than the general had anticipated, with a high ceiling, a gigantic mural against one of the walls, rich carpets and plush furniture.

Against the far wall, the general saw the words *Fais ce que tu voudras* painted in black letters and knew it translated to 'Do what thou wilt.'

Some of the assembled guests – all of them masked – looked up in his direction, and nodded politely. The general acknowledged their greetings, feeling slightly foolish behind his own mask.

"A brandy, perhaps?" inquired Lucian, smiling.

The general nodded, some cheer returning to his face. "Has Dame Lafroste arrived?" he asked.

Lucian nodded and busied himself pouring the general's drink. "She is preparing," he said.

"I was wondering if I might have a moment in private with her. There is an urgent matter I wish to discuss."

Lucian hesitated. "This is an important night for our priestess…"

"That's quite alright, Lucian," a voice said. Margaret Lafroste was standing close by, her face obscured by a shiny silver mask, with an attachment that looked like a bird's beak. She wore a long gown, glittering with intricate designs embroidered in gold, green and red thread. She smiled at General La Fey, and then took his hand. "I'm delighted you have decided to attend; absolutely delighted."

"That is most gracious, madam," said the general. "I hope you'll forgive an old man his concerns."

"Nonsense; you are not old and your concerns will always carry the highest importance for me," said Margaret, and then turned to Lucian. "Lucian, would you mind very much excusing us?"

Lucian, who had already helped himself to a couple of glasses of brandy, seemed carefree. He nodded, and then joined the other guests, greeting them in his usual jovial style.

Once they were alone, the general said, "The young woman, the one we left at the professor's house, remained in my thoughts, which is why I sent you the letter. I hope it was not too audacious. You see, I was concerned for her wellbeing, and thought you might be the appropriate person to—"

Margaret touched the general's arm, and he could feel the warmth of her touch radiate through his sleeve. It was bold, but he knew that Margaret Lafroste was never one to shrink away from expressing her feelings.

"General... Henri," she said. "I understood your concerns the moment I received your letter, and I thank you for your discretion. Can I assume that you have not discussed the matter with anyone?"

The general shook his head firmly. "Naturally, I kept this matter between us," he said.

She hooked her arm into his and walked him towards the door through which he had entered. "Well, I have good news, Henri. I spoke to the professor. He seems to think the young lady in question had made a remarkable recovery – a medical miracle, I think he called it. So, I asked him to bring her here tonight."

The general was surprised. "You should not have troubled yourself over my petty concerns, Dame Lafroste," he said, feeling uncomfortable about the disruption he had caused.

"Not at all," she said, and the general could detect that she was smiling behind her mask. "Unfortunately, she has not yet arrived, as the professor had other important business to attend to. However I expect her to arrive without much further delay."

"There is really no need—" the general began to say, but Margaret Lafroste stopped him with a gesture of her hand.

"I feel that I owe this to you, general. And I hope you'll be willing to accept this arrangement, and that you'll forgive me at my lack of sensitivity about your concerns."

The general was left speechless. An apology was the last thing he'd expected.

"You are most gracious," he said finally, and then allowed himself to be led out of the room, into the passage and into the room next door, which was stark in contrast and had a table and simple set of chairs in the middle of it.

"An awful room, but the best we could do under such short notice," Margaret apologised.

"I beg you, madam. Please do not apologise," the general said.

"Could I ask you to remain here, until the professor's assistant arrives?" said Margaret. "Unfortunately, duty calls, and I have no choice but to proceed with our meeting in the other room."

The general nodded, and bestowed a smile on Margaret,

even though it was partially obscured by his mask.

She nodded and then left the room, leaving the general by himself. He sat down in one of the chairs, and on realizing that his mask served no purpose here, he removed it and put it down on the table.

In the room next door, he could hear excited voices, as Margaret Lafroste joined her other guests.

Margaret's gown caused a stir and light applause among the guests. Once her audience had settled down, she began. "Welcome to our exciting new meeting place. Tonight we have a new guest, who will soon be a new member – and he is sitting somewhere near you, right now."

The guests glanced at one another, hoping to spot the new guest among the masked figures.

"I shall introduce him shortly, but first we must honour the rituals of our founders, and pay respects to the spirits and daemons."

Margaret made a gesture to draw everyone's attention to the back of the room. There, Lucian opened a curtain and revealed a doorway, hidden in the wall panelling.

"As you know, this room was once used by the monks of Medmenham," said Margaret. "What you may not know, is that they have built a hidden temple in this very building, and that is where we shall assemble for the rest of the proceedings. Please follow me."

She walked through the open door, and the guests followed.

The adjoining room was smaller, and had a black ceiling, which gave the impression of a black void hanging directly above them. Oil lamps, mounted on the walls, provided dim, flickering illumination of the gargoyle-like figurines that were mounted on the walls and in the corners of the ceiling. The figurines had fierce animal and human faces, some of them hybrids – half-human, half-leopard or human bodies with bird-like features. At the far end of the room was a small stage, raised above floor level by a few inches, and on it stood an altar, draped in black.

Margaret Lafroste waited patiently until all her guests were inside. She smiled at the way they expressed surprise at the interior of the temple and its unusual decorations.

"Dear friends," she said, her gown shimmering in the dim light. "I hope you like our new meeting place." The small crowd murmured their approval. "I must express my gratitude to someone among you, for telling us about this most exquisite place, and for obtaining it for our use. That person is also the man I want to introduce as a new member of our order tonight. His name is Aleister Crowley – a friend, respected alchemist, and a powerful magician... Aleister, please show yourself."

A man in a dark cloak and wearing a golden mask stepped forward. The mask was animal-like, and showed large fangs protruding from the gaping mouth. Aleister stood next to Margaret Lafroste, and smiled behind his mask as the other members murmured his name, and then shouted "Hail Aleister!"

"May our proceedings here be blessed," said Margaret, and she placed a hand on Aleister's shoulder. "I, priestess of barren lands, guardian of the mist, protector of the ancient arts, propose Aleister Crowley as a new member to this order. Let the ceremony begin!"

A black-haired young man and woman entered from the back of the room, and made their way to the altar. They were naked, apart from a sheet of black silk, wrapped like a giant scarf around their bodies. The young woman carried a staff that glistened gold in the light of the oil lamps, and she handed it to Margaret, with a brief curtsy.

Lucian approached the stage with a small bowl and sprinkled its perfumed contents on to the two young participants. Then he unrolled a scroll of yellowed paper and began reading from it. "There is no part of me that is not of the gods," he said. "The soul is of infinite space, before whom time is ashamed, and understanding dark..."

Meanwhile, General la Fey sat quietly and alone in the room where Margaret Lafroste had left him. He stared at the opposite wall for a period, and then took out his pocket watch to check the time. He could not hear any noises, although he assumed the ritual would go ahead without him. The silence became oppressive.

Finally, the door handle turned.

"Professor..." the general began, rising to his feet. But then, to his disappointment, he saw that it was Riley. "Oh, it's you."

Riley nodded. "The professor gave instructions for me to provide you with an escort to a private meeting place."

"So he's not coming here?"

"Unfortunately, the professor was not able to see his way—"

"Fine, good," said the general, interrupting Riley. "When is this meeting intended for?"

"Right now, if it suits you, General."

"Very well; lead the way," said the general, and he followed Riley out of the room.

In the meantime, the group attending the ritual looked on eagerly as Margaret Lafroste stepped forward and placed a crown, woven out of twigs and leaves, on Aleister's head.

"Welcome, Aleister. Your magical name will be *Frater Perdurabo*: 'I shall endure to the end'." The group erupted in applause, and they stepped forward, each touching Aleister in turn and running their hands over his chest and down his body.

Aleister's eyes glowed with pleasure. He touched the other members of the group in turn, kissing some of them and relishing the status that he has been hankering after for such a long time. Most of the members began disrobing, and several of them appeared to be sexually excited. Aleister approached the young woman at the altar, who played the role of nymph in the ritual, and tongue-kissed her. The young black-haired man, touched Aleister from behind, and Aleister turned and pulled him closer, as he carried on kissing the girl. The threesome stood together and kissed and fondled each other. Soon they were all naked, revelling in their nudity and sensuality.

Margaret Lafroste too, was naked, and she approached a woman who was wearing a cat-like mask. Without hesitation she kissed her on the mouth, and the woman responded by opening her mouth and kissing Margaret eagerly. Margaret lifted the woman's mask with her fingertips. Helen Gartner's face smiled back at her.

Outside the building, General La Fey followed Riley to where a carriage was waiting.

"Where are we going?" he asked.

Riley turned slowly. "To meet the professor... and the woman."

"Where?" the general repeated.

"The professor asked me not to... divulge the details of the meeting," said Riley. He was proud of himself for remembering the proper words.

"Divulge or not. This is highly irregular and I wish to know where I am being taken." The general felt uneasy, and his suspicion increased.

"The truth of the matter is that I'm not sure, sir. The coachman has been told the location, but I have not," said Riley, and shrugged.

"Then I wish to speak with the coachman," said the general. He ignored the carriage door that Riley held open and walked to the front of the carriage. Looking up at the coachman, he said, "I wish to know where we are going!"

The general, slightly deaf from old age, did not realise that Riley was closing in behind him. He also did not see the blade that was concealed in the cane that Riley had carried with him.

Riley withdrew the long blade from its sheath and, before the general could turn around, he plunged it into his back. The general's eyes froze in shock, and his expression of annoyance turned to pain as the blade pierced his heart. The sharp point protruded through the front of his shirt, and a patch of blood spread quickly across his shirtfront.

The general sunk to his knees, his own breathing hissing in his ears.

Riley waited patiently until he was dead.

30

Phyllis Secombe found herself strapped down on a narrow bed, stark naked. Her wrists were secured to the sides of the examination bed, and her legs raised and attached to a pair of stirrups, which forced her legs apart and exposed her pubis to anyone who cared to look.

Riley checked that all the straps were secure. He smiled at her, his yellowed front teeth bared.

"Should keep you out of mischief," he said. He ran his finger from her belly button, down to her pubis, watching for her reaction with an amused smile.

When Professor Simeon Strasberg entered, Riley withdrew his hand and stood aside.

"What are you? Scared of the old man?" Phyllis spat out.

Riley frowned angrily.

"She's trying to goad you," said the professor calmly. "Pay her no attention."

"What do you want with me?" shouted Phyllis, but the professor didn't reply. Instead he sat down at the foot end of the examination table and looked at the area between her legs.

"That will be all for the moment, Riley," he said at last. Riley nodded, and with a poisoned glance at Phyllis, left the room.

"Now let's see," said the professor. "His finger slid into Phyllis's vagina, and he probed her inner private parts, feeling and prodding his way.

Phyllis sweated, and her face felt flushed, even though it was not particularly warm in the room.

"What is it that you want?" she said again, this time without really expecting an answer.

""What I want is your cooperation," said Simeon without apparent humour, "And for you to bear healthy babies."

"Babies? More than one?" asked Phyllis, aghast.

"Possibly," said Simeon. "Let's take it one step at a time, shall we?"

"But why? I don't understand," said Phyllis, on the verge of tears.

Simeon looked at her strangely. "Quite simply, to change the course of history," he said.

"Why me?" Tears rolled down Phyllis's cheeks.

"Because you are here, and reasonably healthy. Both important factors," he replied. Simeon placed a bugle-shaped metal instrument against her belly and pressed the other, narrow end against his ear, listening intently. After a few moments of silence, he said. "There is movement. That is good; strong action. Do you feel anything?"

Phyllis didn't reply, but stared at him angrily.

"You look after this baby with great care, and I shall do the same for you," he said.

"Why should I believe a single word you utter?" said Phyllis, the anger boiling inside her.

"If this baby fails, I shall have no further use for you. You can believe that."

Phyllis didn't respond, but felt an uncomfortable lump in her throat. She was afraid, terribly afraid. And she realised anew there was nothing she could do to get herself out of this terrible situation.

The professor turned away for a moment, and then picked up a different instrument from a large wooden tray. This one Phyllis recognised.

"Oh no," she groaned.

Simeon pinched the one end of a rubber tube between his fingers and then unceremoniously began pushing it into her anus. Phyllis groaned loudly, and then a growl of frustration and pain escaped her lips.

"Enemas are good for you," said Simeon. "It will help to keep disease away."

Phyllis closed her eyes as the rubber tube wormed deeper inside her.

31

Helen Gartner arrived unannounced at Jack Lightfoot's door, rapping lightly with the door knocker on the front door. There was no reply, and she repeated the knocking. When the door eventually opened, a surprised-looking Jack stared back at her.

"Miss Gartner, I had no idea—" Jack began, confused but pleasantly surprised.

"I must apologise, Jack. It was my intention to arrange a meeting, but when things happened so fast, well, I was so excited I had to see you at once."

Jack was delighted, and ushered her inside, glancing back at the street to check if any of his neighbours had noticed Helen's arrival. There was no sign that they had. He noticed that she was carrying a large, flat leather wallet, bound by a leather strap.

When they sat down in the library, Jack said: "Tea? You prefer Earl Grey."

"None of the ceremony, please Jack," said Helen. "What I have to tell you is far more important than a cup of tea."

Jack leaned forward eagerly. "Please."

"A friend, a dear friend, was looking for someone of unique talent. Someone who could build something quite extraordinary – something that has never been built before, Jack. When I heard what my friend had in mind, I immediately thought of you – your astonishing skills at creating something that is functional, and beautiful at the same time."

Jack blushed, but he made no comment. He was eager to know what she was talking about.

"I hope you can forgive me, Jack. I mentioned your name, and the fact that you produced for me one of the most exquisite machines yet devised," she said.

"Well of course I am pleased, but..."

Helen Gartner opened the leather wallet, and extracted from it a sheaf of papers. New, good quality paper with fresh ink on it, Jack noticed. The first page had some lettering on it, and with a lightly smudged thumbprint in one of the corners, as if the page had been written in some haste.

Helen dampened a finger on her lips, an action that Jack found to be utterly charming and somewhat erotic. He watched as she began searching through the pages and finally found the desired one, which had a drawing on it.

But instead of handing it to Jack, she held it up against her chest and spoke earnestly. "Jack, it is vital that you do not tell a soul of this. I swore that I would keep this a secret."

"Of course, but—"

"It is of the utmost importance that no part of this is divulged. Will you have a look at this, Jack, but will you undertake an oath that you will not whisper a word of it to anyone?"

"An oath?" said Jack uncomfortably. "Is that really necessary?"

Helen nodded vigorously.

Jack had never taken an oath with such a beautiful woman in attendance. It felt awkward.

"I... most solemnly... swear to keep this information secret—"

"Excellent," she interrupted him excitedly, and promptly put the chosen page in his hands.

Jack looked at the strange drawing on the page and frowned. It looked like a machine of some sort, alright, but nothing recognisable.

"What is it?"

"My... friend has created detailed drawings of everything you'll need," Helen replied. "At present, I am not at liberty to give you any more information. I hope you'll understand, Jack."

"Hmm." Jack examined the drawing closely. The 'machine' looked a little like a pot-bellied stove, clearly made of metal. It had a small window in front, probably meant to be made of glass, and tubes extending out on all sides. To Jack's eye, it appeared as if the tubes extended to the inside – but there was no way of determining what they were meant to connect to.

"It's difficult to judge the size of it," he finally remarked.

"Can you do this work, Jack?"

Jack was hesitant, but agreed. "I'm sure it can be done. How much time would I have? The materials would be important—"

"I knew you could do it, Jack. I didn't have a moment's doubt." Helen was beaming, and she briefly clutched his hand in her own. Jack felt a warm glow spread throughout his body. "Because of the nature of this project, Jack, because it is so special, and so hush-hush, the work will need to be done in the highest level of secrecy. Do you understand?"

"Secrecy? Certainly, yes."

"Jack," she said, smiling warmly at him. "My dear friend would like to meet you, in person, to discuss this. Are you willing? Please say yes, Jack."

Jack nodded. "Yes. Of course, yes."

Helen smiled, and Jack noticed that her smile brought out the cutest dimples in her cheeks.

32

Bates and Henley Chemist Shop had a single, street-facing window, in which was displayed a number of apothecary items, including jars of salts, and a large, but old scale with weights and measures. Inside, the wooden shelves carried a large array of jars, all of them labelled and some bearing the inscription that marked them as poisons.

Bates and Henley took pride in preparing its own tinctures, which attracted customers from all over London. One such regular customer was Sheriff Emilio Ducanti, who stopped by the chemist shop again that day, limping slightly from an old injury that kept him awake at night. He waited patiently as the pharmacist mixed a preparation. He watched as the man's slender, nimble hands used a mortar and pestle to crush unidentified crystals and add them to the mix.

The pharmacist sported a smartly separated middle path, slicked down with hair oil, as well as a small but proud handlebar moustache, which he wore with considerable pride. The powdery mixture was eventually transferred to a small glass bottle, and duly labelled, before being passed over the counter to the sheriff.

Ducanti smiled at the pharmacist, trying to hide the stabbing pains in his leg.

"As always, thank you," he said.

"A delight, as always," the pharmacist replied, and bowed his head briefly.

Ducanti slipped the little bottle into his coat pocket and was about to leave the shop when he noticed a familiar face at the shop window, looking in. The face belonged to Nadia Barossa. Ducanti sighed.

Outside, the street smelled of horse manure. It matched Ducanti's mood. "How did you find me here?" he asked.

"By good fortune," Nadia said. "What ails you?" Her eyes glanced briefly at the tiny pin Ducanti wore on his lapel.

"An old injury... the wars," said Ducanti, grimacing slightly as he began walking. Nadia walked alongside him. "And I assume there is something that you wish to discuss?" he said. He deliberately avoided looking at Nadia.

"There is something that you may wish to have knowledge of," she replied.

"And what would that be?"

"I heard that Reginald Lafroste is dead," she said.

"I've heard the same thing. You may consider that rumour confirmed."

"Rumour has it that a select group of guests remained behind for a special ceremony, after the funeral had been concluded," Nadia said. She watched for a reaction on Ducanti's face, but saw only a small flicker of the eyelid.

"That is perfectly acceptable," he said.

"Curious though, that the entrance to this ceremony appeared to be closely guarded..."

Ducanti stopped, a blush of anger colouring his cheeks. "Your insistence on investigating the private affairs of the Lafroste family is becoming tedious," he said. "As I recall, I asked you to refrain from it."

"The Lafroste funeral was a public affair. The man was well known. Many citizens of London attended."

"Including you?" said Ducanti.

"Yes."

"Should I prepare myself for further... revelations?" he asked.

"A private ceremony was held in the mausoleum afterwards," said Nadia. "After the other guests had left."

"Which naturally aroused your suspicions…"

"It happened behind closed doors. Locked doors, guarded by none other than Raskovic, the garrotter from the prison."

Ducanti showed an interest in this piece of news. "The garrotter was there?"

Nadia nodded. "Right by the entrance, to ensure that nobody else could enter."

"That merely proves that he was in the employ of someone who had arranged the funeral," Ducanti said.

"He was in the employ of Dame Lafroste, of that I am certain," said Nadia.

"Even if he was—"

"I suspect he had been in her employ all along."

"Which proves absolutely nothing," said the sheriff.

"It was what I saw at the private ceremony afterwards that was particularly revealing."

"You were at the ceremony?" Ducanti sighed. "Uninvited, I assume?"

"I wasn't inside, but found a way to look at what was happening inside."

"Miss Barossa, if you were acting illegally, I may have to pursue the matter, as part of my duties."

"Your pin," said Nadia, and she touched the little pin on his jacket lapel. "Why are you wearing it?"

Ducanti appeared reluctant to reply at first, but then he responded. "I wanted to see if I could get a reaction from someone. My thoughts were that it might be a club, or society or something. A failed attempt on my part, I'm afraid."

"I saw it – the same design," said Nadia. "At the funeral."

"Someone wore the same pin?"

"Pin? No," she said. "I saw a larger version of the same thing. But it was unmistakable."

"Now, Miss Barossa, don't keep me in suspense."

"It was a marking, a tattoo in a person's skin. I didn't recognise it immediately, but later I remembered that it matched the design on the pin."

"Whose skin?"

"At the funeral, at the private event that happened afterwards, I peeked through the keyhole. What I saw was people taking part in a ritual," said Nadia, watching Ducanti's expression closely. "They removed their clothes – exposed their skin. That's when I saw it."

"Whose skin?" Ducanti repeated.

"Dame Margaret Lafroste," said Nadia.

The outburst she had expected finally arrived.

"I am thoroughly convinced that you are conducting a vendetta against Dame Lafroste – a nasty, vindictive campaign to discredit one of the pillars of our community!" Ducanti bellowed. He lowered his voice as he noticed that other people on the street were staring at him. "I will hear no more of this ridiculous speculation."

"Every word is true," said Nadia steadfastly.

"Miss Barossa," said the sheriff. "Our discussion is over. Have a good day." He began walking away, and Nadia remained behind, unable to think of any other way of convincing the sheriff that her testimony was true.

As he walked, Ducanti was bristling with so much anger that he hardly noticed his aching leg. Yet something was nagging at him. The troublesome thought in his head was that Nadia Barossa was not telling lies. But how could it possibly be true?

33

Jack paced up in down, fidgeting with a pocket watch that he had removed from his waistcoat pocket. Where was she? Why didn't she tell him where she was going? He felt Nadia's absence in the room. The silence was oppressive, and with the shutters drawn, the library felt isolated. But Jack's mind soon leapt back on to something else altogether; a machine. He imagined that it was a magnificent machine that he would be asked to build. Finally, a client with a job worthy of his skills, he thought.

He waited for another five minutes and then glanced, for the fourteenth time that day, at his silver pocket watch. Jack knew that it was approximately 840 steps to the railway station, and that it would take him about nine minutes – just one of the many obsessive details he had stored in his memory.

He opened a leather case and checked its contents: a set of tools mainly, along with a canister of oil, a number of bolts and screws in a jar, cloth, and string of various thicknesses, rubber tubing, and electrical wiring – everything he had considered important for working away from his own laboratory.

Then he sat down to write Nadia a short note, and sealed it in an envelope. He wrote her name on it and positioned the envelope near a flower vase in the entrance hall.

With one last look at the note, he picked up his bag and walked out the door, closing it firmly behind him.

Clapham Road Station was bustling. Jack dodged hawkers, newspaper salesmen and commuters to get to the main entrance. He rolled his newspaper and held it pointing upwards, as if he was carrying a torch. He felt a little foolish at first, but continued to wait at the pavement's edge. Horse carriages came and went until Jack heard the rhythmic rumble of a motor car engine. The car was unlike anything Jack had seen before. It was a motor cab, which had the driver sit in the open in front, and with an enclosed cab for passengers at the back.

The car stopped next to the pedestrian walkway, and the driver signalled to Jack. Jack hesitantly lowered his newspaper and walked towards the vehicle. He didn't recognise the driver, and wanted to confirm that the car was intended for him, but then it occurred to him that he didn't know his client's name.

The driver hopped out of the driver's seat and opened the passenger door. Curiously, the windows of the motor cab were blacked out with a thick curtaining material.

"Sorry, guv, there no scenic view on this drive," said the driver. "Orders from my employer."

Jack nodded slowly. His new client was certainly very secretive. He stepped into the cab and sat back in the comfortably upholstered seat. Moments later, the door closed and Jack was enveloped in near-darkness. At the same time, the outside noise was muffled, and Jack felt as if he was captured within a cocoon.

The strange trip in the motor cab took Jack halfway across London. He waited patiently as the cab swayed gently from side to side, and occasionally stop-started through the denser horse-and-cart traffic. He could occasionally hear crowd noises from outside, as well as the typical clip-clop noises of horses on cobbled roads, but as the journey progressed, it grew quieter. Jack leaned his head against the back of the seat, and closed his eyes.

The motor cab entered the grounds at Harrows Gate, but instead of stopping in front of the entrance, it pulled round and stopped at a half-hidden entrance near the back of the building.

Jack squinted against the outside light when the door opened, and found himself quickly ushered into the building, and then led to an expansive library.

There was something familiar about the house, although Jack didn't recognise it at once. The first thing he noticed about the library was a peculiar smell, as if someone had released chemicals of some sort in the room. While he waited for his client, he took the time to admire the paintings on the wall. He recognised Francesco Francia's *Madonna and Child with Angel*, hanging in a gilded frame, and was immediately impressed by his host's wealth.

"Not the original, unfortunately, but a twin," said a voice behind him.

Jack turned and instantly recognised his secretive host. "Professor Strasberg. I didn't recognise your home."

Simeon walked towards him with a hand outreached in greeting. "I must apologise for the secrecy, Mister Lightfoot," he said. "Unfortunately, this project is highly sensitive, and it must be kept out of the public eye at all cost."

Jack shook his hand warmly. "May I say it's an honour, sir. I never expected—"

"I've heard excellent things about you, Mister Lightfoot. The honour is mine, entirely."

Simeon gestured towards a seat at the large table, which dominated the centre of the room. "We have much to discuss, Mister Lightfoot. That is, if you are willing to accept this most delicate and important assignment."

Jack nodded. "Well of course. How could I refuse?"

Simeon sat down in the chair next to his. "Then I shall tell you everything. However, there is one very important consideration. The work will need to be done here, at my house. I cannot risk the plans leaving these premises. It is of immense importance that you remain here, in this house, until the work is done."

"But... my clothes. I may need some things."

"Everything you need will be provided, Mister Lightfoot."

"And I would need to tell—"

"Your associate? Miss Barossa?" Simeon interrupted.

"Exactly."

Simeon slid a sheet of paper towards him on the table, and tapped with his fingertip on it. "Write her a note, Mister Lightfoot, and I will see to it that it gets delivered to her personally. You have my word."

"I... I er..."

"Mister Lightfoot, I would not have considered inconveniencing you in this way, if it wasn't of the greatest importance. This project needs to be completed in absolute secrecy. Some of the most prominent figures in this country, including the Minister of War, have a personal stake in this – and they rely on me to appoint the right person for this work. You, Mister Lightfoot, are that person. I have never been more certain of anything in my life."

"I... I am honoured, sir," Jack said, feeling slightly bashful. He felt sorry that he had ever questioned the professor's demands. "Of course I shall do as you ask."

The professor smiled, his gaunt face appearing ghostly in the gaslight. Then he rose from his chair and walked to a cabinet against the wall, near the bookshelves. He unlocked it with a small key, then turned to Jack. "Brandy, perhaps?"

Jack shook his head. "I don't. Thank you."

Simeon nodded, then removed a large book from the cabinet, brought it to the table and placed it in front of Jack.

Simeon donned a pair of white gloves and slowly turned page after page. Jack caught glimpses of a weird text and drawings – of plants, astrological symbols, the female form, and what appeared to be human bodies, dissected for examination.

Simeon finally stopped on a page that had a drawing of a machine on it. The ink was slightly faded, but Jack could still make out most of the detail. The machine looked like a pot-bellied stove, with many tubes protruding from it, similar to the one he had been shown by Helen Gartner.

"I need you to study this with great attention to detail, Mister Lightfoot," said Simeon.

Jack peered at it closely, so closely, that for a moment, his nose nearly touched the page. He could smell the mustiness of the pages, an earthy smell that was unfamiliar to him.

"What is it?" he finally asked.

"The machine of miracles," Simeon replied, his eyes shining.

34

Nadia Barossa returned to the South Bank later than she had expected. When she unlocked the front door, the interior was so quiet that she paused for a moment, waiting to hear the familiar noises of Jack working in his lab, or cooking up a strange concoction in the kitchen. But there was nothing. Jack didn't leave the house by himself very often, but Nadia was sure that he was out.

Then she noticed the note he had left for her, propped up against the vase. Nadia opened it slowly and carefully, as if she didn't want to damage it. He had never mentioned an appointment, Nadia thought. And it's strange for Jack to venture out on his own, without telling her the details.

The note was in Jack's neat, slanted handwriting.

> *Dear Nadia,*
> *I have been called out to meet with a client.*
> *Cannot provide details. Very hush-hush.*
> *Shan't be long. Must leave now.*
> *Fondly,*
> *Jack.*

While reading, Nadia became aware of a hint of a fragrance lingering in the room. A perfume, flowery and light, yet distinctive. It seemed familiar. And then Nadia remembered. "Helen," she said to herself.

There was a slightly muffled thump on the door, then a steady knock. When Nadia opened the door, she saw Deke Dunberry standing there.

"Good evening to you, Miss," he said, wiping his nose lightly with the glove that he held in his hand. "Just coming on duty, and I was wondering if you and Mister Lightfoot... well, if you needed any help at all." Jack had begun giving Deke small jobs to do, which added to his meagre salary as a nightwatchman.

"Funny you should say that Mister Dunberry. Mister Lightfoot has left on an appointment, but I don't know his whereabouts. He didn't... mention anything to you, perhaps?"

Deke shook his head. "Not a thing, Miss. But I can ask the others. They're just coming off the day shift and, who knows, they might have seen Mister Jack somewhere."

"That would be very kind, Mister Dunberry. Please let me know if you hear anything."

She closed the door as the large man turned around and left.

—•—

Margaret Lafroste interrupted her crochet work and dropped her hands into her lap when Raskovic entered. She sat in the informal lounge, in front of a large window that allowed the sun to warm her ageing bones. Her white hair shone, creating the appearance of a halo.

She looked the large man up and down, taking in his worn jacket with the scuffed sleeves, and the slightly dirty cotton shirt that pulled at the buttons. The garrotter was a man of very few words. He stared at her blankly, blinking now and again.

Margaret didn't bother to ask him to sit.

"I have a special request – a favour, if you will," she said. "The woman you have been watching – she has become a thorn in my side. And you know what we do with thorns, don't you? We remove them."

The garrotter gave a barely perceptible nod.

"When you followed her the last time, what exactly happened?" she asked.

"That missy try to trick me," said the garrotter, his voice gruff and apparently unused to making sounds. "But I saw her, from on high." He lifted his hand, to illustrate.

"But she got away."

The garrotter nodded, but made no excuses.

"So, do you know where she goes every day? To meet with her associate? Her working partner?"

The garrotter remained silent. It was clear that he didn't.

Margaret placed a hand gently inside her needlework bag, and then withdrew a small scrap of paper.

"No matter," she said. "I have done your work for you. Here is the address."

She handed him the piece of paper.

The garrotter held the note at arm's length, attempting to focus his eyes on the small written words. The difficulty he had with reading words on paper frustrated him.

Margaret waited patiently until he looked up at her.

"Now I want you to listen carefully," she said at last.

35

Jack stood alone at the centre of his new quarters. The room was comfortable enough, with a single bed, wash stand, and a writing desk with a lamp, along with an ample supply of paper, ink, pens and pencils for his drawings. Jack opened a window and peered outside. The steep drop to the ground discouraged any attempt to escape. He also noticed, with growing unease, that the door did not have a handle on the inside.

Did that make him a prisoner? Nadia certainly would have thought so, Jack told himself. And he had no choice but to come to the same conclusion – business client or not.

Of course he had access to a bathroom, but he had to ring for one of the staff to let him out of his room, and Jack was sure the staff had been instructed to keep a close eye on him. Walking around the rest of the house would be out of the question, of that he was certain.

There was another doorway, to his workshop, as Simeon had called it. It was an impressive large room, and was equipped with metal cutting tools, and all the accessories he could ever need; tubing, an array of tools, as well as small and medium-sized sheets of glass, and metal rods and connectors of various types. Jack was impressed with the detail in which the room was fitted out.

Near the wall stood a table with a display of some of the pages that had been carefully removed from the Book of Transmutation.

The precious pages were covered by sheets of glass, to prevent damage. Jack sat down and stared at the drawings in front of him, then set about making notes and taking in the detail of the drawings.

He had an additional page with translated terms, and saw a signature at the bottom of it – *Tennison B. Abbywick*. The page provided a translation of each of the labels that explained the different parts of the drawing. Jack could not make head nor tail of the ancient script, but the English labels were clear, if somewhat cryptic. 'Connect blood vessel' read one of the labels. 'Placenta fluid' read another.

At first, the machine looked as if it would be implanted inside a large animal, such as a cow – but it gradually dawned on Jack that it was a stand-alone machine, perhaps meant to operate without the co-operation of a live host. That explained the two small pumps that were attached; the pumps were meant to circulate fluids within the machine.

However, there was one part of the original drawing that puzzled Jack. There appeared to be a fleshy part inside that could be seen through the little window at the front of the machine. The label simply read 'Generative female parts', without explaining what it was. However, the overall picture became clear, and Jack knew that he was meant to create some sort of breeding machine, and assumed it was for a farm. But why then would the 'most prominent figures in the country', as the professor called them, take such a keen interest in the machine? A breeding machine for humans? Surely not, thought Jack.

Jack suddenly felt tightness enclosing his throat, and fear settled like a heavy weight in his belly. The little hairs on his neck stood up, as if there was another, unseen presence in the room. To Jack, the room, the entire house, suddenly took on a different appearance. The comfortable room suddenly felt much more like a prison cell, and the house sounded as quiet as a morgue.

But the silence did not last long. It was shattered by a loud, wolf-like cry. Jack rushed over to the window and peered out, but there was nothing unusual to be seen outside. He realised then that the sound came from inside the house. It sounded as if a wounded beast was being held captive and tortured in another room.

An involuntary shiver ran down Jack's spine. He watched the door, gripped by fear – but nobody entered, and he didn't hear the animal-like noise again that day.

———•—•—•———

In another room in the house, Tennison Abbywick heard the same sound. He had heard it before and had asked Simeon Strasberg about it, but the professor's reply had been evasive. It had something to do with an asylum that allowed Strasberg to examine some of their patients. There was no further information – and the matter was never discussed again.

Abbywick put down his magnifying glass and rubbed his eyes. He had been staring at old texts, drawings and inscriptions day after day. He was exhausted, his eyes bloodshot and sore. He sat back in his chair and sighed.

There was a light knock on his door.

"Enter," said Abbywick. He had recognised the knock as belonging to Simeon Strasberg. "Good evening, professor," he said as the grey old man entered. "I'm relieved to see you looking much better."

Simeon nodded, and then sat down in a chair near Abbywick's. "You rang?" he said. His voice sounded tired.

"I've completed it," said Abbywick. He handed Simeon a sheaf of papers with the translation written in a consistent hand, the large letters flowing in a confident, almost decorative handwriting style.

Simeon flicked through the notes, stopping here and there to take in the detail. "Great God, this is excellent," he said finally. Then he looked up at Abbywick. "Do we know that it is all... correct?"

Abbywick looked at him curiously. "Professor, I cannot bear to produce work that does not match my own highest standards."

Simeon nodded, and then smiled briefly at Abbywick. "I thank you."

It was Abbywick's turn to nod an acknowledgement.

"I wonder if I could ask you to remain... perhaps for a day or two? I may have questions. I may need clarification," said Simeon. "You will be paid, of course."

Abbywick nodded. "If you wish."

"Perhaps a brandy or a sherry, in the library later, to celebrate?"

Abbywick shook his head. "I regret that I must decline," he said. "I am a teetotaller."

With a final nod, Simeon Strasberg left the room.

Abbywick remained in his chair, deep in thought. He was conflicted between the reward of finishing the work, and the anxiousness about how it would be used.

To take his mind of these worrying thoughts, Abbywick too, left the room. He was allowed to wander in a small section of the house, including the library, and that is where he headed.

He opened the heavy oak door to the library and found it quiet. He was alone. He had been there several times before, but simply to find books that may have helped in his translation. Now he merely browsed. He walked past the extensive section of medical volumes and, on another shelf, found several books on the topic of architectural design. Abbywick touched the spines of the books, stroking them lovingly and opened one or two.

Then a particular book caught his attention. It was about Harrows Gate.

36

The sound of repeated thumping on the front door reverberated in the entrance hall. Nadia tried to catch a glimpse of the front porch, but was unable to, because an awning blocked her view. She quickly descended the stairs, thinking that it might be Jack, but as she approached the door, she heard the thumping again and slowed down.

Visitors to Jack's lab on the South Bank were rare, and Jack wasn't one to thump the door in such a manner, not even if he had lost his key. Nadia was suspicious, and opened the door at a crack at first. She heard a groan and looked down. A man in a scruffy jacket lay face-down in front of the door, his one arm extended.

Nadia opened the door wider, with caution, and then recognised the man. It was Deke Dunberry, and he was lying in a small pool of his own blood.

"Deke!" Nadia kneeled down next to him, and tried to help him to sit up. But Deke was a large man and it was difficult to move him. Nadia saw a wound in his chest, and then realised that someone had stabbed him from the back, and that the weapon had passed through Deke's chest.

"What happened to you? Who did this?" Nadia felt the panic rise in her. Was this connected to Jack? Where was he, when she needed him?

Deke tried to say something, but was unable to speak.

Instead, bubbly, frothy red blood flowed over his lips. There was a gurgling noise in his throat and chest.

"Deke, what happened? We must get you a doctor!"

Deke's hand suddenly gripped her wrist, as if he was trying to keep her close to him. Nadia noticed a trail of blood on the footpath behind him. Deke Dunberry had dragged himself along the ground to reach the door.

Deke shook his head resolutely. He tried to speak again, but then slumped forward and lost consciousness.

Nadia stood up, and realised that her sleeve and part of her dress were stained with blood.

There was no one else on the street – nobody that Nadia could ask for help.

She heard a noise from inside; a loud thud, as if something heavy had landed on the floor. She controlled her urge to scream out aloud in panic. For a moment, she returned her attention to Deke. He was quiet now, and no longer struggling. With tears in her eyes, she turned him on his side and tried to prop him up against the wall.

Deke's head sagged to one side, and his face appeared ashen grey. Nadia pressed three of her fingers against his neck to check for a pulse. There was none.

She left his body at the door, and entered the building, her senses alive and searching for any movement or noise. It was quiet inside, but to Nadia it felt as if there was something else present – something malevolent.

Her first instinct was to fetch her sword from upstairs, but as soon as she stepped on the first wooden step, it creaked loudly and Nadia stopped, realising the noise would give her away. She turned to the umbrella stand in the hallway and picked the largest umbrella, holding it in front of her like a sword. It gave her little confidence, but she moved forward anyway, her eyes scanning room after room for any activity.

She inched her way towards the kitchen, stepping lightly to avoid making a noise. Then she noticed grit on the floor, where there was none before. Nadia froze in her tracks and stared at it. It was dirt, trodden in from the garden. Unless Jack was particularly careless, the chances were that it was brought in by an intruder.

Nadia moved quietly closer to the kitchen bench, where she saw a cast-iron frying pan, possibly left there by Jack. As she gripped the handle, she saw a blur of movement on her right. It was a large figure, and Nadia recognised the intruder instantly. It was Raskovic, and he had a garrotting wire clutched in one hand.

Nadia swung the frying pan wildly, even though its weight was considerable. The edge of the pan caught the garrotter on the side of his face as he moved in – and deflected his movement, sending him reeling to the side. His full weight crashed against the wall, then bounced back and Raskovic landed on his back on the floor. Nadia lost her grip on the frying pan handle and the pan fell on the floor, clattering loudly.

She scrambled to the far end of the bench, where she wrenched open a drawer and grabbed a large carving knife. As the garrotter staggered to his feet, shaking his head, she charged. The garrotter tried to push her away, but he was dazed, and too late to respond effectively. Nadia stabbed him in the abdomen – and his eyes widened in surprise. He stumbled backwards, but then steadied himself against the wall.

Nadia watched, horrified, as the garrotter grabbed the knife with both hands and pulled it out. He bellowed like an animal as the knife came out, coughing up splatters of blood, and then stood there, as if in a daze, with the bloody knife in his hand. The wound was gushing blood.

Nadia retreated, looking around for an escape route. Trying to run for the front door was risky, as the garrotter could easily block her path and grab hold of her. Running in the other direction might cause her to become trapped in another part of the building. So, instead of running, she waited for a response. Her heart was racing as she watched every twitch, every movement the large man made.

He began stumbling towards her, still holding the knife. Nadia retreated further, keeping well clear of him. He was sweating now, and seemed eager to reach her.

As he stepped forward, his boots skidded in the pool of blood on the floor. He fell down heavily, groaned, and then tried to get back on his feet. Nadia took the chance to slip past him, and to head for the door. But then she spotted the frying pan on the floor, and stopped to pick it up.

Holding the heavy frying pan in both hands, she cautiously stepped towards the garrotter. He was still down on the floor, groaning, and for a moment, Nadia hesitated. She realised that another blow to the head could kill him. In the next moment, the garrotter twisted around and grabbed the edge of the frying pan. Nadia tugged at it, both hands clasped tightly around the handle. But the garrotter held on with an iron grip, his face a mixture of agony and rage. He trembled violently as he began to pull her closer. The next moment, Nadia slipped in the pool of blood on the floor, and she fell down hard, immediately scrambling to get up. As she tried to get away, he grabbed her foot and tried to pull her closer.

Nadia cocked her other leg and let fly with a hard kick, hitting the garrotter in the face. The kick barely affected him. His bloody hand tightened its grip and he inched her towards him.

Out of the corner of her eye, Nadia spotted the garrotting wire that he had carried with him. She grabbed it with one hand, and pulled it closer.

Instead of trying to get away from the garrotter, she moved in closer, and slipped the garrotting wire over his head. With her other hand, she began pulling, tightening the wire around his throat. The wire was looped at one end, and Nadia pushed her foot into the loop, then extended her leg until the wire tightened. She began throttling him.

As the wire tightened around his neck, Raskovic loosened his grip on her and clawed at the wire with one hand, but his large fingers wouldn't fit inside the loop.

For the first time, there was panic in the garrotter's eyes. Nadia saw more blood gushing out of his chest, and watched in horror as blood dribbled out of his mouth. His mouth widened, as if he was about to shout. But instead his throat produced strange gurgling noises.

His eyes took on a fixed stare and then he slowly sagged to the floor. Nadia's arms ached from holding the tension on the wire. She was desperate to let go, but held on nevertheless, keeping up the pressure.

After several minutes, the garrotter's body was finally still; the last resistance was gone. Nadia released the garrotting wire and stood up, panting heavily from exertion. She stared down at Raskovic, unable to believe the events of the past few minutes.

37

Emilio Ducanti was sitting in his corner office, watching the early-evening grey sky through the window, when a young duty constable burst in.

"I'm sorry, sir," he immediately apologised. "I didn't mean—"

"What is it?" Ducanti was not in the mood for idle talk.

The constable was aware of Ducanti's dark mood, and it made him nervous. "There was a... they found a body, sir. At a Mister Jack Lightfoot's premises—"

Ducanti rose to his feet and frowned.

"When?" he barked. "Who was found dead?"

"They have yet to... identify..."

Ducanti held up his hand to stop the constable. His heart felt icy cold. He hesitated before asking: "Male or female? Was the victim male or female?"

"Male, sir. So I hear."

Ducanti almost sighed in relief, but retained his composure.

"I need the team," he said. "And get me the doctor. We don't know what else we may find."

———◆—·—◆———

Ducanti stood with his legs apart, over a pool of congealed blood. Deke Dunberry's body lay at his feet. The body had already entered the early stages of *rigor mortis*. Blood smears covered part of the wall and doorway, which suggested that the body had been moved.

Ducanti bent down, careful not to allow his coat to touch the blood. He turned the body face-down, which revealed a stab wound in the back, with blood caked around it.

There were one or two gasps among the onlookers, who had gathered to view the gruesome spectacle. Ducanti appeared not to notice them. He lifted the back of Deke's tattered coat, to get a clearer view of the wound. Blood had soaked through the dead man's shirt, and it was difficult to make out detail, but it was clear he was stabbed – with a short sword or a large knife.

Rather unkind, Ducanti thought, being stabbed in the back.

There were some footprints and scuff marks near the body, but Ducanti suspected they were old, and would be of no use to the investigation. Instead, he followed the blood smears across the narrow laneway and found another spot where blood had formed a small pool.

"Sir," a voice said next to him. "We found something, sir." Normally Ducanti hated being interrupted, but this time he found it a welcome relief. He looked at the police constable next to him, and raised an eyebrow.

"Broken glass, sir. The killer may have forced his way inside."

"That side?" Ducanti asked, pointing at the side of the building that provided more convenient cover for someone who was trying to remain unseen.

The constable nodded. "Precisely, sir."

"Get someone to stay with the body," said Ducanti. "And get me O'Malley. We're going to break the door down."

The constable nodded hastily. O'Malley was a large policeman with a penchant for opening things by brute force, including doors, and he was the obvious choice for this task.

He was about to rush off, when Ducanti stopped him. "Before you go, get these people to move further away. The blood, there – that's where he was stabbed."

The constable nodded.

It took O'Malley three tries to break the door lock. At the third attempt, the door groaned under his considerable weight until there was a loud snap when he crashed with his shoulder against its veneered surface. The wood around the lock and handle splintered and the door swung open. O'Malley wiped the sweat out of his brush-cut red hair, and then wiped his hands together, looking satisfied with himself.

"There ya go," he said.

Ducanti stepped inside, pausing and listening for a moment before moving on. He walked through the entrance hall, and into a reception space that had a passage leading off to one side. He saw a contraption of sorts against the far wall, and presumed it was one of Jack's creations. Ducanti had heard that Jack was a prolific inventor, and something of a collector of strange mechanical objects.

He ignored it and moved into the passageway. At the entrance to the kitchen, he paused again. Blood smears were visible on the floor and, when Ducanti entered, he saw kitchen utensils strewn across the floor.

The garrotter's body lay beside the kitchen table near the wall, his dead hand still grasping the table leg. His normally pale face had turned a purplish colour, and his tongue protruded obscenely through his open lips. Ducanti could clearly see the lacerations around his throat, where the garrotting wire had cut into his flesh. The garrotte lay nearby, discarded on the floor. The garrotter had been garrotted. Ducanti could scarcely believe his eyes.

O'Malley had entered the kitchen and peered over Ducanti's shoulder. "God almighty," he said loudly. "I recognise that man, sir. He was—"

"—the executioner at the jail," Ducanti completed his sentence.

"But how?"

Ducanti ignored his question. "Call them in, O'Malley. We have some work to do. We have to search this entire place."

38

The name 'Harrows Gate' was written on a brass plaque at the gate of the manor house. Nadia glanced at the name and shivered. It was still bitterly cold at night, even though spring was on its way. She opened the latch on the gate and stepped through. Once inside, she chose a garden path that led past the large lawns and behind a row of trees.

The house looked spooky in the moonlight, its grey-tiled roof and shutters creating a dark, forbidding impression. Nadia advanced swiftly behind the line of trees, her movements cat-like and quiet, except for the occasional rustling of leaves underfoot. She wore dark clothes; a pair of masculine, dark-grey pants, a black cotton shirt, and flat shoes. Not a good fashion statement, she thought, but the unusual clothes gave her a sense of lightness – of freedom. Nadia's sword, in its scabbard, was strapped to her back so that it didn't restrict her freedom of movement.

There was nobody outside, and she allowed herself to breathe a little easier as she approached the house. The west wing, shrouded in the moon's shadow and with ivy covering large parts of the wall, was the darkest. As Nadia edged closer, she noticed that a light was on in one of the rooms on the second level. There was no movement, and it was difficult to tell if the light was left on by mistake.

She finally reached the wall, and grabbed on to the ivy, to test if it would carry her weight. It couldn't. The intricate branches immediately broke away, and Nadia was left holding a handful of ivy plant. The guttering, on the other hand, presented a far better option. She gripped the gutter with both hands and lifted herself slowly off the ground, the toes of her shoes looking for grip on the down-pipe. Moments later, she was slowly edging upwards, her hands moving smoothly and her fingers searching for little crevices and hand-holds which allowed her to climb higher.

A third of the way up, Nadia paused, out of breath from the exertion. She slowly turned her head and noted with satisfaction that she had already advanced a respectable distance up the gutter pipe. She felt a small measure of satisfaction, but when she looked upwards, the roof seemed so far away as to be out of reach.

Testing the muscles in her arms, Nadia continued climbing. Her feet were more assured now, finding toeholds more easily, and moving her along at a good pace. Her right arm was starting to throb, and Nadia realised she had used it for most of the heavy lifting.

At last she was high enough to be able to reach across to a window ledge on the upper floor. She clutched on to the ivy, while gingerly taking a step across to the window ledge. Once her foot found a secure position, she reached out for a handhold on the window frame and then moved her other foot across, until she was standing freely with both feet in front of the large window.

The window was not shuttered, and it was open at a crack. Nadia inserted her fingers and slowly edged the window handle upwards, until it slipped out of the notch that kept it from swinging open. She grabbed hold of the window handle before it could drop down, and then slowly opened the window, peering into the darkness inside the room. She listened, but there was no noise to be heard.

Nadia opened the window still further, then lifted one foot onto the windowsill. Leaning her weight on the front foot, she moved into a sitting position with both feet together. Ever so gently, she lowered one foot onto the floor inside the room. She felt solid timber under her sole. Easing forward, she placed her second foot onto the floor, watchful and alert. She crouched down, her eyes attempting to penetrate the darkness. A little moonlight filtered in from the window, and as her eyes adjusted to the darkness, she could make out a bookshelf, and the edge of a bed.

She heard a creaking noise; a bedspring, perhaps? Immediately, she stiffened, every muscle coiled. She gripped the hilt of her sword, preparing to draw it from its scabbard. Was the sound her imagination? Why didn't she hear anything before?

There was a slight groan, and then she could hear breathing. Someone was in the bed. Sleeping perhaps... or just waking up.

Nadia's ears picked up every breath now. She remained on her haunches, quiet as a cat, and listened.

Then she heard the breathing again, this time settled into a steady rhythm. It was a man, of that Nadia was certain. After listening to the sound for a few seconds, she craned her neck and rose up slightly. She could make out a shape in the bed; a figure covered in blankets, the only visible movement being the gentle rise and fall of the bedding.

Painfully slowly, Nadia edged towards the door. She turned the door handle so slowly that it felt as if it was taking hours to open. Some of the passage light spilled into the room, and Nadia squeezed out through the narrowest of openings.

In the meantime, the man's eyes opened. His head shifted slightly, and two eyes peered out, squinting. As Nadia closed the door behind her, the man suddenly sat upright in the bed. His eyes were wide now, and he seemed fully alert. It was Tennison Abbywick.

39

Instead of police transport, Ducanti decided to take a late-night cab to visit Professor Strasberg's house. If Nadia's suspicions were unfounded, he didn't want to embarrass the entire Metropolitan Police Force.

The cab dropped him off at the gate, and he walked down the long gravel pathway, towards the manor house. The night was chilly and quiet. Despite renewed pain in his leg, Ducanti kept up a brisk pace, breathing steam into the night air.

Two windows were illuminated, and Ducanti took this to mean that someone in the house was still awake. When he reached the imposing front door, he used the brass knocker to knock loudly. The house was silent for several minutes, and it took several more knocks before another light came on, this time in the reception hall. Ducanti straightened his back, and waited for the door to open. There was a rustling of keys at first, then he could hear metal crunching in the lock. The door finally swung open.

Ducanti didn't recognise the man at the door, and assumed him to be one of the servants. The man had an almost-bald, bullet-shaped head, and as he spoke, Ducanti saw metal fillings flash in his teeth.

"I apologise for the lateness of the hour, and my unannounced visit, but I must speak to Professor Strasberg. It is urgent," said Ducanti, his voice carrying a commanding tone.

"And who shall I say—" Riley began.

Ducanti expected the question. "I'm the sheriff of the Metropolitan Police in London," he replied smoothly.

Instead of inviting Ducanti inside, Riley closed the door in his face. It took a moment before Ducanti's surprise turned to anger. His moustache twitched and a light blush spread to his cheeks.

After what felt like an eternity, the door reopened and Riley stood aside, allowing Ducanti to enter. "The Professor said to wait in the library, if you please," said Riley. The words were polite, but his tone was not. It was clear that he despised policemen.

Ducanti didn't bother to thank him. Yet, he was grateful to be inside, and warmed himself by the low-burning fire in the library hearth. In the furthest corner of the room, Ducanti noticed a collection of African paraphernalia: a shield covered in animal skin, three spears of differing lengths, a calabash used as a water gourd, and a detailed painting of a native African warrior holding a spear, his naked torso gleaming.

Ducanti examined the weapons more closely, and found that the metal tips of the spears were pitted, and that the handles were well worn – signs that they have been used in fighting, or perhaps hunting.

"Ever been to Africa, Sheriff?" said a voice behind him. Ducanti turned.

Professor Strasberg had entered the room, wearing a plush dressing gown tied at the waist. He appeared older than Ducanti had anticipated, and frail, leaning on a walking stick and walking rather slowly.

"I did service there, in the military," Ducanti replied.

"Did you kill many?" Simeon Strasberg asked, with an amused look.

The question took Ducanti by surprise. "In the line of duty, yes," he said.

"Duty. Ah yes," the professor said, walking towards one of the nearest chairs to take a seat. "We are bound by duty, all of us. Duty to society. Duty to civilisation."

Ducanti put out his hand in greeting, but the professor ignored it and instead sat down slowly.

"I am dreadfully sorry, Professor Strasberg. It is very late but is a matter that simply couldn't wait," said Ducanti.

"Not an emergency, I hope," said Simeon Strasberg.

"Two people have died at South Bank tonight, Professor," Ducanti said, his face serious and tense. He too, sat down.

"I'm sorry to hear that, Sheriff. Did you need my help in the investigation?"

"I have some questions, and I hope that you'll be willing to help me answer them," said Ducanti.

"My dear fellow, if you are looking for a murderer, I might suggest you are looking in the wrong place."

"Professor, do you know a person by the name of Nadia Barossa?"

The professor smiled and shook his head. "Doesn't ring a bell."

"Perhaps you have heard of the name Jack Lightfoot?"

The professor shook his head again, but Ducanti picked up a tiny flicker of hesitation in the old man. He felt a sudden unease. What was Strasberg hiding?

"Mister Lightfoot mentioned to me, that he had met with you on a previous occasion," Ducanti said, feeling uncomfortable about telling a lie.

The professor seemed unperturbed. "Did he? It might be so, Sheriff. I meet lots of people. Surely you don't expect me to remember all of them?"

"No sir," said Ducanti. "I'm merely trying to get to the truth."

"I fail to understand your questions, Sheriff. Have these people committed a crime?"

Ducanti shook his head. "I expect they may have tried to stop a crime," he said, and took a photograph from his inner coat pocket. He handed it to Strasberg, and waited for the old man to take a good, close look at it.

"It was taken a few years ago," said Ducanti.

The photograph was slightly yellowed, and had a pinhole near the top edge. Ducanti had removed it from a wall in the prison warden's office. The photo was of a man, sitting in the garrotting chair, and with Raskovic standing behind him.

Simeon squinted at the picture to make out the fine detail, and then said, "And who was this unfortunate fellow?"

"A jewel thief," replied Ducanti. "But do you recognise the man standing behind him?"

Simeon Strasberg took another look at the image. "It seems to be the man responsible for the garrotting executions at the prison," he said. "I remember meeting him while I was working there, doing my research."

"He was found dead," Ducanti said. "Strangled."

There was a glimmer of a smile on the professor's face. "Some would call that justice, for a man who has killed so many by choking them to death," he said.

"Quite. It was rather surprising, however, that his body was found in Jack Lightfoot's workshop."

The professor appeared genuinely surprised by the news. "I don't understand," he said.

"Neither do I, Professor. Put that together with the fact that Mister Lightfoot cannot be located, and that his assistant, Nadia Barossa, is nowhere to be found, and the entire affair becomes rather... unsettling."

"Forgive me, sheriff. I agree with you, but I fail to understand why you have arrived at my doorstep, seeking information."

"May I ask what, exactly, your business was at the prison, professor?" asked Ducanti. "What research did you conduct?"

Simeon Strasberg shrugged lightly. "It was somewhat experimental, I'm afraid," he replied. "I'm a man of medicine, and the aim of my work was to find out if some people were better able to tolerate... foreign matter. To put it bluntly, I wanted to know if one person's flesh could be transposed on to another."

"Can I be similarly blunt, Professor? Why on earth would you want to know that?"

Strasberg smiled. "Your reaction comes as no surprise, Sheriff. Most people fear science, because they do not understand it. Experiments like mine help us to understand whether one can remove the limb of one man and transfer it to another. If such a thing can be done, it may be possible to save an important man's life, sheriff, even if that means that a newly-executed criminal may be used as a... donor."

Ducanti felt vaguely sick. "And how did your experiments turn out?"

"Successful, to a degree."

"To a degree?" Ducanti repeated.

"Some people make better test subjects than others, Sheriff. However, we did accomplish some promising results."

"I believe you are acquainted with Dame Margaret Lafroste?"

The professor's grey eyes were cold, and stared unwaveringly at Ducanti. "I trust you didn't disturb me late at night, simply to ask for a list of my friends and acquaintances. Yes, I do know Margaret Lafroste. I was a friend of her husband's, and his physician."

"I've heard that he is recently deceased," said Ducanti.

"You heard correctly, Sheriff. A sad loss. Is this line of questioning leading anywhere in particular?" Simeon was abrupt now, unwilling to extend further courtesies to his uninvited guest.

Ducanti decided to push his questioning further. "As you have been a friend of both Margaret and Reginald Lafroste, I suppose you must also be aware that Raskovic, the executioner from the prison, has been in their employ?"

The professor was quiet for a moment. He studied the sheriff's face closely. "I do not interfere in the staffing decisions of my friends, Sheriff. I simply have no interest in such matters."

"Then perhaps you can tell me about Fryman Sellers," said Ducanti.

"Who?"

"Fryman Sellers. A convict, who took part in your experiments at the prison, Professor. The warden tells me he has been... a good subject."

"Ah, yes," Strasberg said finally, pretending that he had forgotten. "Not much to tell. He was one of many at the prison."

"The remarkable thing is that he disappeared. Vanished without a trace," said Ducanti.

"Oh? I heard he was executed."

"So you do remember him. The unfortunate truth is that there has been a plot to remove Fryman Sellers from the prison, and to make it look like an execution. Sadly, someone died in his place – one of the prison guards."

"A plot, you say? I'm sure convicts plotting to escape is nothing new, Sheriff."

"Not convicts, sir. This escape plan was orchestrated from the outside, by people in positions of authority."

The professor gave a dry laugh. "To help a convict go free? Rather far-fetched, don't you agree?"

"Not if the convict had some value for his... benefactors."

"Value? What value?"

"I was hoping you could enlighten me, Professor."

"Now you have me utterly confused," said Strasberg, but he suddenly appeared more cautious, and uncomfortable.

"Fryman Sellers is accused of a crime by Margaret Lafroste, and he lands in prison. But then he turns out to be a highly-valued subject in your experiments. You and the Lafrostes are well acquainted. The garrotter at the prison is employed by the Lafrostes, and he is implicated in the strange disappearance of Fryman Sellers. Such a series of coincidences seem... quite remarkable, don't you agree?"

Simeon Strasberg was suddenly quiet, and he appeared to be considering Ducanti's words. When he looked up, his grey eyes seemed clearer, more alert. "Funny you should mention that, Sheriff," he said. "I have my own suspicions, but I dare not cast aspersions on an old and dear friend..."

"Pardon?"

"The entire matter concerning Dame Lafroste," he said. "Facts have come to light that I have found deeply troubling. But I am an old man, Sheriff, and the whole thing seemed so... unlikely."

"Are you confirming that Dame Lafroste was involved?"

The professor grinned. "I think I may have the proof you are looking for, Sheriff – now that you have explained your suspicions."

"What is it, Professor?"

The old man slowly rose from the chair. "I think it would be better if I showed you," he said.

Ducanti rose to his feet, but the professor held up his hand. "I shall bring it to you, Sheriff, if you'll allow me a few minutes."

"But of course," Ducanti said and awkwardly sat down again. He watched as the old man walked out of the room and closed the door behind him.

40

Nadia paused at the top of the stairs, her senses alive and her ears picking up the tiniest of noises. She could hear the front door being unlocked and low voices – male voices – having a brief discussion. The words were indistinct, and she was unable to make sense of them.

The front door closed, and Nadia could hear movement. At first she was afraid that someone might walk up the stairs, but no-one did.

Her curiosity piqued, Nadia stepped cautiously down the first few stairs. A floor board creaked here and there, which caused her to pause and listen. But then she heard someone walking back towards the front door. Nadia scrambled back up the stairs and remained still at the top, listening intently.

The visitor was ushered into one of the downstairs rooms, and she could hear a heavy door close. She was unaware, however, that the door behind her opened at a crack. An eye peered through the crack, and gazed inquisitively at Nadia's figure standing motionless near the top of the staircase. After a few moments, the door closed without a sound. Nadia felt the hair on the back of her neck stand up. She turned quickly, but there was no one behind her. The passage was also clear.

Gathering all her courage, she decided to venture downstairs, and gingerly stepped down one step, then another, and another, until she found herself halfway down the stairs. She crouched down and peered through the balustrade, hoping to catch sight of whoever was entertaining a guest at such a late hour. She was particularly eager to learn the identity of the guest.

Nadia reached the bottom of the stairs undetected, and quickly made her way to a set of heavy curtains that covered the large window at the northern side of the entrance hall. Then she wriggled in behind the curtains to hide herself from view.

She heard footsteps, and as they passed, she peered out through a part in the curtains to see who it was. She recognised Simeon Strasberg, wearing a dressing gown and leaning on a walking stick. He entered one of the rooms and she could hear him speaking to someone inside. There was a reply from another male voice, and Nadia thought there was something familiar about the other voice, although she wasn't certain.

As she was about to abandon her hiding spot and look for another, she heard different footsteps coming in her direction. She waited and listened. The footsteps stopped mere feet away, and Nadia held her breath, keeping absolutely still. Did someone know she was there? But how?

Long, anguish-filled minutes passed, then she heard a door open and close again. Nadia could hear Strasberg walking out of the room, the walking stick punctuating his steps.

"With me, Riley," she heard him say.

The walking stick tapped its way further down the passage, and Nadia could hear Riley's booted footsteps following on behind. Strasberg said something, but his voice was indistinct. Nadia thought she heard the word 'problem'. When the footsteps disappeared, she came out from behind her cover, and quietly moved to the closed door. For a moment, she stood and listened, but there was no sound inside the room. Nadia was sure, however, that it wasn't Jack inside the room. She would have recognised his voice instantly, she reasoned. Whoever it was, it was not worth the risk of finding out.

Nadia reconsidered her position. If Jack was in the house, where would he be kept? *Kept?* She realised she was considering all the possibilities, including kidnapping. Perhaps a basement or cellar, she thought, and immediately started her search for stairwells and passages leading downwards.

She soon found a doorway that led to a descending staircase.

Nadia moved noiselessly down the stone steps, her soft shoes cushioning her steps. A gaslight halfway down illuminated the steps, and as she progressed, Nadia became aware of a strange chemical smell.

At the bottom of the stairs, a wide passageway led towards the western corner of the house. Pools of light pointed the way to the far side. Nadia could see several doors, most of them solid looking. She tip-toed down the passage, listening, but all was quiet. The only occasional noises came from the ground level, above her.

As she progressed along the passage, Nadia became aware of another sound – light snoring. She tip-toed closer to a door that stood ajar, and when she peeked inside, Nadia could make out a man sitting at a table, resting his head on his arms, fast asleep. His face was flattened on one side by its own weight, and Nadia could see that the man's pudgy hand was holding a set of keys, the knuckles clenched as if the man knew that he was holding something of great importance.

The risk of trying to remove the keys from his grasp would be great, Nadia realised. She glanced down the passageway one last time, just to be certain that she would be undisturbed. Then she gently stepped towards the sleeping man. He remained fast sleep, blissfully unaware of her presence. Nadia allowed herself a tiny smile. Maybe this was possible, after all.

She spotted a metal cage in the adjoining room and stopped abruptly. It looked somewhat like a prison cell, with bars criss-crossing the front, forming a formidable barrier. Was it Jack's prison? For a crazy moment, Nadia had the urge to whisper Jack's name. She was desperate to know if he was held there. But that was lunacy, she decided. What if it was a cage for an animal? But then, wouldn't it be outside?

Before Nadia could decide what to do, an ear-splitting sound filled the air. A howl rose from the cage, so ferocious that Nadia felt herself unable to respond immediately. She stood on the spot, before realising she was an open target and a long way from cover.

As the man at the table began to lift his head, Nadia retreated swiftly, trying to remain on tip-toe as she raced for the open door, and back to the passage. Behind her, she heard the man shout, "Stop! Damn you!" The voice was so forceful that Nadia almost obeyed. But she pushed on and narrowly escaped around the corner, taking once glance backwards, frantically reaching for the sword that was strapped to her back.

"Fucking animal!" the man shouted. "Stop that noise! I will have no more of it!"

Nadia stood out of sight, her heart racing and with her back pressed hard against the stone wall. He wasn't speaking to her. Hopefully he hadn't seen her. She enjoyed a moment of overwhelming relief.

She heard a chair being shifted. The man was getting up from the desk. For a moment, it sounded as if he was coming nearer. Nadia held her breath and bulged her fists. The man was big, she realised – too big to fight, even if she did have the element of surprise.

Then she heard a loud clanging noise. The man was beating against the cage with something, perhaps a stick of some sort. She heard the sound reverberating loudly in the room and down the passage.

"Shut up you fucking animal!" the man shouted.

It was Nadia's opportunity to escape, before the noise attracted anyone else. Without wasting a further moment, Nadia made her way down the passage and back to the stairs as fast as she could. She was less careful about making noise now, and after a moment or two, broke into a run.

When she finally reached the stairs, Nadia raced, jumping two or three stairs at a time. Once she was at the top, she was able to slip into the cover of darkness and disappear.

41

Jack Lightfoot was awakened by the sound of a fist thumping on his door. Moments later, the door opened and Riley entered.

"Begging your pardon," Riley said, but it was clear he wasn't begging for anything. "The professor wants to have a little chat, so he sent us to fetch you."

The gatekeeper, Duddo, was standing behind Riley, his face red with agitation. First his sleep had been disturbed by that animal, Fryman Sellers, and then he was summoned to do the professor's bidding at an ungodly hour.

Jack was wide awake, and stood up, reaching for the metal-rimmed spectacles on his bedside table. "Why on earth would he—"

"Well, the professor doesn't tell us all about his comings and goings, does he?" said Riley with a sneer. "Now let's be quick-smart about it."

"Good lord, it's two o'clock in the morning," said Jack. "What could be so important that it couldn't wait—"

Riley, with a short wooden club in one hand, stepped forward and delivered a quick blow to Jack's stomach. The blow took Jack completely by surprise. He doubled over and clutched his stomach, sinking slowly to the floor.

"Chit-chat's over," Riley said to Jack, then he gestured with his head at Duddo, and together they lifted Jack and carried him out of the room.

———•———

Sheriff Ducanti stood up as the professor entered the room. Following on behind Strasberg were his two henchmen, Riley and Duddo. They carried a large chest, which appeared quite heavy, into the room and placed it at the side of the room, near the bookshelves. Duddo withdrew to the far end of the room, while Riley stood guard over the chest.

Ducanti watched, puzzled, as Professor Strasberg stepped up to the chest and spoke. "This is a rather delicate matter, Sheriff, and I do not wish to besmirch the names of people that are held in such high regard by the public. I am hesitant to tell you more if you have already discussed your theories..." his words tapered off.

"So far, my 'theories', as you call them, are my own, professor," said Ducanti. "Any evidence that you provide, will of course be treated with the utmost discretion."

"Very well then," said Strasberg. "I suppose there is no further need for secrecy." He nodded at Riley, who responded by opening the large metal clasp on the chest. As he opened the lid on the chest, Jack's head popped up, and he looked around the room, bewildered.

"Sheriff?" Jack said, now thoroughly confused. "You too?"

Jack stood up, but was unstable on his feet.

"Good heavens, man," said Ducanti. "What are you doing here?" He turned to Simeon Strasberg. "What is the meaning of this?"

"I thought I would show you the evidence, Sheriff – just as you wanted."

"I don't—" Ducanti began, but he stopped dead. Behind him, Duddo had driven the African spear into his back with great force, and Ducanti looked down in surprise at the spear-tip that emerged out of his chest. He could taste the blood flooding his mouth, and in an instant, it all became clear.

Ducanti sunk to his knees. "Not like this," he tried to say, but only gurgling noises escaped from his mouth. He propped himself up with one hand, while the other reached inside his pocket and withdrew a small pistol. Without taking proper aim, he lifted it and fired at his attacker. Duddo managed a look of alarm as the bullet penetrated his eye socket. He stumbled backwards, trying to hold on to one of the chairs for support. It didn't help. He fell down, as heavily as an ox.

Ducanti's supporting arm gave way and he fell on his side on the floor. He still held the weapon in his hand, and tried in vain to take aim at the professor. Riley stepped forward quickly. "I'll have that," he grunted, and removed the pistol from Ducanti's hand. Blood was pooling around him, and Ducanti's world faded into blackness.

Jack watched the unfolding horror in disbelief. He stumbled forward, trying to reach out to Ducanti, but it was clear that the sheriff was dead.

42

Riley led Jack back to his room, holding him by his collar. Jack meekly obeyed, realising that his own life depended entirely on the whim of his captors. They took to the stairs, with Simeon Strasberg following behind, his pace much slower and more laborious.

Once they were in the room, Jack sat down on the bed. He looked confused, and was disorientated. The professor entered the room and looked him up and down.

"We sometimes must do brutal things, for the greater good," said Simeon.

Jack slowly looked up. "What greater good could there possibly be for this?" he said. "You killed a decent man."

"An ambitious man, who thought he could stop the unstoppable," said Simeon.

Jack had tears in his eyes. "And what would that be?"

"Do not worry yourself about the final outcome, Mister Lightfoot," said Simeon. "It will become clear soon enough. I would like to get some rest. Tomorrow we will embark on a most important project." He turned towards the door.

"What if I refuse?" Jack asked defiantly.

Simeon paused to look back at him. "I think we are well beyond that point, don't you?" Then he spoke to Riley. "Leave Mister Lightfoot to rest. He will need his energies tomorrow."

Riley grinned, and then followed Simeon out of the room.

The heavy door closed behind them, leaving Jack sitting alone on the bed.

He felt overwhelming hopelessness. With Ducanti dead, there was little hope that he'd ever be rescued. He sat silently, staring at the opposite wall and replaying the moment of Ducanti's death over and over in his mind.

It was then that Jack heard a faint sound at the window; a scratching noise, and then a slow tick, tick, tick, as someone was lightly tapping against the glass. He turned as he saw a shadow at the window. It took him a moment to realise that it was Nadia. Jack leaped to his feet so quickly that he felt momentarily faint, and had to hold onto the bedpost for support.

"How—" he started saying, but then he saw that Nadia was gesturing for him to keep quiet.

Jack quickly moved over to the window and opened it further. "Nadia," he whispered excitedly.

Nadia squeezed through the opening, and moments later, stepped onto the floor inside the room. She hugged Jack tightly, and despite the outside cold, he felt her warmth flooding through him. He hugged her back, ignoring years of Victorian conditioning about things that are considered improper for a gentleman to do. Tears of relief welled up in his eyes. Then he felt the scabbard strapped to Nadia's back. "What's this?" he said in surprise.

"Jack, we don't have much time," Nadia whispered urgently. She held him by the shoulders and looked him in the eyes. "We must get you out of here, but it's very slippery out there. Perhaps there is another way."

"Ducanti is dead," Jack whispered back. "I was such a fool. I believed him. I believed Strasberg, everything that he said."

"That's not important now," said Nadia. She took his arm. "We must go now. Let's see if—"

She was advancing towards the door when it suddenly opened. Riley stood there, sneering, with Simeon Strasberg standing beside him.

"Now that would be rude, leaving without saying goodbye," said Strasberg, wearing his awful grin. "Unfortunately, you have been spotted, Miss Barossa. As I recall, this is the second time you have entered this house uninvited. You clearly lack the proper manners."

Nadia retreated, and she pushed Jack towards the far end of the room, away from his 'hosts'. She unslung the scabbard and withdrew her sword. The blade made a faint metallic sound, which resembled a note played on a flute. It glistened in the gaslight, and she flicked the tip of the blade towards Riley.

"I warn you to stay clear and let us pass," she said.

Riley picked up a small footstool, and held it in front of him like a shield, the feet pointed in Nadia's direction. He grinned confidently. "Come now, my pretty," he said in a soft, but venomous tone. "Don't make it harder on yerself."

Nadia's sword sliced the air between her and Riley. It was a quick cutting movement; a final warning.

Riley grinned. He held the stool high, ready to block any blows. Then he suddenly thrust the stool forward, towards Nadia, as if trying to scare her. She heard him chuckle. She could feel Jack's presence behind her. He had shrunk back against the wall, and was watching them with an expression of dread.

Nadia stepped lightly to the side, and Riley responded immediately, changing his stance and readying himself for her next move.

But Nadia's next move took him completely by surprise. She dipped down, bending her knees slightly, and then sweeping the sword quickly from left to right, delivering a cut above Riley's knee. It ripped his trousers and drew blood. The blood quickly soaked into the fabric and discoloured it.

Riley was surprised at first, and mumbled an unrecognisable swear word. Then his surprise turned to anger, which quickly flamed into rage. Instead of retreating, he stepped forward, trying to jab at Nadia with the stool.

Nadia deftly side-stepped him, and delivered another cut, this time to his calf.

"By God, I will rip your skin off, whore!" he shouted, with spittle flying out of his mouth.

He threw the stool at her, and it hit Nadia against the arm, although she managed to deflect most of the blow. Riley, turned and headed for the door.

The moment Strasberg realised that Riley was leaving the room, he shouted. "Wait! You have to fight her!"

But it was too late. Riley was already out of the door, walking fast and purposefully. Nadia knew that the fight was far from over.

In the meantime, Simeon Strasberg edged towards the door, and followed Riley. But he was much slower, and could only hobble along with his cane. By the time he reached the top of the stairs, Riley was already nearing the bottom.

"Riley, come back at once!" Strasberg shouted, but it was in vain. Riley ignored him.

Back in the room, Nadia looked at Jack. "He'll be back, with a weapon. We must leave now," she said urgently. Jack nodded his head energetically.

She grabbed Jack's hand, and pulled him along as she stepped out of the room.

Simeon Strasberg had made his way halfway down the stairs, when he looked nervously over his shoulder and spotted Nadia and Jack at the top of the stairs. He tried to hurry, his weak leg buckling, and then he suddenly toppled forward, and crashed down the stairs.

Nadia and Jack watched as the flailing body of the professor rolled and thumped down the stairs. His head hit the balustrade and blood spurted against the wall as he rolled further down the stairs. At the bottom, he finally came to a stop, his body motionless.

"Dear God," Jack whispered.

"Come, we must take the stairs. It's the only way out," said Nadia.

But they stopped when a door at the far end of the passage opened. A man came out of one of the other rooms, holding a revolver in one hand and pointing it at them. He looked down at the broken body of Simeon Strasberg and then back to Nadia and Jack.

"You killed my brother!" he said.

Nadia and Jack were speechless. They were looking at Simeon Strasberg's identical twin.

43

Simeon Strasberg's twin stood tall, and without the support of a cane. He grinned – the identical ghastly grin of his brother – as he took aim with the pistol.

"My brother was the weakling, destined to be replaced," he said. "I am the Simeon Strasberg you need to fear."

He pressed the trigger and a shot reverberated in the house. It ripped a chunk of plaster off the wall between Nadia and Jack. Nadia instinctively dropped to her haunches, trying to shield herself behind the balustrade. Then she noticed that Jack was running for the stairs.

"Jack! No!" she shouted, but he had already gone too far. Jack was at the top of the stairs, holding on to the handrail, and pausing the moment he heard Nadia's voice.

A second shot rang out. There was a loud crack as the bullet splintered the wood of the balustrade, not far from where Jack was standing. Frantic, Jack took to the stairs, feverishly gripping the handrail here and there as he descended as fast as he could.

Nadia noticed that Simeon's attention was drawn back to her. As he swung the pistol around to take aim, she ran back into the room, just in time to hear the bullet hitting the timber doorframe, chipping the paintwork a few centimetres from Nadia's head. She instinctively ducked, but it didn't stop her forward movement.

Inside the room, and momentarily shielded, Nadia searched

frantically for something she could use as a projectile of sorts. She found a vase that was small enough to throw, but by the time she was readying herself near the door, Strasberg drew closer, the pistol held in front of him and aimed at the open door.

She hurled the vase through the open door and at Strasberg, but it missed its target completely, crashing against the wall and shattering into hundreds of pieces.

Simeon Strasberg was grinning now.

Nadia was breathing fast and irregularly. She realised she was trapped. The window was a possible escape route, but it would take too much time to climb down – and she knew Riley would be waiting for her to do just that. And jumping from such a height would seriously injure her. A sense of helpless panic rose within her chest.

When Jack reached the bottom of the stairs, he was heading for the front door when he ran into Riley, who was carrying a hunting rifle. Riley was taken by surprise, and he reacted almost instantly, using the rifle butt to push Jack backwards, up against the wall.

"Well now," he said, when he realised that Jack was by himself. Then Riley noticed Strasberg's body at the bottom of the stairs, the corpse's neck twisted at an awkward angle.

"Did you do that?" he asked. Jack shook his head. He could hear his own heart drumming in his chest. Riley was a big man, and Jack knew he would not hesitate to kill. He stood still, not daring to make a move.

"Riley!" the other Simeon Strasberg shouted from upstairs. "Fetch a can of kerosene from the cellar. We have an unwelcome guest. We'll burn her out."

"I have the other one down here!" Riley shouted back.

"Good," Strasberg replied. "Make sure he doesn't run away, but keep him alive!"

Riley reacted swiftly. He lifted the rifle, and smacked the rifle butt hard against Jack's head, knocking him unconscious. Jack fell to the floor and lay dead still.

Riley left him lying there and headed for the cellar.

In the meantime, Nadia had latched and barricaded the door. She heard Strasberg's words, and knew that her time was limited. Her only hope was to clamber out the window and into one of the other rooms, and then rely on the element of surprise to make her escape. Nadia felt a sudden chill at the thought of leaving Jack behind in the house. If they were willing to set fire to the room, what hope did he have?

She heard a creaking noise behind her and snap-turned around. One of the wooden panels mounted against the wall was moving, sliding to the side. Nadia picked up her sword, which she had left on the floor, and swiftly but quietly moved towards the opening panel, her sword held in front of her, ready to stab or slice at whoever was about to enter.

She pressed herself against the wall to remain out of sight, and waited. Her senses were alive and her muscles twitching in anticipation. Then she saw movement. A face appeared in the opening left by the sliding panel, and a man stepped into the room. He was small in stature, and rather peculiar looking.

Nadia responded, grabbing him by the lapel and throwing him down on the floor, her sword ready to stab him through the heart. The large book that the man had held in his hands fell heavily onto the floor, and the man held up his hands in a feeble attempt to protect himself. He looked terrified.

"Speak. Now," Nadia said, her voice sounding like a growl.

"My... name..." the man stammered. "My name is Tennison Abbywick," he managed, finally.

The name didn't ring a bell, and Nadia didn't relax her guard.

"And?" she said.

"I'm just a translator. I translate books," he said, his voice trembling with tension. He glanced at the book that lay on the floor beside him. Nadia looked at it. The words 'Harrows Gate' were printed on the cover.

"What is that?"

"A book," Abbywick said nervously, "About this house. That's how I found the secret passage. When I heard the commotion—"

They heard footsteps outside the door, and then a sloshing noise, as someone poured liquid against the door frame. Some of the liquid leaked through under the door and began to soak the corner of the carpet. Nadia recognised the smell of the kerosene instantly.

She grabbed Abbywick by the lapel and pulled him upright, holding his arm until he was standing up and supporting himself.

"They will set this place on fire," she whispered to Abbywick. "We must leave now."

Abbywick's eyes were wide with fear. He too, smelled the kerosene.

She pushed Abbywick ahead of her towards the once-hidden entrance and followed him through. Then she closed the panel behind them, just as flames began flickering near the door, and quickly spread over the floor to the carpet.

44

The Earl of Whittlecast stood at the bay window, which offered a view over the pristine gardens of his exquisite home. He fidgeted with his gold pocket watch, then replaced it in a pocket in his waistcoat. Sighing deeply, he turned and sat down at his desk. Opposite him sat the Commissioner of Police.

"And you are absolutely sure it was Simeon Strasberg," said Edmund Faderley, leaning back in his chair to give his voluminous stomach room to expand.

"Yes m' lord," said the Commissioner. "He was badly burnt, truth be told, but part of his face was somehow shielded, possibly because he lay on his side. But it was him. His body was formally identified."

"How did it happen?" asked Faderley. "How did you come to investigate this?"

"It was the fire, m'lord. The fire brigade was called by a concerned neighbour, and they notified the police when nobody could be found on the property – nobody alive, that is."

Faderley wrinkled his nose at the mention of the deceased.

"So you arrived at the house, and..."

"Well, the sergeant arrived at the scene of the fire, with his men, m' lord. As soon as he realised that two men had died – and that one of them was the Sheriff – well, he didn't hesitate to contact me, m'lord. You see, I made it clear to the men that I should be contacted, day or night, in the event of—"

233

"Yes, yes, I fully understand, Commissioner," Faderley cut him short. "Did the Sheriff, at any opportunity, tell you of his intention to visit Professor Strasberg?"

"No, m'lord. I expect he needed the professor's advice on a matter of police work."

"And you have no idea what that may have been?"

"Unfortunately not, m' lord," the commissioner admitted reluctantly. "Naturally, I was kept informed of the high level cases, but in this instance—"

"Commissioner, I must inform you that the Sheriff has previously conducted some investigations at the behest of the Crown – investigations at the highest level of secrecy. These are matters of national concern, Commissioner, the details of which simply cannot be divulged under any circumstances."

"But m' lord, I was not informed of such—"

"Exactly, Commissioner. It has been so requested by the Ministry of War. Do you understand?"

"Of course, sir... m'lord. I shall ensure—" the Commissioner stammered. But he was cut short again.

"Commissioner, all documents pertaining to the work of Sheriff Ducanti must be submitted to my office without delay, and must, under no account, be shared with any other departments, whether on police business or not. Do I make myself clear?"

"Most certainly, m'lord. I shall see to it personally," the Commissioner said, his face reddening.

Faderley looked pensive for a moment, before he spoke again. "I think it would be for the best if we make no mention of the Sheriff when we discuss this matter with members of the press."

"I beg your pardon, m'lord?"

"Considering the... delicate work in which our Sheriff had been involved, I think it would be unwise to make mention of it to the gentlemen of the press, don't you agree?"

"Most certainly, m'lord. I shall instruct the men not to mention a word of it to anyone, least of all the newspapers."

"Very good," said Faderley and he smiled. Then he stood up from behind his desk, causing the Commissioner to scramble to his feet. "I appreciate your discretion, Commissioner. And I shall be sure to pass on just what a... sterling job you have done in this regard. Thank you."

"Nothing gives me greater pleasure than to serve the Crown, m'Lord."

He bowed towards Faderley, but couldn't help noticing that the Earl of Whittlecast was looking slightly impatient.

"Now if you'll excuse me. There are so many demands on my time," Faderley said.

"But of course m'lord," said the Commissioner, "and may I say what an honour it is—"

"Stafford!" Faderley called out, causing his butler to enter moments later. "Be so kind as to show the Commissioner to the front door."

The butler nodded, and held the door open for the Commissioner, who meekly did as he was told.

Once they had left, Faderley opened another door, which led to an adjoining room. Dame Margaret Lafroste, her voluminous skirts swishing, entered his office. She looked composed and at ease.

"You're a skilled diplomat," she said with a smile.

"The man is an insufferable bore. But at least he does what he is told," said Faderley, grinning.

"I am in your debt, Edmund," she said. "The Sheriff's mind had been poisoned by rumour and innuendo, spread by none other than the two troublesome individuals that I had been telling you about. At least some good has come from this tragedy."

"And what about these upstarts?" said Faderley. "This Jack Lightfoot and his associate, Nadia Barossa?"

Margaret smiled. "They have no power without the Sheriff," she said. "I expect we'll hear no more of them."

Faderley looked relieved. "There it is then. Problem solved."

"That is exactly why I admire you so, Edmund. A man of prompt action and resolve."

Faderley felt elated, receiving such praise. For some reason, he had the inclination to impress Margaret Lafroste at every opportunity. For a woman in her later years, she still held a feminine charm that he found difficult to resist.

"Just another day in the corridors of power, my dear lady," he said proudly. "Do you have time for tea?"

45

A morning breeze carried the smell of fish and rotten fruit, which, by early morning, permeated the air at the docks. At the eastern dock, between Wapping and Shadwell, a steam barge slowly sailed past a tangle of ships, some of them carrying corn and timber cargoes, for shipment to the Mediterranean.

A number of sheds and warehouses crowded the northern end, some of the smaller sheds displaying signs such as 'Superintendent's Office' and 'Principal Dock Master's Office'.

Nadia walked along the docklands, side-stepping puddles of water that had accumulated overnight. Tennison Abbywick followed, about three paces behind her, looking warily at the dockworkers, and holding a handkerchief over his nose to filter the pungent air.

"This appears to be the place," he said in a handkerchief-muffled voice, peering at the sheet of paper in his hand. "Warehouse number ten." Abbywick's cheeks appeared rosy in the cold breeze, and he looked at Nadia with watery eyes.

"Perhaps someone can help us," said Nadia absently. Her eyes were misty and sad, and Abbywick was uncertain whether it was the weather, or her anguish about Jack Lightfoot that was to blame.

Together, they approached a dockworker, who busied himself over a consignment of wool bales.

"Pardon me, sir," Nadia said, her voice almost drowned by

the noise from the docks. "Do you know the vessel *Mariblanca*?"

The dockworker, a burly, red-haired man in a filthy singlet and tattered pants, looked at her suspiciously, then at Abbywick. "What's your business with her?" he asked.

"We wish to find out about a shipping consignment," she replied.

"This be no place fer wimmen such as yerself," the dockworker said with a lecherous grin, and an accent that Nadia could barely decipher. "You best speak to the clerk then, haven't yer?" He nodded towards a nearby office.

"Thank you, sir," Nadia said, and followed his vague directional nod to a small office that had the words 'Customs Free Goods Office' painted in stencilled letters on a sign above the door. Abbywick followed.

The door of the office was an unlikely combination of iron framework and timber, with thick layers of paint covering the outside. Nadia opened the creaking door, and inside the office found a young man attired in a starched shirt and button-up waistcoat, and wearing a small set of silver-rimmed glasses that balanced precariously at the tip of his nose. Somehow, he looked out of place in a shipyard. He looked up from a sheaf of paperwork, revealing a thin, waxed moustache on his upper lip. He seemed affronted by the intrusion.

"I am so awfully sorry to interrupt your work, sir. I was hoping you might help us with an inquiry," said Nadia.

"That depends what your inquiry is about," he said, peering at Nadia, and then at Abbywick, over his spectacles.

"We are looking for a friend, and have heard he left on board the *Mariblanca* two or three days ago. It is a family matter, and we need to contact him urgently. If you can give us any information—"

"A passenger then?" said the clerk.

"...Yes."

"Odd, in that case, since the *Mariblanca* is a freighter," he said sharply.

"Perhaps he was offered passage?" said Nadia, her voice a little thin.

"We discourage that sort of thing," the clerk said, his eyes wandering to a large logbook on a nearby table. "There are more than enough passenger vessels." He flicked through the pages of the book and then ran his finger down a list of entries.

"His name?" asked the clerk.

"Jack Lightfoot," said Nadia. She edged closer to the clerk and tried to peer over his shoulder at the neatly written lines in the book. He glanced sharply at her, as if to warn her not to step any closer, then retuned his attention to the list.

"Hmm," he said finally. "Name's not registered here."

"Perhaps Strasberg, Simeon Strasberg," said Nadia quickly, encouraging him to continue looking.

"He has two names?"

Nadia shook her head. "A friend. They might have travelled together," she said. "Please, if you can provide any information at all…"

The young man looked up at her with the slightest glimmer of sympathy. But then his expression changed, and he shut the book. "I'm sorry."

"Can you tell me where the *Mariblanca* was heading?"

"Calais," he said curtly. "That's its regular run."

"Is there perhaps anything else that—"

"I'm sorry, madam. Your line of questioning is… irregular, to say the least, and, as you can see, there's plenty of work to be done."

Nadia drew away from him, feeling the weight of disappointment on her shoulders.

"Thanks for your assistance," she said softly, and turned towards the door.

The clerk shook his head briefly, and then returned his attention to his work.

Abbywick followed Nadia outside, catching up with her as she walked aimlessly towards the nearest dock.

"Nadia," he called softly. But she didn't respond. She looked distraught, her sadness enveloping her like a cloak.

"Nadia," said Abbywick, louder this time. She stopped and turned.

"There is something you ought to know," said Abbywick. He stopped when he saw the tears in her eyes. "I'm sorry. I didn't mean to…" he began.

Nadia shook her head and dabbed her eyes. "What were you about to say? There's not much hope, is there?"

Abbywick held up his hand, and moved closer to Nadia, then leaned in to whisper in her ear. "I suspect he – the man in there – is not telling the truth, entirely."

"What on earth do you mean?"

"The book he was holding – it wasn't a ship's manifest," said Abbywick.

"But, it doesn't make sense. How do you—"

"I've read passenger and cargo manifests, many of them, I assure you. He was looking a different book, a log book perhaps. But only the ship's manifest has a list of the passengers—"

"Are you absolutely sure, Tennison?"

Abbywick nodded. "Ship's manifests were a… pastime for me. I imagined that I would go sailing to strange lands."

The briefest of smiles appeared on Nadia's face, but then she said, "But how do we— Where do we find the real manifest?"

"It is customary to keep a duplicate," said Abbywick. "In the Dock Master's office."

Nadia was suddenly excited. She grabbed Abbywick's shoulders and squeezed them. "You are a gem, Tennison. I am in your debt."

Abbywick was taken by surprise by Nadia's exuberance. His face was serious when he responded. "Nadia, he may not have been on that ship. If Jack's name does not appear, and it is likely that it will not, then we may never know…"

Nadia smiled at him. "Tennison, you have given me hope. That is the greatest gift. Will you come with me? To the Dock Master's office?"

Tennison smiled shyly, and nodded. "I have an acquaintance with a person working there," he said.

Nadia rewarded him with a radiant smile.

46

Nadia had never seen such a large moustache. It was a bushy patch, lined with grey hairs, that concealed the man's upper lip and somehow managed to hide the lower lip as well, spreading out sideways towards his cheeks. Portions of it above the lip were stained from tobacco smoke. Nadia couldn't stop staring at it, and only disengaged her stare when the man cleared his throat loudly.

"Nathanial Barnes," Abbywick announced in his usual, soft voice, introducing the man to Nadia.

"I'm... I'm very pleased to meet you," she said, purposefully averting her gaze from his moustache and locking it on to the man's grey eyes instead.

Nathaniel responded with a grunt, and with the barest nod of his large head.

"We met... well, I was collecting ship's logs," Abbywick added. "It's a hobby." He sounded bashful about it.

Nadia, who didn't want to waste a moment, said, "A dear friend of mine has disappeared, Mister Barnes, and I was hoping you might be prepared to help us, even if it is—"

"Where did he go?" asked Nathaniel. He didn't seem particularly curious, just gathering information.

"I think, I heard, that he might have left London, on board the *Mariblanca* – a few days ago," said Nadia.

"By himself?"

Nadia shook her head. "In the company of... others," she said. "Possibly Professor Simeon Strasberg."

Nathaniel cleared his throat, loudly. "I don't mean to pry, miss, but why would he have disappeared? What if he left of his own volition?"

Nadia shook her head firmly. "I was his assistant. I arranged things for him, most of the time. Jack was not the adventurous type. He would have said something, especially leaving on a ship for another country."

Nathaniel raised an eyebrow.

"Eh... I put her on to the *Mariblanca*, if that was your next question," said Abbywick. "Strasberg rented a warehouse, near the river. When we inquired, it appeared he left... moved out, lock, stock and barrel on the day of the voyage. It coincided with the departure of several ships, but the *Mariblanca* was the most likely."

Nathaniel nodded. He knew Abbywick's obsessive nature, and his uncanny ability to predict the unpredictable.

"Very well," said Nathaniel at last. He stood up with a groan, and walked towards a large cupboard and unlocked it with a key from a large keychain.

"He transcribes the ships' records," whispered Abbywick.

"That's his job?"

"Yes, young lady," Nathaniel's voice boomed from the other end of the room.

"I apologise," she said quickly.

"No need to," he said. "We had two fires here. They destroyed hundreds of documents before our eyes – nothing we could do. So the harbour master gave me the job of keeping duplicate records."

Nadia nodded. "I see."

Nathaniel pulled one of the large books off the shelf, and set it down on the table. He paged through the book until he found the last transcribed page while Nadia and Abbywick moved closer for a better view.

Nathaniel paged backwards, then stopped, his fingers caressing the page. "Here she is," he said finally. "Left a week ago, and made for the port of Calais. She was a cargo steamer. I seem to remember she had a fire in her coal bunker, just on three years ago. They restored her good and proper."

Nadia nodded impatiently as Nathaniel reminisced, and held her tongue.

"Hmm," he said, peering at the page. "Full complement of crew, but only a handful of passengers..." Nathaniel looked up at Nadia with a curious expression: "Your friend," he said. "Was he involved in some circus act?"

"Pardon?" Nadia said, surprised at the question.

The big man shrugged. "The ship's papers mention a circus troop. An ape, and a 'wild man' in cages, it says. Both were loaded into the cargo hold."

Nadia was puzzled. "Does it mention anyone else?"

Nathaniel shook his head, and ran his finger down the rest of the text. "This is a black-cross entry," he said suddenly.

"Pardon me. What does that mean?" asked Nadia.

"It means someone died on board," said Abbywick quietly.

"What? Who died? Do they record that?" Nadia's voice was suddenly shrill with anxiety.

Nathaniel looked up the reference further down the page. "A Mister Jack Lightfoot," he announced.

Nadia's world turned. She tried holding on to the table nearest to her, but failed. She fainted and fell to the ground before Abbywick had the chance to support her.

47

Almost a year later, about three miles outside the village of Günzburg in Bavaria, the air was still chilly but the snow had melted and an early spring was in the air. It meant that the inhabitants of Günzburg could look forward to pleasant weather and flowery fields, and the prospect put nearly everyone in a good mood.

Simeon Strasberg stood in front of the window of his mountain cabin. From the hill, he enjoyed a distant view of the Danube. He sucked the air deeply into his lungs, feeling energised by the sun and the fresh morning air.

"Marvellous," he murmured. He turned when he heard a noise behind him. It was Riley, dressed in a clean, white shirt and wearing a waistcoat. Strasberg had insisted that he dress in a more gentlemanly fashion in the countryside, where tattered clothes and bad behaviour often drew stares.

"And where is our miracle maker?" said Strasberg, grinning.

Riley nodded towards the door.

Strasberg opened the door and took the stairs down to the large, thick-walled cellar, which had been constructed as a hiding place during the Franco-Prussian War. Deprived of daylight, except for a narrow window and air vent on the eastern side, the cellar was darker and had a strange smell to it. It was divided in two large sections – one of them now used as a makeshift laboratory.

In the laboratory, low lights hung over two large tables on which stood tall, tubular glass containers, some of them connected with an array of rubber tubes. A gas burner was boiling a strange dark liquid in a smaller glass beaker.

In the corner stood something that looked like a small, pot-bellied oven. Jack Lightfoot sat beside it, his hair prematurely white-grey and his eyes staring at the opposite wall. His mouth hung slightly open, and his hands fidgeted uncontrollably.

Strasberg walked up to Jack and squeezed his shoulder lightly. "I'm in your debt, Jack," he said. "You have helped me to create history; not an easy task."

Jack did not reply, but simply continued staring at the opposite wall. His arms were trembling slightly. Strasberg bent down and looked through the small window that provided a view inside the little iron, pot-bellied instrument. A fleshy substance, connected to a multitude of tubes, floated in a yellowish liquid. To outsiders, the fleshy substance would have been difficult to identify, but to the professor's eye, it was as unmistakable as it was familiar. It was the reproductive parts of a woman – the ovaries, fallopian tubes and what remained of a uterus. The flesh was connected to the tubes, and fed from an external machine through small tubes, while being suspended in the viscous liquid.

"Of course our experiment was not a complete success, Jack, but it was nevertheless a giant leap forward... a giant leap," said Strasberg, still peering intently at the fleshy bits suspended in the liquid. He seemed genuinely pleased. Then he stood up and patted Jack's shoulder. "Don't take it too hard, Jack. Think of the possibilities. We are exploring a new frontier – discovering new worlds of possibility."

Jack didn't respond. He looked disorientated, his eyes unfocused and watery.

"We must not lose momentum," said Strasberg. "We must pursue our goals with vigour, with energy." There was still no response. Strasberg shook his head. "You need rest, Jack. Some rest and perhaps some fresh air. Would you like that?"

Jack's head nodded, in what appeared to be agreement.

◄—·—►

In the other part of the cellar, Riley delivered bowls of food to two cages, made of criss-crossed metal bars and secured to the wall with large bolts. The cages each stood almost two metres tall. Large iron brackets held them together for stability. The room was dimly lit, and the rudimentary bed in each cage was barely visible.

"Time to eat, breeders!" said Riley loudly.

His voice roused the inhabitants of the cages, but they merely stirred, and remained in their beds.

"You best keep your strength up, or you will be of no use anymore," said Riley with a sneer. "And you know what happens to useless things..." He glanced at the wall of the cellar, where the head of a gorilla was mounted on a wooden board.

There was a loud groan from one of the cages. Riley turned up the gaslight, and illuminated the inside of the cage. On the bed, a naked man turned over to face him. The man was large and animal-like, his muscled, hairy body glistening with sweat. Between his legs hung an engorged penis and grotesquely enlarged scrotum, reddened with irritation, and swollen almost beyond recognition.

The animal-man's eyes were bloodshot, and his bushy eyebrows and long hair gave him a wolf-like appearance. He opened his mouth to speak, but he could utter only guttural sounds.

"What's the matter Fryman?" said Riley. "Lost your appetite?"

Fryman Sellers, or rather the creature that he had become, sat up slowly in his bed. It was clear that he was suffering pain.

Riley peeked into the cage next door, where a naked woman covered herself with a sheet that was dirty and torn.

"Morning, darlin'" said Riley, grinning.

Although dirty, Phyllis Secombe was in much better condition than Fryman. Now fully awake, she reached over to the crib that was standing next to her bed. She reached out and gently touched her baby's body, caressing its hair.

"Sooner or later you'll have to give up that other one," said Riley. "I have a good mind to take him right now..."

Phyllis immediately reached for a small bundle in her bed, and held it tightly to her chest. The bundle was tightly wrapped, mummy-like.

"That thing stinks to high heaven. You've had it here for long enough!"

"No!" shouted Phyllis loudly, and clutched the bundle tighter.

Within a moment, Fryman was on his feet, grunting so loudly that spittle flew from his mouth. His arm was outstretched, his hand trying to grab at Riley. But Riley was faster. He anticipated the attack and quickly stepped further away from the cage.

"Dear, dear," he said. "Papa is angry."

He placed the bowls of food near Phyllis's cage and then turned back to the door, pausing for one last moment. "Play the happy family if you want," he said. "I'll soon be back, for both the babies."

Fryman's body shook with rage. His arm was still outstretched towards Riley when he had a sudden convulsion. He staggered backwards, hitting his head against the cage, and then fell to the ground, grunting and foaming at the mouth, his body trembling.

Phyllis sat up and looked at Fryman with alarm. "He's dying!" she shouted.

"He'll survive," said Riley with a sneer. "For now."

48

Tennison Abbywick sat motionless as the woman in front of him dabbed her eyes.

"Me mother, God bless her soul, was the kindest woman to walk this earth, Mister Abber-wick," she said.

Abbywick wanted to correct her, but he held back. He did not want to interrupt the woman's story.

"And they treated her like a slave, they did. The scrubbing, the tidying, every moment of every day. She worked her fingers to the bone." She sighed, then looked up at Abbywick, her eyes glossed with tears. "It was only on her deathbed that she told me... about those monsters. Finally, she was free to speak."

"What exactly did she say, if I may ask?" prodded Abbywick gently.

The woman leant forward, her plump hands flat on the table. She whispered, but her voice carried clearly. "On the night of the birth, they discovered there were two..." she said. "Two, there were."

"I don't understand," said Abbywick.

"Twins," the woman said. "Two little boys. Scrawny little things. Hardly alive, they were." She shook her head, her eyes filled with the memory of her mother. "They could afford a governess, of course, but they didn't want anyone to know. Not a soul. So me own mother had to take care of him."

"They kept the twins a secret?"

"The one of them, they did. The old Mister Strasberg said twins were... unnatural, evil," she said. "They hid one away, and pretended there was only the one boy."

"Hid him away? For how long?" said Abbywick.

The woman leaned closer to him: "Forever. That boy was taken away, to another country."

Abbywick was aghast. Could someone make up such a macabre tale?

"Years later," the woman said, "After the old man died, he came back one day. The two brothers met, but they were like strangers... never together."

Did they ever... reconcile?" asked Abbywick.

The woman shrugged. "After those years, the sickness overtook my mother. She couldn't work anymore. They made her swear never to tell a soul," she said.

———•———

A thick grey fog hung over London, turning buildings into ghosts and monsters emerging from a twilight world. Nadia stood in front of the window, peering out. She held the hilt of her sword in one hand, occasionally turning it and lifting the sword slightly to feel the weight of it.

Abbywick entered the room and sat down at a large, polished oak desk, the papers from his latest project organised in neat piles in front of him. He looked up at Nadia, and then at the sword that she had balanced with its tip on the floor.

"How long have you... done that?" asked Abbywick.

Nadia half-turned towards him. "Pardon?"

"The sword. It's unusual."

Nadia smiled. "For a woman, you mean," she said. "My father was an excellent swordsman, in the military. But he couldn't stand the horror... of war. He left home one day, and joined a travelling circus – 'the man with the golden blade', they called him. He could throw his sword and hit a target."

Her voice trailed off. Nadia looked misty-eyed into the distance.

"This was his sword, in the army," she said, turning the blade so that the light from the window gleamed on its surface.

"You have a special... affinity, for men in the military," said

Abbywick hesitantly.

"You refer to Sheriff Ducanti, I take it. I suppose I have," she said. "I remember my father's uniform with fondness." She smiled unexpectedly. "In the circus he had a uniform too, or a costume, more accurately: A red jacket with golden epaulettes and gaudy braid."

"You saw him perform?"

Nadia nodded. "He wrote to me, at home, about his adventures in the circus. Letters came from all over Europe. So, when my mother died, I wanted to join him. I travelled with the circus for a while, doing acrobatics and climbing up tall poles to balance on top... I was fourteen." Her voice faltered for a moment, and then she said, "Jack would have told him."

"Pardon?"

"Jack would have told Strasberg my story – about being in the circus. Do you think that's where Strasberg found his idea? To pretend to be a circus troop on the ship?"

"I... I'm sure he could have..." Abbywick stammered.

"He taunted me," said Nadia.

Abbywick shook his head in dismay. "The man is without conscience," he said quietly, but in his mind he saw two young boys, staring at one another, without uttering a single word.

"Poor Jack," said Nadia, her eyes misty and sad.

"You did all you could," said Abbywick, but he knew that his words offered little comfort.

49

Summer had begun in Günzburg. As the young man approached his house in *Feinwasser Strasse*, he could see his wife at the door, beckoning him.

"Karl, come quickly. Doctor Strasberg is here!" she called out excitedly.

"Coming" he said, picking up his walking pace. His wife was smiling; no, she was beaming. So this was the big day. Karl felt the excitement bubble up inside him. For two years now, they have hoped and prayed for a child of their own, and then, by God's grace, they had met Doctor Strasberg. He was so kind, considerate. He understood them so well.

As he entered the house, he headed straight for the humble but cosy sitting room. He saw Strasberg sitting in one of the armchairs, and the doctor rose when he entered the room. In his arms he held a small bundle; a baby wrapped in a light, fluffy blanket.

"I arrived early. I am sorry," said Strasberg.

"Doctor, you are most welcome in our home at any time," said Karl.

"We are delighted," added his wife with an excited smile, yet she seemed nervous at the same time.

"As I explained before, the baby's twin brother... was not as fortunate. They were born after a tragic accident, and I fear the mother will not live out the year."

Karl's wife held her fingers over her mouth. "The poor woman," she said.

Strasberg nodded. "These are unfortunate circumstances. But the news – that her baby would go to such caring, loving parents – was a comfort to her. She told me to give you her most sincere thanks."

"Is there something we could offer her in return? Invite her to our home, perhaps?" said Karl, and his wife nodded in agreement.

Strasberg shook his head. "She is in no condition to travel, and seeing the baby again… it would be most upsetting. I hope you understand."

"Of course," said Karl, "Of course we do."

"We will treasure this gift, always," said his wife.

Simeon Strasberg smiled. He lifted the baby slightly higher in his arms, then held the little bundle out towards them.

The couple stepped gingerly forward, hardly able to believe their good fortune. Karl allowed his wife to take the baby in her arms. It mewled softly, and she smiled and said, "This child is a gift from God."

"The child has not yet been baptised. He doesn't have a name," said Strasberg.

"We have been thinking of a name," said Karl, and his wife added, "We want to call him Josef." She looked lovingly at the little baby boy. He had dark hair, and his face was that of an angel.

Strasberg smiled. "A fine name," he said.

"This is a day of celebration," said Karl. "Doctor, we cannot thank you enough. Will you have some wine with us? I have some delicate sweet wine that I have saved since the day we wed."

Strasberg shook his head with a smile. "Friends, unfortunately duty calls me. I am unable to stay."

"If there is anything—" Karl began to say, but Strasberg held up his hand.

"Knowing that Josef is in the best of hands is my reward," said Strasberg. He picked up his hat from the arm of his chair – a hat commonly wore by Bavarian hunters – and placed it on his head.

"I wish you and your dear wife all of the best, Mister Mengele. I hope little Josef will cause you great pride one day," said Strasberg. Then he nodded goodbye, walked to the front door and, with a final look back at the happy couple and their baby, took his leave.

What's next?

If you have enjoyed this book and have a moment to spare, I would greatly appreciate a review.

You can also sign up to be notified of book releases, news and giveaways, at:

neilcolby.com/sign-up

Emails are sent out infrequently (no more than once a month), so they won't clutter your email inbox, and you can unsubscribe at any time.

About the author

Neil Colby lives in Sydney, Australia.

A former scriptwriter, he now focuses on writing books in his spare time, while doing an eight-hour daily stint in a corporate pod and dreaming of being a full-time writer and traveller.